I0731408
VERTICAL

INCUBUS 1

Written by Brandon Varnell
Art by Orendi Laran

DEDICATION

This page is made in dedication to my amazing patrons. Without them, my characters would never get lewded by so many wonderful artists:

Aaron Harris
Alarinnise
C.L. Holgrahm
Chase Corso
Charming_TR
Clifford Solonas
DNAnime
Domonique Q Roddan
Edward Lamar Stephenson
Emery Moore
Feitochan
Forrest Hansen
Jacob Flores
James Leon-Moore
Kevin
Lane Watkins
Lucid Fayt
Mathew Wallace
Max A Kramer
Michael Moneymaker
Peter Barton
Phillip Hedgepeth
Rafeal Eriksen
Sean Gray
Seismic Wolf
Syed Hamdani
Thomas Jackson
ToraLinkley
Travis Cox
William Crew

CONTENT

PROLOGUE

Anthony Amasius stepped out of the sliding doors to the hospital and into the brisk midnight air. The scent of salt mixed asphalt hit his nose as a chilly breeze blew through the street. Tall buildings loomed over his head, though none of them were larger than four or five stories. Larger buildings stood in the distance, however, some of them tall enough to reach into the sky. Lights from the buildings played off his face. There were a lot of signs, though fortunately, none of them were neon and gaudy.

He looked behind him, at the large building with numerous windows and a sign hanging over the front that read "Academy Island Hospital for Catastrophes," then turned back around and began walking off. His jeans ruffled against his legs, and his slightly baggy shirt hid his emaciated torso. He was wearing a large jacket to further conceal his rail-thin frame.

As he was passing a store with several mannequins displaying the latest in women's fashion in front of a large window, Anthony caught a glimpse of his face in the window's reflection. His pale face was gaunt. There were bags under his eyes. His dark brown hair was a mess. Even though he was clean shaven, it didn't change how terrible he looked. At nineteen years old, Anthony could honestly state that he was in terrible shape.

Just as Anthony looked away and was about to continue walking, his wristwatch alerted him to a telepathy call. He raised his left hand. Attached to his wrist was a small band. It was silver, but there was a small black section, which was currently glowing. He waved his hand and a screen appeared in front of him. Selecting the communication app from the many programs on his screen, the name of the person calling appeared before him.

Professor Incanscino.

Anthony narrowed his eyes as he pressed on her name.

"You're calling at an awfully late hour, Professor. I'm guessing there's trouble?"

"*I love how perceptive you are,*" a voice said. It was soft and girlish, like the voice of a girl in middle or high school, but there was a sharp edge to it that banished the sense of it belonging to a child. It also wasn't coming from any speakers. The voice sounded like it was coming from inside of his head. "*Yes, there is trouble. We have a rogue werewolf who has infiltrated Academy Island. We don't know what she wants, but she isn't listed anywhere on the demon registry.*"

"Another one? This is the fifth rogue therianthrope I've dealt with in the last month. Is the Academy Island Private Security Force even doing their job?"

"Let's just say they have had their hands full dealing with other matters and leave it at that."

"Whatever. I'm guessing you want me to take care of this woman?"

"I wouldn't be calling you if that wasn't the case."

Anthony grimaced as he realized he would likely be getting home a lot later than he wanted, but it wasn't like he could tell his professor "no." He owed her too much to just dismiss her requests.

"Can you give me her location?"

"I'm uploading it now."

Anthony looked at his wristphone as the screen projected above it changed from Professor Incanscino's name to a map of Academy Island. It quickly zoomed into a street, which showed a red dot moving through it. He recognized the area the dot was traveling through. It was the government district. This particular area was where the Academy Island Board of Directors met to make economic and political decisions. Their headquarters was a several dozen story building in the shape of an oval.

Now what could she be doing over there?

Well, he supposed what they were up to didn't really matter. He'd been asked by his professor to help out, so that was what he was going to do.

After ending his call with the professor, Anthony bent his knees, took a deep breath, and began channeling mana through his body. He winced when his nerve endings flared with pain, but he had grown used to his own magical circuits hurting when he activated body enhancement magic. It was just how things worked with him.

His body lit up as blue lines of power appeared on his skin, partially hidden by his baggy clothes. Not all the lines were hidden, however. There were several blue lines that traveled along his neck and face. Had anyone seen them, he was sure they would have said these lines looked like the power circuit of a supercomputer's motherboard.

Once his powers fully activated, Anthony was off. He shot forward with an incredible burst of speed.

The world around him became little more than a blur as he ran. The government district of Academy Island wasn't located too far from the hospital he'd just left. Anthony didn't bother taking to the streets. He leapt onto the roof of a building in a single bound and began traveling in a straight line over the roofs, using his magically enhanced physical strength to leap from one building to the next.

From this high up, Anthony could see a good portion of the city as it spread across the landscape like a vast jungle of steel. Tall skyscrapers rose into the sky. Some were so tall they looked like they might reach the stars. Of course, the stars were invisible here, blotted out by the innumerable lights from the city.

Academy Island was a city that had been created after the San Andreas Fault ruptured some time at the end of the twenty-first century, turning a large section of what had once been called California into an island.

Academy Island stretched on for about 150 square miles in all directions. Most of the island was composed of large buildings that contained numerous schools and research facilities. The reason this place was named Academy Island was because of the numerous magical academies that had sprung up, which taught everything from advanced magics to magical sciences. The research facilities, which were owned and operated by large corporations and companies that dealt with magic and technology, were also often associated with many of these schools.

It wasn't long before Anthony reached the government district, and he looked down to see if he could find the werewolf who was running around here. He couldn't. Looking at his wristwatch again, he saw that the figure on the map had moved. They were traveling toward the government headquarters, where the Academy Island's Board of Directors worked. He frowned, but adjusted his course and soon discovered the werewolf in question.

They were traveling very quickly through the streets. Had he been a human, all he would have seen was a blur. As expected of a werewolf, her body was covered in brown fur that only just hid her powerful physique. Most of the fur was located along her arms, legs, and back. He couldn't see much else, however, because her body was covered in what appeared to be... a patient's smock?

Still wearing his frown, Anthony leapt off the latest building he'd been running across and dropped to the ground. His knees buckled a little when he landed in front of the werewolf. He bent them to help absorb the impact, but even so, he couldn't keep from wincing when he felt the powerful force jarring his knees. If only he wasn't using a pseudo power granted to him through a magic he hadn't mastered. If only he had several women who could...

He shook his head and dispelled the thought.

Meanwhile, the werewolf had stopped running when she saw him appear in front of her. Like most werewolves, this woman's face resembled more wolf than human, though he knew werewolves could shape shift into a more human form if they wanted. Most actually preferred their human form because it allowed them to insert themselves into society more easily. He wondered why this woman was not in her human form.

"I don't know what an unregistered werewolf is doing on Academy Island," Anthony said to the woman. "However, you should be aware that being an unregistered demon is illegal according to the Demonic Covenant. I would rather not have to get violent, so could you please surrender yourself to the nearest demon detention facility?"

Anthony thought his words were well-thought out. However, the werewolf before him didn't appear to have even heard what he said. She snarled at him like a rabid beast, then reared her head back and unleashed a ferocious howl at the moon. It was a sign of impending danger. The hairs on Anthony's arms prickled as, seconds after unleashing what sounded like a cry for blood, the werewolf rushed toward him.

He sighed. "So much for having a peaceful resolution."

As the werewolf charged forward, Anthony bent his knees and adopted a simple fighting stance. He reared his left fist back and watched as the woman came closer. By this point, he could see the werewolf's shaking eyes and dilated pupils. The frown he'd been wearing since the beginning grew larger. It looked like she was terrified, or like she'd gone insane. He wondered if she could even understand him. Perhaps she was one of those feral werewolves who refused to interact with human society. But if that was the case, then what was she doing in Academy Island of all places?

These thoughts and more left as the werewolf reached him. She raised her massive left paw, sharp claws glinting in the moonlight, and brought them down quicker than a bullet.

Anthony was faster.

Before the woman's strike could land on him, he delivered a punch to her torso. A loud, concussive *bang* echoed across the street as the werewolf was lifted clean off her feet and sent flying. She hit the road, skidded across the blacktop, and stopped several yards away from him. Anthony waited to see if this woman would stand back up. When she didn't, he relaxed his stance.

The glowing lines covering his body faded away as if they'd never existed. As they did, the mana enhancing his physical strength left, and exhaustion took its place. It felt like his bones that had been filled with strength had suddenly become brittle, like his muscles brimming with power were now weak like a kitten. His shoulders slumped.

"Professor? Are you there?" Anthony asked after using his wristwatch to call Professor Incanscino again.

"I'm here. I'm guessing you dealt with our furry problem?"

Anthony snorted. "She's unconscious and ready to be picked up."

"Good. I'll have the Academy Island Private Security Forces come by and pick her up. Can you wait there until they arrive?"

"Do I have a choice in the matter?"

"You do not."

"Then what's the point of asking?"

"True enough. Anyway, I still expect to see you in class tomorrow. Don't be late."

As the woman hung up, Anthony lowered his arm and looked over at the werewolf, who was still quite unconscious. While he didn't look it, he was quite powerful when using the magic ability Physical Enhancement.

He walked over to the woman and noticed that even while unconscious, her body had not reverted back into her human form. That was… odd. He gave the woman a pensive stare, but then shrugged and sat down next to her. It would be awhile before the Academy Island Private Security Forces arrived. He was tired, so he didn't want to continue standing.

As he looked at the night sky, he released a soft sigh.

"So much for getting a good night's sleep…"

CHAPTER 1

Beep! Beep! Beep!

Anthony stifled a groan as he lifted his face from the pillow. He glared at the alarm clock sitting on the nightstand beside his bed, wishing he had the power to shoot laser projectiles from his eyes so he could incinerate the damn thing.

It was 8am, and Anthony felt like his head had just hit the pillow before the alarm clock began going off. He hadn't even gotten home until around 4am this morning thanks to the events of last night. Not only had he gotten barely four hours of sleep, but this was the second time he'd stayed up late. Last night he'd had to stay up to study for an upcoming test.

Stupid werewolf. Stupid professor.

He shut off the alarm clock and sighed. It looked like today was gonna be another inglorious day.

Stumbling out of bed, Anthony wandered out of his bedroom and into his bathroom, where he took a quick shower in the small shower unit. It was just a small square space with enough room for him to stand. His soap and shampoo were sitting in a small alcove next to his head. If his shower head wasn't detachable, Anthony didn't doubt that washing himself off in this dinky little shower would have been impossible.

After showering, Anthony went back to his bedroom. He found a clean pair of baggy black jeans, an equally baggy T-shirt, and a jacket with a hoodie. He put the socks on last and made his way into the kitchen/living room.

Anthony lived in a small one-bedroom apartment. It wasn't more than maybe 300 square feet, had a single bedroom, a living room attached to a kitchenette, and a bathroom with a toilet and a shower.

Because he didn't have much space, Anthony didn't decorate his residence with anything. The white walls were mostly barren. Only a few pictures hung from them, and most of the pictures were located in his bedroom. His living room featured a single small couch with a holographic television. Meanwhile, his kitchen had a very small stove, an even smaller fridge, a microwave, and a few cabinets attached to the ceiling.

Anthony went to the fridge.

A glance inside revealed several square boxes; each had the logo of a fox plastered on the side and the name Kitsune Kitchens underneath it. He grabbed one of the boxes labeled Eggs & Ham, peeled open the top, placed it in the microwave, and pressed Auto Cook.

It only took about two minutes for the food to cook, and then he was sitting down on his couch and eating a quick meal of processed eggs and ham. He wolfed his meal down as he watched the news. The newscaster was reporting on something that caused his mind to turn to last night's events.

"And in the latest news, several rogue demons were spotted on Academy Island late last night. According to reports, they attacked one of the research facilities owned and operated by

Nametech, a company well-known for their creation of advanced prosthetics that are said to feel as real as your own limbs. Nobody knows where these rogue demons came from or what they wanted. However, the Academy Island Private Security Forces were able to swiftly arrive on the scene and apprehend all of the rogue demons, which are now being detained inside of the North Island Academy Detention Facility. Back to you, Sheral."

It sounded like the werewolf he'd fought wasn't the only rogue demon who had been running amok on Academy Island. He wondered where all these rogue demons had come from, but he didn't have long to ponder these thoughts. A glance at the clock revealed that half an hour had passed. He needed to be at school before 9:30.

Anthony threw away his now empty box of instant breakfast, cleaned his teeth, grabbed his laptop case, and slipped his converse on at the front door. The apartment door slid open and locked behind him as he left. He glanced at his wristwatch just to confirm that the door had indeed locked. Then he moved toward the elevator, took it down to the first floor, and walked through the mostly empty lobby, out onto the street, and merged into the mass of people that surged through the bustling city like a school of fish.

Academy Island was incredibly busy. There were all kinds of people located within this massive island city, and not all of them were human.

A young woman was walking to his left. She had blonde hair and blue eyes and looked relatively normal—until he noticed the fuzzy tail sticking out of her pants and the triangle-shaped ears on her head. It looked like she was a nekomimi, a catgirl variant of therianthrope. Several meters to his right were a group of young men around his age. Their skin was even paler than his, their eyes glowed with an inhuman vibrancy, and they carried themselves with incredible grace. Vampires.

The apartment block Anthony lived in was located about thirty miles from the Institution of Magical Sciences. To get there, Anthony traveled to the maglev station, which was even more crowded than the streets. He pushed his way through the throng of people and clambered into one of the maglev's long cars along with a horde of other people.

Maglevs operated on the principles of magnetic levitation. The maglev levitated several dozen centimeters above the railway and used magnetism to propel itself forward. Not only was the ride incredibly smooth, with not the slightest bit of jostling, it was also fast.

That was a very good thing. Anthony did not enjoy being squashed between so many people.

As he stood in the maglev, he noticed how several people glared at him. All of them were men. Of course, he didn't know any of them. They were just glaring at him because of their natural instincts, something that he didn't blame them for, though it still made him uncomfortable even after dealing with these looks for more than a year.

The women on the maglev ignored him.

The maglev soon reached his stop, and Anthony checked his wristwatch as he got off. It was 9:15am. He would have to hurry if he didn't want to be late.

It was fortunate that the maglev station was literally right next to the Institution of Magical Sciences. He walked across the street and toward a series of massive buildings at least ten stories tall situated together. The structures were a blend of modern aesthetics. Many of them featured asymmetrical shapes, or had strange extensions protruding from them. All of them were also connected via a series of walkways at several story intervals. The largest building was the one in the very center, which reminded Anthony of a helix spiral.

Walking along the winding walkway, Anthony did his best to ignore the looks sent his way as he made it to the large building in the very center. It was easier with so many people. Even if men felt threatened by his existence, his presence was so weak right now that most of them could easily ignore him. He was even more fortunate that none of the women were drawn to him—at least, he told himself that was a good thing.

Entering the building through a sliding door, Anthony traveled through a lobby filled with people, reached the elevator, and took it to the third floor. He exited the elevator and entered a hallway with several doors. The door he entered through was room C-2. Underneath the room name, which flashed on a screen, were the words Theoretical Principles of Magic Catastrophes.

The room on the other side was a lecture hall. There was a stage backed into a wall and shaped like a half-circle. A podium sat in the center and a holographic projector was located on top of it.

Anthony made his way up the tertiary seats, which were already filled with men and women of both the human and non-human variety, and sat near the very back of the class in the top row of seats. He placed his case on the desk and pulled out his laptop. It was a sleek black model with glowing red lines and a logo that looked like an atom. That was the Institution of Magical Sciences' logo.

He turned it on. A holographic screen appeared and asked for his password. He typed it in, then watched as the screen changed to his main page, which featured several apps and programs that he used for school like his ebook library, word processor, calculator, and so on.

At that very moment, the doors opened and in walked a small woman. Standing at a height of about 4'10", the woman who walked into the room possessed a young face that would have caused most people to mistake her for a girl in her teens. Of course, the moment they looked into her eyes and noticed the sharpness present, they would probably think otherwise.

Professor Incanscino's cute face was framed by locks of blonde ringlets the color of honey, which complimented her soft skin, pale blue eyes, and small pink lips. She wore a sharp white business suit that contrasted with her youthful appearance. As she walked onto the stage and moved over to the podium, she set her expensive-looking purse on the podium and turned to face the students.

"Good morning, class. Today, I am going to give you all a general overview on Magic Catastrophes. In a show of hands, how many of you know what a Magic Catastrophe is?" Nearly everyone raised their hands, which caused Professor Incanscino to snort. "I'd be very worried if even a single one of you didn't know about Magic Catastrophes." A number of people chortled. However, they were silenced by her dark glare. "To put it bluntly, Magic Catastrophes are the term we use to describe magical events that create widespread chaos and changes within the world. A good example of this is the event from one and a half years ago known as the Lilith Incident."

As she spoke, Professor Incanscino's eyes landed on Anthony, causing him to shift in his seat. Her eyes fortunately didn't stay on him for long before they swept across the rest of the class. He shuddered and released a weary sigh.

"Magic Catastrophes are relegated into a ranking system. There are seven ranks that Magic Catastrophes fall under. They go from F to S, with F being the weakest and least dangerous Magic Catastrophe, and S being the strongest and most dangerous. Can anyone here tell me what ranking the Lilith Incident was?"

As she finished speaking, Professor Incanscino looked around at all of the people present, as though expecting one of them to raise their hands. No one did. However, Anthony didn't think it was because no one knew about the incident. Everyone and their mother had heard of the Lilith Incident. It had been all the news would talk about for several months.

"Mr. Amasius," Professor Incanscino called him out.

With a sigh, Anthony stood up and ignored the men glaring his way as he looked at the woman. "It was an S-rank Magic Catastrophe."

"And why was it an S-rank Magic Catastrophe."

"Because over one hundred thousand people died. The level of damage done to the surroundings was also on the same scale as a large earthquake. Not only did the event cause a lot of damage, but the environment changed significantly, transforming a once prosperous city surrounded by countryside into a desolate wasteland."

When Professor Incanscino continued to look at him like she expected him to say more, Anthony looked away. This caused the woman to sigh.

"You are close enough," she said as he sat back down. "Generally speaking, the number of deaths doesn't actually matter to the Magic Catastrophe Classification System, but bigger Magic Catastrophes that cause more destruction are always ranked higher because they affect a higher number of people. The Lilith Incident is one that happened when the Succubus Queen Lilith fought against the Vampire Warlord Cane in a battle that wiped an entire city and the surrounding countryside off the map. However, the widespread destruction is not the reason this incident was listed as an S-rank Magic Catastrophe."

The professor raised her left arm, revealing a purple wristwatch, which she activated, creating a holographic image that she tapped on once. When she did, the projector inside of the podium suddenly lit up. An image was projected above the podium. This image was of a massive crater that had a strange black miasma drifting through it. In the very center of this miasmic crater was a black dot, a sphere hovering several feet off the ground.

"When Lilith and Cane clashed, their mana erupted between them and not only created a ghastly poison that is toxic to both humans and demons, it created a quantum black hole. Even though a year has passed, you can see how the miasma inside of this crater remains. Also, while the quantum black hole has not grown at all since it was created, it still remains present. Even the best magical scientists have been unable to figure out how to close it, though several theories were proposed. One theory actually states that closing it would require a being with two times more magical power than Lilith and Cane combined. Of course, there are no beings with such power in existence, and thus the black hole remains."

As he typed on his laptop, taking notes, Anthony could only sigh and ignore the sharp pain in his chest as he listened to the woman speak.

***

When class ended, Anthony traveled down the staircase alongside the other students. Before he could leave, Professor Incanscino called out to him.

"Mr. Amasius, stop by my office after school."

Anthony turned around and looked at the short professor, but then he nodded. It was about that time.

"Will do, professor."

"Good. See you then."

Professor Incanscino dismissed him after getting a confirmation that he would stop by her office. Upon leaving her classroom, Anthony took a walkway that led to Building #2, which was located on the north side of the school campus. This building did not have any classrooms. Instead, it was a massive shopping center. It was, in many ways, a mall filled with places to buy items and food. There were all kinds of shops, restaurants, and also a library where people could check out electronic books.

Anthony took an elevator and traveled to a small restaurant called Italiano Pizzeria. As he entered the shop, the scent of cheese, sauce, and freshly baked garlic bread hit his nose. He might have remained by the front door, smelling the delectable combinations of mouth-watering scents, but someone called his name.

"Hey, Anthony! What are you standing around like an idiot for? Come over here!"

The person who spoke to him was a woman with curly dark hair, smooth skin, and a wide smile. Dressed in the latest fashion, the young woman's somewhat short skirt revealed almost all of her long, lean legs. She was wearing white platform shoes that gave her an extra few inches. Her shirt was stretched taut across her large chest, to the point where Anthony could see the straps of bra—not that it mattered since she was also wearing a short-sleeved jacket, which adequately covered her.

She was waving him over.

Sitting next to her was a young man who wore a somewhat cocky-looking grin. His blond hair was swept back from his face. He had green eyes, pale skin, and several earrings. His rumpled clothing and piercings made him look like a delinquent. Like Anthony, he wasn't muscular but thin and a bit boney. Unlike Anthony, he still looked healthy and not emaciated.

"Secilia. Alex," Anthony greeted the pair as he sat down next to them. They had already ordered a large pizza, which sat on the table. One half was pepperoni and sausage, while the other was just cheese.

"You look half-dead," Secilia joked. "Long night?"

"Something like that," Anthony admitted.

"You went to the hospital again, right?" She continued prodding him with questions. "How's your brother?"

Anthony gave her a pained smile. "Same as always, I'm afraid."

"That's good, though, right?" Alex said in an upbeat voice that was at odds with his delinquent appearance. "If he's the same as always, it means he hasn't gotten worse."

"You idiot!" Secilia scolded the man. "It also means he hasn't gotten better."

"That might be true, but if he hasn't gotten worse, then we can only consider that a good thing," Alex rebutted.

Anthony smiled as he listened to the pair argue. Alex and Secilia were his only two friends right now. He had met them bickering just like they were now. At first, he had assumed they were a couple because of how close they seemed, but he eventually found out they were half-siblings. Same father. Different mothers. Both of them were attending college for a degree in magical engineering.

As the scent of pizza continued wafting into his nose, Anthony felt his stomach gurgle. He reached over and grabbed a slice of the meat pizza. Taking a bite as the pair continued to argue, he enjoyed the taste of mozzarella, tomato sauce, sausage, and pepperoni. No matter the day or age, pizza would always be one of the best foods in the entire world. Hands down. Anyone who said otherwise was fooling themselves.

"Oh! Did you hear about what happened last night?" asked Secilia, turning to Anthony.

"Are you talking about the rogue demons?"

"Yeah. That. It's crazy, isn't it?" Secilia said, continuing before he could answer her. "I managed to hack into the Academy Island Private Security Forces's database, and the reports claim there were over a hundred rogue demons that just randomly showed up out of the blue. They were all therianthropes too. No one knows where they came from, but all of them appeared out of nowhere and began attacking a Nametech research facility."

"You really should use that brilliant mind of yours for something other than illegally hacking into private databases," Alex said with a sigh.

"Oh, stuff it." Secilia stuck out her tongue and blew him a raspberry.

"Did the reports say what the Nametech facility was researching?" asked Anthony.

Secilia shook her head. "No, but there is a rumor about that." She leaned over, turquoise eyes lighting up with a conspiratorial look as she cupped a hand to her mouth. "The rumor that's been going around is that the Nametech research facility was experimenting with cloning technology."

"Isn't cloning illegal?" Anthony asked with a frown.

"It is," Alex confirmed. "Ever since the now defunct Kurōn Conglomerate was discovered using clones for inhumane experiments, cloning has become illegal. Every cloning facility has been shut down. The fines for being caught cloning even single-celled organisms is astronomical and can land you with life in prison."

Cloning was considered one of the four biggest magical felonies. It was different from felonies like assassination, murder, and even genocide. A magical felony was a felony that involved inhumane magical research. The four biggest ones were cloning, inhumane and non-consensual experimentation, experiments involving the replication of Magic Catastrophes outside of theoretical application, and necromancy. Each one of these four would cause a person caught doing them to spend their entire life in prison and any company or research association to be forcibly shut down.

"By the way, Anthony, what are you doing after school ends?" asked Secilia as she placed her elbows on the table, leaned forward, and twirled her hair between her fingers.

"Professor Incanscino wanted to speak with me," Anthony said.

Secilia clicked her tongue.

"What's this?" Alex chuckled. "Feeling threatened by everyone's favorite lolita teacher?"

"Don't be stupid," Secilia said as she took a vicious bite of her pizza. A long trail of cheese connected her to the slice as she moved back. "Why would I be threatened by a woman who looks like a child?"

"I don't know." Alex plastered a smug grin on his face. "You tell me."

Secilia looked toward Anthony, then looked away.

Anthony sighed when he saw this look, but he didn't say anything because there was nothing he could do about it. He continued speaking with the pair until it was time to begin his next class. Then he made his way to his classroom, where another professor he had taught them about the creation and application of medicine.

School lasted for about four hours after lunch. When he finished all of his classes, he traveled toward the south building, known as Building #4, and headed to the top floor.

The top floor was Professor Incanscino's office, though it looked more like a penthouse suite to him. The soft carpet looked expensive. Furthermore, this office had several paintings from famous and long dead artists hanging from the walls. A sweeping staircase with an extravagantly decorated balustrade led to an upstairs area where Anthony assumed his teacher slept.

Professor Incanscino was sitting behind her desk when he entered. She looked very tiny behind the large desk, which had numerous nick knacks and magical implements, along with a large holographic screen that the professor was currently using to read. He couldn't tell what she was reading. Even though he could see the contents (which were viewed by him in reverse), he didn't know what the strange symbols covering the monitor meant. It looked like a magic formula.

"I'm glad you showed up," Professor Incanscino said as she flipped off the holograph and hopped off her chair. She walked around her desk and over to him. "You're nearly out of mana, right? You should have had enough to last you for at least another week."

"Yeah…" Anthony rubbed the back of his neck. "Sorry. I didn't think chasing down that werewolf last night would use so much mana."

"It's because your body is growing an immunity." The professor sighed as she gestured for him to follow her. She continued talking as she led him into a hallway. "Your body has a very unique composition. Because you are no longer human, mana transfers don't work on you like they would for a regular person. This ritual I devised is one that was made specifically for you, but I suspect it won't be long before even this ritual becomes useless."

Anthony grimaced as he heard that. "Is there anything we can do?"

Professor Incanscino stopped in front of a wooden door. He'd noticed that none of the doors in her office/residence were automatic. They were all made of an expensive wood that made her residence resemble a noble's small manor.

"There is nothing *I* can do," Professor Incanscino said as she opened the door. "However, there is something *you* can do."

"I'm not going to have sex with anyone," Anthony said. "I won't betray Lilith."

Professor Incanscino cast him a dark glance. "Stubborn as always."

Anthony shrugged as he walked into the darkly lit room, which used candles instead of lamps to illuminate the space. It wasn't a large room. He estimated it to be no more than 100 square feet. As he walked in, Anthony moved to the very center of the room, which contained a large-scale magic circle. It looked like a circle with a decagon followed by a ten-pointed star inside. Numerous symbols were drawn inside of the circle. He didn't know what any of them did since magical hieroglyphs were not something he ever studied, but he knew what they were used for.

"Take off your shirt and sit down," Professor Incanscino instructed.

Doing as instructed, Anthony removed his shirt and threw it out of the circle, then sat down as Professor Incanscino came up behind him. He steadied his breathing as her scent drifted into his nose. The short professor smelled of lilacs and lavender. It was a very soothing scent, or it normally would be, but Anthony had trouble because he understood this scent came from a very cute woman.

He did his best to ignore that as a pair of small, soft hands found their way to his shoulder blades. Anthony didn't know what Professor Incanscino did to keep her hands so smooth. They sent an electric jolt through his body, though again, he tried to pretend he felt nothing.

"Are you ready?" asked Professor Incanscino.

"Yes," he said.

"Good. I'm starting now."

The hairs on Anthony's scalp prickled as energy washed over his body like an electric current creating static on his skin. All the symbols inside the magic circle began glowing a bright blue. The incandescent light illuminated the dark room more than the candles did. As the symbols lit up, the mana filling the room suddenly paused, then sank into his body. For a moment, Anthony felt like he was getting younger, like time was being rewound. It caused the empty feeling from his nearly exhausted mana reserves to disappear.

As the ritual magic died down, the glow disappeared, and Professor Incanscino took a step back.

"All done," the professor said with a sigh. She sounded tired. "I hope you appreciate what I'm doing for you."

"I do appreciate it." Anthony stood up, found his shirt, and slipped it back on as he turned to face the diminutive woman. "I understand that I would be dead right now if it wasn't for you. I appreciate everything you've done for me."

"If you really appreciate what I'm doing, then hurry up and build a damn harem," Professor Incanscino said with an irritated scowl. "I don't like being your personal mana battery."

Anthony gave his professor a pained smile. He knew he was being selfish by not doing as she asked, that he was forcing her to use up her own mana to keep his sorry ass alive, but he just couldn't bring himself to bind a woman, any woman, to him. Maybe it was stupid, but he didn't want to betray his feelings for Lilith.

He didn't want to betray the woman who had saved him and his younger brother from their own personal hell.

***

Anthony looked at the moon as he stood outside of the hospital. A full moon was out that night. The sky should have been dotted with stars, but the pollution and lights from the city blocked out almost everything. While a lot of the pollution had been clearing up thanks to new innovations in technology that relied on mana instead of fossil fuels, it didn't change how humanity had been screwing up this world for hundreds of years.

He'd just finished visiting his younger brother, but nothing particular or special had happened. His brother was the same as always.

Anthony turned on his heel and began walking toward the nearest maglev station. It was late, but the station should still be open for another half an hour.

As he was walking along, a strange sensation came over him, like eyes were drilling holes into his back. Anthony was used to this feeling. Normally. The eyes he felt on him right now were different. They weren't at all like the angry glares of men who felt like he was threatening their territory. A trace of killing intent caused a shiver to run down his back.

He turned around and looked left, then right. He didn't see anyone. However, when he looked up, Anthony discovered a dark figure standing on a building next to him. He couldn't see who they were because all he noticed was a dark silhouette, but it looked like they were carrying something long in their right hand.

"What the—who are you?!" he shouted.

The figure said nothing as they leapt from the building and fell toward him like an avenging angel. As the light from street signs played off their body, Anthony finally caught a good glimpse of the person flying toward him.

It was a woman. She was more of a girl really. Her red hair was long and looked like streamers of fire as each strand whipped through the hair behind her head. Vibrant blue eyes were narrowed in concentration and determination. Her voluptuous body was clad in a tight black suit with glowing blue lines. Mana was running through that suit. As she descended toward Anthony, she spun the object in her hand around, and he finally saw it for what it was.

A double-bladed sword.

"Holy—!"

Anthony didn't have much time, so he used what time he did have to activate Physical Enhancement and leap back. Blue lines of power similar to the ones on this woman's suit appeared on his body. With his strength enhanced, he was able to leap far enough back to avoid her attack. The blade in her hand slashed into the ground, cutting straight through it and leaving a perfectly straight line with smooth edges in the road. He grimaced. If he'd been cut with that, his body would have been split in half.

"Tch. I can't believe you dodged that," the woman finally muttered, and she sounded… young. Actually, she looked to be about his age or maybe even younger. She wasn't that tall, and while she did have an impressive figure, her face was youthful, with full cheeks and a smooth chin.

"Who are you?!" Anthony demanded. "Why are you attacking me?!"

"You don't need to know my name," the woman said as she spun her double-bladed sword around and adopted a fighting stance. "All you need to know is that I'm here to kill you, Incubus!"

Anthony's blood ran cold as the woman finished speaking. She had called him an Incubus. However…

"No one should know about that except Professor Incanscino and a few others," Anthony said. "How do you know what I am?"

The woman scoffed at him. "I don't need to tell you anything. Now hurry up and die!"

As the woman rushed forward, Anthony realized that trying to talk his way out of this was pointless, so he assumed a fighting stance and got ready.

The woman was on him in an instant. She swung her sword around, attacking him with one of its blades. He jumped back, but then she spun the sword and thrust the other blade out, and Anthony nearly found himself impaled through the chest, though he managed to avoid it at the last moment by stumbling left. Even so, he nearly lost his balance, which gave her the opportunity to attack again.

As the woman launched more attacks at him, Anthony found his eyes drawn to her sword. There were several symbols etched onto the surface that he recognized as a magical formula. Each formula resembled runes he'd seen in some of the ebooks he read. They glowed a vibrant blue.

It looked like this weapon was using mana to increase its cutting power. He didn't know what sort of magical principles it relied on, though. He wondered if it was similar to a surgical knife that used magic to sever the bonds between molecules. If that was the case, then getting cut with that would slice him open with ease.

"Ha… ha…"

Anthony's breathing became heavy as he evaded this woman's attacks. A dull throb appeared in his chest. Sweat covered his face. Meanwhile, his attacker wasn't having any troubles at all. Her breathing was even, her expression composed, and her arms apparently incapable of tiring even as she swung that massive weapon around her body like a gymnast twirling around a baton.

Pressing his back against a wall, Anthony thought fast before rolling across the ground as the woman swung her sword. He skipped back to his feet and gawked when he saw how her weapon had cut through the wall like it was nothing. These walls were made of a composite material that was resistant to flames, electric, and physical damage. Even an explosion wouldn't break these walls. That her sword did proved it was no ordinary weapon.

I can't afford to let that cut me even once!

"I don't suppose… we can talk about this…?" Anthony asked as he gasped for breath.

The woman frowned at him like he'd said something stupid. "There's nothing to talk about. I'm here to kill you."

"Right… I figured as much." Anthony backed away. "In that case…"

Turning on his heel, Anthony bolted down the street, dove through an alley, and emerged on another street. He raced across the road, toward the maglev station. His attacker had attacked when he was alone. That meant she didn't want any witnesses. If he could just get to the maglev station, he should be safe.

Those were his thoughts when sirens blared inside of his head. Instinct kicked in and Anthony stopped running and leapt to his right, and it was a very good thing he did because the woman he'd tried to leave behind landed in the spot he'd been standing. She bent her knees and crouched low. One end of her sword was impaled into the ground all the way up to the long handle, though it slid out easily as she stood up and glared at him.

"Coward. Do not run away and face your death with dignity!"

"If it means staying alive, concepts like dignity and honor can kiss my ass."

The woman didn't take kindly to his words as she leapt forward and swiped at him with her weapon. Anthony bent his body to avoid it, but then she planted a foot on the ground, spun around, and slammed her other foot into his chest. He gasped in asphyxiated agony as her heel crashed against his ribs. It felt like a freight maglev had rammed into him. If he hadn't been reinforcing his body with mana, that would have snapped his ribcage like it was made of toothpicks!

Anthony wasn't even given time to recover as the woman came at him again, her sword appearing as mere flashes of light and streaks of silver. Despite being clearly outclassed, Anthony tenaciously hung on as he shuffled along the ground, avoiding her attacks by the barest of margins. A swing sliced several strands of hair off his head. Another one cut open his cheek. As blood ran down his pale skin, Anthony bit his lip as he realized he might actually have to use most of the mana he had recovered.

Professor Incanscino was going to be so pissed off.

Leaping back several times, Anthony raised a fist into the air and channeled the mana he possessed into it, causing his fist to emit a bright blue glow. The woman's eyes widened as he brought the fist down. She tried to reach him, but he slammed his fist into the ground before she could.

The road erupted in front of Anthony. It was like a self-contained earthquake. Large chunks of upturned road broke into fragments as a massive chasm opened between him and his attacker. The woman stumbled at the unexpected maneuver, which caused the ground to shake and forced her to stop running so she wouldn't fall.

Anthony felt his vision dim as the lack of mana running through him caused his body to begin shutting down. He had saved a bit to keep his body functioning properly. However, he'd been forced to use almost everything he had in that last attack.

Despite how tired he felt, how sluggish his body now was, Anthony stumbled to his feet, turned around, and began running again. He raced all the way to the maglev station, not daring to look back. There were several people present when he arrived.

This included a security guard, which caused him to sigh in relief. But he didn't stop, not for anything, not even for the security guard asking if he was okay, and made his way toward the platform and hopped onto the next maglev.

As the door shut behind him, he pressed his back against it and slid down until he was on his butt, gasping for breath as sweat ran down his face.

His destination was no longer home.

He needed to see Professor Incanscino.

CHAPTER 2

Lucretia Incanscino had come home late and too hyped to sleep. Mana coursed through her body as she sat on a couch in her large office, which also seconded as a living room and entrance hall. She stared at the massive window that spanned nearly the entire wall on her left. It offered a great view of Academy Island, showing the millions of blinking lights from buildings, cars, and signs. She could even see a massive holoscreen—one of several dozen—located throughout the city, which constantly reported on various happenings around the world.

Holding an expensive teacup with both hands, she raised the cup to her lips and took a gentle sip of the warm liquid within. It wasn't tea. It was coffee. While the caffeine would keep most normal people up all night, she was currently using it to soothe her frazzled nerves. All the work she'd been forced to do had really done a number on her.

"Damn lazy bums. Can the Academy Island Private Security Forces not do anything without me?"

Just as she was bringing the cup back down to rest on a small plate, a loud bell echoed throughout her residence, causing Lucretia to furrow her brown. Who could be coming at this late hour? How did they even get through the school's door? The Institution of Magical Sciences was closed right now. She set the cup on the expensive glass table in front of her, stood up, and wandered to the front door.

Like all the other doors in her residence, the front door was not an automatic one. It was a wooden door made of bocote. She'd had this double door along with all the others installed after moving into this place. Lucretia didn't care for the automatic doors. They were just too inelegant.

She opened the door and nearly leapt back in shock when a body fell through and landed on the ground with a dull thud. Lucretia blinked several times as she stared at the body. It wasn't long before she recognized who it was.

"Anthony!"

Shock coursed through her body as she studied the young man, whose pale and clammy skin was covered in sweat. His breathing was labored, coming out in thick gasps, as if he was suffocating but doing his best to intake oxygen despite that.

Her left eye began glowing crimson as a small magic circle appeared within it. She blinked once as his body suddenly became invisible and glowing blue lines appeared within his body like veins. Aside from the veins, there were also seven small orbs, but they were all gray like stone. As she studied his magic circuits, a shudder ran through her.

"Mana Depletion," she muttered with a scowl.

There wasn't much time. She could already see that the remaining mana within his body was leaving him. If she didn't help him in the next few minutes, it was very likely that he would die.

"Damn it… Anthony… you are such a pain in the ass."

Lucretia tapped her foot against the ground, creating a glowing blue magic circle underneath Anthony's body. The circle faded as the glow from the mana encased Anthony. Soon, the young man was being lifted into the air by a seemingly invisible force. With a huff, Lucretia walked out of the long hallway and toward the ritual room, the floating and unconscious figure following after her.

Her ritual room where she performed the magic ritual to replenish Anthony's mana was already prepared. The large-scale magic circle on the floor was an impressive work of art she had spent nearly a month creating. Lucretia normally didn't use such arcane methods of magic like old-school magical rituals, but for something like this, modern magic simply didn't work.

She set Anthony in the middle of the magic circle and sighed. Cracking her back several times, Lucretia knelt before the young man, closed her eyes, and concentrated as she put her hands above him. Mana flowed through her fingertips and into his body. Images flashed past her. She saw Anthony waking up, taking a shower, and getting dressed. She paused after he put on his pants and shirt, then waved her hand, removing his shirt by singling out the moment in time when he put it on and making it so that event never happened in the first place.

The shirt vanished.

For just a moment, Lucretia gazed at Anthony's emaciated body, at the ribs visible beneath his skin, and his rail thin arms and legs. Her chest ached. It pained her to see someone like this, but no matter how many times she had suggested Anthony build himself a harem, the boy refused. His loyalty to Lilith was indeed admirable, but it came at a cost so great she was sure Lilith would have smacked him over the head for his stupidity.

Now that Anthony was topless, it was time to begin the ritual. She placed her hands on his chest, closed her eyes once more, and began channeling mana into her magic ritual.

"I hope you appreciate what I am doing," Lucretia muttered in a strained voice. "Reversing the flow of time like this is not easy."

Of course, Anthony didn't answer her.

Not that she had expected one.

Anthony opened his eyes as rays of morning light shone into them. He blinked several times and felt out his surroundings, groping around with his hands, wondering where he was and how he'd gotten there. The soft mattress underneath him was not his. It was too soft, too comfortable. Also, the white ceiling above his head was not the worn out ceiling of his apartment.

Sitting up, Anthony took in the room, gazing at the large chamber that was furnished with expensive furniture. The dresser immediately in front of him was an example of classic furnishings. It was something he would expect to see from the renaissance period. Likewise, the desk, coffee table, couches, and armoire were all furnishings that had a classic aesthetic and looked more expensive than his entire apartment.

"Where…" Anthony shook his head. "Is this Professor Incanscino's place?"

Last night, Anthony had run from a woman who was trying to kill him and took a maglev that went all the way to his college in an attempt to reach the professor. However, he had blacked out at some point. There was a large blank space within his memories. He remembered hopping on the maglev, getting off, and nothing after that.

Anthony stood up and realized he was shirtless but not pantless, which he guessed was a good thing. He'd be worried if he woke up without his pants. That said, he couldn't find his shirt anywhere even as he looked around. He wondered what happened to it, but… well, he was more interested in figuring out where he was than what happened to his shirt.

There was no clothing within the dresser or armoire. Anthony ended up leaving the room shirtless. The chilly air hit his body, causing his skin to break out in goosebumps.

He ended up in a hallway that was actually vaguely familiar. He didn't recognize this particular hall, but he knew the style from the times he went to see Professor Incanscino. Now that he realized he truly was at her residence, had somehow made it safely to where she lived, a sigh of relief involuntarily left his mouth as he began walking down the hall, which eventually revealed the sweeping staircase that led down to the professor's office.

Professor Incanscino was sitting behind her desk when he wandered down the stairs. She was reading something from her holographic monitor, but she glanced at him when he stepped onto the tiled floor and wandered over to her desk.

"You're finally awake," she said in a dry voice. "I was wondering how long you planned on sleeping."

"Thank you for saving me last night," Anthony said.

"You missed your first class of the day," the professor continued as if she hadn't heard him. "Professor Callahan was most aggrieved by this. Don't worry, though. I called in for you and let him know you had an emergency situation and would be indisposed."

"Um… thank you," Anthony said again.

With a flick of her hand, Professor Incanscino shut off the holographic screen on her desk, then fully turned to face him. She placed her hands on the wooden surface and stared. It was a stare that made Anthony rather uncomfortable, and he soon looked away and focused on the view outside the window.

"Tell me what happened last night."

It was not a request.

Anthony sighed but nodded. "Last night… I was on my way home from the hospital when someone attacked me. I don't know who she was. She wielded a double-bladed sword that had some kind of magic attached to it. Her weapon could cut through anything, even buildings, with ease. I tried fighting her for a while, but she was clearly stronger than me, so I used the remaining mana I had to create a distraction and run."

"And then you came here," Professor Incanscino concluded with a nod. Anthony shrugged and gave her a half-smile, causing the woman to sigh. "Well, you made the right choice to come here. Had you gone home, you'd probably be dead by now. You were suffering from Mana Depletion." She gave him a firm stare. "You realize you cannot afford to be so reckless with your mana, right? If you were just a regular human, Mana Depletion would not be a big deal. You'd eventually replenish it on your own. But you aren't human anymore. You are an incubus. Supernatural beings such as yourself need mana to live. Without it, you would die."

"I am aware of that," Anthony said defensively.

"If you're aware of that, then try to be more careful from now on," Professor Incanscino rebutted.

Anthony nodded before asking, "Do you have any idea who attacked me or why? She called me an incubus, so she knew what I was, but nobody except you should be aware of this, right?"

"That isn't necessarily true," Professor Incanscino admitted. "You realize that on top of working as a college professor, I also work for the Academy Island Private Security Forces, right? Do you honestly think I could allow you to live on Academy Island without them knowing what you are? At the very least, the top brass working for Academy Island, the Board of Governors, are aware of your identity. The only reason you haven't been detained is because I told them I was going to watch over you."

He had actually not been aware of this at all. As he stared at the woman, who all but admitted she had stuck her neck out to let him live a relatively normal life, warmth suffused his heart. His eyes softened.

Professor Incanscino must have noticed this because she looked away.

"Thank you," he said, his voice thick with emotion.

"You shouldn't thank me." The small woman dismissed his thanks with an irritated wave of her hand. "I only helped you because I owe Lilith a great debt and this was the only way I could repay her. I didn't do it for you."

"That's all the more reason I should thank you." Anthony shrugged.

"Tch. Cheeky brat." A soft pinkish hue sprang to the woman's cheeks, but she quickly mastered it by coughing into her hand and returning to what they had been talking about before. "As for that woman who attacked you… I cannot be sure because I haven't seen her for myself, but just from the description you gave me, I believe she is a War Maiden working for Custodes Daemonium."

Anthony let out a slow breath after hearing her words. He closed his eyes to calm his racing heart. It felt like it was slamming into his chest. At this rate, it might even burst out of his ribcage!

"So I have an international organization whose purpose is impeding large-scale Magic Catastrophes and magical terrorism after me?" He let out a hollow laugh. "That's not funny at all."

Professor Incanscino shrugged. "Considering what you are, I believe that organization has come to the conclusion that you are a walking, talking, large-scale magical disaster. It wouldn't surprise me if they've already ranked you as an S-class Magic Catastrophe. There have been cases of other incubus appearing throughout history, you know? And each time one has appeared, disaster has inevitably followed. It would not surprise me if they believe the same thing that's happened in the past will happen again, so they've decided to take a proactive stance and take care of you before that can happen."

Anthony would have grimaced, but he felt like he'd been doing that a lot lately, so he refrained. Even so, the idea that an organization as massive as Custodes Daemonium was trying to kill him did not invoke pleasant feelings.

What made this whole situation worse was that he'd never done anything to warrant being attacked—unless someone took what happened during the battle against the Vampire Warlord Cane into consideration. However, the battle against Cane had been mostly Lilith's doing and not his own. His contribution at the time wouldn't be enough to warrant ranking him as an S-class Magic Catastrophe.

As these thoughts raced through his mind, a loud gurgling erupted from Anthony's stomach. He looked at Professor Incanscino and blushed.

"Go get something to eat," the small woman said with a sigh. "Also, I had someone fetch a spare shirt for you. It should be in the bathing room. Take a shower, get some food, and I'll see you in class."

With a meek nod, Anthony turned around and went back up the stairs. However, just as he reached the top, he realized something, went back downstairs, and stopped in front of Professor Incanscino's desk. His cheeks were hot.

"Um… where is the bathroom?" he asked, rubbing the back of his neck.

✳✳✳

Anthony was sitting in a small coffee shop later in the afternoon, his laptop turned on. The holographic screen in front of him displayed page upon page of words, which he added more to by typing away on his keyboard, writing up a report for one of his classes. His eyes felt tired. He had to blink several times when they threatened to sag shut. He wondered if this was because he'd suffered Mana Depletion, but it could also just be due to how he'd been staring at this screen for the past hour.

The coffee shop was fairly busy. He wasn't the only college student sitting at a table, typing away on a laptop. In front of him were a pair of girls doing the same thing he was. It looked like they were trading notes, or perhaps reading each other's essays and offering pointers. Behind him was a man who was using a sleek tablet to read something. It was an older model and didn't have a holographic projector, but those were fairly popular because it meant no one could read over your shoulder without you knowing. Holographic monitors like his could be viewed from both sides.

A cup of coffee sat in front of him, though Anthony hadn't touched it in the past fifteen minutes. It was probably cold by now.

As he kept working, the door opened and a woman walked in. He recognized the dark curly hair, nearly black eyes, and cute face. The woman had a small nose, which wiggled slightly as the scent of coffee beans hit it. After looking around for a moment, she spotted him, smiled, and made a beeline in his direction.

Anthony found himself only slightly distracted by the swishing of her skirt. It was high enough that a spirited twirl would probably reveal her panties.

"Anthony, sorry I'm late," she said.

He shrugged as Secilia sat down across from him. "Don't worry about it. I'm guessing your engineering class kept you busy, or was it your work?"

"School this time," Secilia replied with a smile. "Work has been kind of slow lately. I haven't actually had much to do on that front."

Anthony nodded but didn't inquire further. He actually didn't know what she did for work. There was a time when he had asked her once, but Secilia had replied with a vague answer about how she did this and that. Literally this and that, as if using those words in conjunction somehow explained everything they needed to. He assumed she worked for a company that built magical appliances since she was in the magical engineering department. However, he only assumed as much because of the degree she was attending college for.

"Alex not with you?" asked Anthony.

Secilia scowled a bit, then shook her head. "He was called into work."

"Ah."

"Right. So, anyway, what are you working on?"

"A report for my Magical Maladies class," Anthony said as he stared at his currently five-page long essay. "I have to write a ten page essay on the different types of mana poisoning and how to treat them when you aren't anywhere near a hospital."

"Sounds like some tricky stuff." Secilia placed her elbows onto the table and propped her chin onto her hands. "You know our research team recently tried to invent a device that could cure Sanguinitis?"

"I did not know that," Anthony said.

"It was supposed to be a compact device that people could take with them when they traveled," Secilia continued. A somewhat sarcastic smile crossed her face. "However, curing Sanguitis is no simple task, and the devices used in hospitals are all large enough to fill a walk-in closet. There are a lot of parts needed to build such a device, and so it's impossible to make something smaller with our current level of technology."

Sanguinitis was something his professor for Magical Maladies had lectured them on before, so he was well-aware of the equipment needed to cure it. He'd even toured a medical facility where they showed off the different equipment used in hospitals, and the large, tank-like device had been one of those objects they showed.

"Sanguinitis is classified as a potentially deadly magical malady," Anthony said. "It requires the use of a tank because you can't cure it without curatio gel, which has the effect of cleansing the body of magical impurities and can even remove excess mana from the bloodstream. To create a compact device that can cure Sanguinitis, you'd need to either find something that can replace curatio gel or maybe turn it into a spray that can be applied to the skin, but there's a problem with that…"

"A spray wouldn't work because curatio gel becomes contaminated the moment it's placed in an open atmosphere." Secilia nodded. "Yes, that's exactly the problem we've been having. There currently isn't a replacement for curatio gel, and we have no way of applying it to the affected areas without subjecting it to contaminants from the atmosphere. It also requires a special container. Of course, we can make a small container that can contain the curatio gel, but we can't actually use it for anything because of the aforementioned reasons."

Anthony spoke with Secilia for almost an hour as he worked on his essay, which he was actually able to complete thanks to some ideas his friend gave him. After they finished talking, he bade her goodbye and traveled to his next class. He only had two more that day.

Classes ended in the late afternoon. When they were finished, Anthony hopped onto a maglev that took him to a station close to the Academy Island Hospital for Magical Catastrophes. It was the same station he'd scrambled through after his fight against that woman. As he hopped off, he glanced at the afternoon sun before making his way toward the hospital.

It looked like the area where he fought that woman was being repaired. Holographic caution signs had been placed around the damaged area, workers were moving about inside of it, and some large-scale construction equipment was being used. It looked like they were clearing away the cracked street and replacing it.

He was about to continue on but paused when he felt eyes lock onto him.

Turning around, Anthony saw the woman who had attacked him walking several yards behind him. She was no longer dressed in a skintight black suit… or so it seemed. He assumed she was wearing it underneath her current outfit, a simple white skirt, a white shirt, and a red blazer that matched her hair. The shirt looked a little loose around her waist, but it stretched across her chest, which just went to show how large those two melons hanging off her were. He wondered what bra size she wore. He didn't see her double-bladed sword, but she had a music case strapped across her back, so her weapon was probably hidden in there.

When the woman saw him staring, her eyes widened and she froze. It looked like she was about to duck behind a building or maybe hide in one of the stores, but she seemed to realize how pointless that would be now that he had seen her, and so, after a moment of indecision, she simply turned her head.

Anthony frowned but kept walking. As he did, the woman followed him. He took a turn down a street. She took the same turn. He walked into a store. She walked into the store seconds later. This woman wasn't even trying to hide the fact that she was following him now that she'd been caught.

For a moment, Anthony wondered why she was following him around in broad daylight. Her job was to assassinate him, wasn't it? If so, wouldn't it be more prudent to wait until nightfall and attack him again like she'd done the night before? Such thoughts only lasted for a moment before he sighed and walked over to the woman.

The woman froze when he stopped in front of her. She warily eyed him like he was a rabid beast she needed to put down, which only caused him to sigh again.

"If you're going to follow me, you might as well just walk with me," he said.

She twitched. "Why would you let me walk beside you when you know I'm trying to kill you?"

Anthony shrugged. "Since I know you're trying to kill me, isn't it a better idea if I have you close by where I can keep an eye on you? Haven't you ever heard the saying 'keep your friends close and your enemies closer'?"

"I have heard that saying, but it doesn't mean much in this instance." Her eyes narrowed. "You're pretty weak. I could easily kill you right now, and you wouldn't be able to do a thing about it."

"True, but you are currently in a public place, in broad daylight, and there are several thousand witnesses all around you. Custodes Daemonium might be an international organization that defends people against Magic Catastrophes and magical terrorism, but even you guys can't kill someone in broad daylight when they haven't done anything wrong."

"Who told you I was from Custodes Daemonium?" asked the woman, her body stiffening as she leapt back. She slid her left foot forward, dropped her music case into her right hand, and glared at him as she reached for the latches like she was going to open it and pull something out.

"Who told me that you're a War Maiden for Custodes Daemonium?" Anthony chuckled a bit. A sly smile appeared on his face. "Let's just say I know some people who are knowledgeable about you and your organization. Don't forget where you are. This is Academy Island. There are a lot of powerful people and companies who have made this place their home, and it isn't under the jurisdiction of any government." The woman said nothing, which caused him to shrug and turn around.

"Anyway, if you want to follow me, be sure to stick close. I'm visiting the hospital again."

The woman didn't respond to him at first, didn't even move, but she eventually rushed to catch up to him and walked by his side.

Anthony glanced at the woman in profile as they walked. Now that she wasn't attacking him and the sun was out, he could see that she was a rather extraordinary young woman. Her hair really did remind him of fire as it caught the sunlight and blew behind her back like streamers in the wind. The vibrant glow of her blue eyes appeared a bit duller than last night, but he assumed she'd been using mana to enhance her vision. She had pale skin the color of pure snow, with a few cute freckles dotting her small nose, delicate pink lips, and a soft face that made her seem younger than he believed she was.

"What are you looking at?" the woman asked with a scowl.

"You," Anthony stated bluntly, causing her to blush. He smiled. "I was just wondering what I should call you. Do you have a name? Or should I keep calling you assassin?"

She didn't speak at first, but after a moment, she said, "Brianna. You can call me Brianna."

"No last name?" asked Anthony.

Brianna shook her head. "I do not have one."

Anthony nodded as they turned a corner, moved aside to avoid several people walking in the opposite direction, and then merged together again. They walked shoulder to shoulder for a time before he spoke once more.

"I've heard most War Maidens of Custodes Daemonium are orphans they picked up." He glanced at her out of the corner of his eye. "Is it the same with you?"

"You're asking some awfully personal questions." Brianna frowned at him. "What makes you think I'm going to answer you?"

"I'm just trying to make conversation," Anthony said.

"Getting to know your enemy?"

"Sure. Let's go with that."

Their conversation stopped after that, but it didn't matter because they had reached Academy Island Hospital for Magical Catastrophes. While Brianna looked up and read the sign, Anthony walked straight through the automatic doors, which led into a large waiting room with chairs, tables, and even a place for children to play, though no one was using it right now. There were a few people sitting in the chairs, but Anthony ignored them as he walked up to the front desk.

"Afternoon, Clarissa," Anthony said to the woman who sat behind the desk. She was moderately pretty, with dark brown hair drawn into a bun near the top of her head, dark skin, and violet eyes. Her eyes contained a glow that couldn't be found on a human, and when she smiled, Anthony noticed her sharp fangs.

"Anthony, here to see your brother again?"

"Of course."

"You've come here every day for the last year since he was admitted here. That's very admirable of you." As she spoke, Clarissa turned to look at Brianna, raised a single eyebrow, and looked back at him with a sly smile. "Are you planning to introduce your brother to your new girlfriend?"

"That's an awfully funny joke," Anthony said without laughing. "This is just a friend I made at school. Her name is Brianna. No last name apparently. I'm hoping that maybe having someone new around will cause him to react."

Clarissa's smile turned sad. Meanwhile, Brianna was giving Anthony a strange look, making him wonder if she was upset about his lie or if she was staring at him for another reason. He did his best to ignore it either way.

"Okay." Clarissa typed on her computer, then glanced at him. "I've added you to our visitors list, so you and your friend are free to visit your brother. I hope…" Clarissa hesitated for a moment before continuing. "I hope your brother has a positive reaction toward your friend."

"Me too," Anthony said as he turned around and walked away from the desk. After a moment of standing there in indecision, Brianna followed him.

"What was that about? Your brother is in this hospital?" asked Brianna as they walked down a white hall. There were several men and women in lab coats walking down it as well. Some of them carried a strong scent of anti-sceptics that made Anthony's nose wrinkle.

Anthony nodded. "My brother has been here since we first came to Academy Island."

"For what? Is he sick?"

"In a manner of speaking."

Anthony didn't say anymore on the subject, and while it was clear from the expression on her face that she wanted to ask, Brianna stopped talking too. She would learn about it soon anyway when she saw his brother.

They took an elevator to the third floor, which was emptier than the first. The third floor was dedicated to more serious injuries and incurable diseases. Since there weren't as many people suffering from this kind of problem, there were less doctors present, though that did make the halls feel a lot more empty.

Anthony led Brianna to a room numbered 343, which opened when he stepped in front of it. He walked inside. The room that spread out before him was not big, about the same size as the bedroom in his apartment, but it was a lot nicer than his room. There wasn't much furniture, but it did contain several potted plants that added color to the room, a window on the far side, and a bed with three padded chairs next to it.

The bed was not a typical bed. It looked more like a giant cryotube with a bed placed inside of it. Medical equipment was hooked up to the bed, including a heart rate monitor, a mana meter that showed fluctuations in a person's mana levels, and an oxygen tank. The oxygen tank had a long clear tube that traveled from it to the cryotube. A soft whirring sound emitted from it, mixing with the beeps and thrum from the other equipment.

Lying on the bed was a boy several years younger than Anthony, with similar pale skin and facial features, though the boy's face was a lot fuller than his own. His eyes were closed. He wore a patience smock. As Anthony walked over to one of the chairs and sat down, he saw that the young boy's chest rose and fell at even intervals. He supposed the fact that his brother was still breathing was a good sign.

"Hey, Calvin," Anthony said with a soft smile. "It looks like you haven't changed since the last time I saw you. Still… still sleeping. I've got quite the story to share with you today. You won't believe what happened to me the other night after I left the hospital."

As Anthony regaled his younger brother with the tale of how Brianna had attacked him, the woman in question sat down in one of the chairs, though she sat with a chair between her and Anthony. She looked at his younger brother for a moment. Then she looked at him. Her expression was… odd. He couldn't quite figure out what kind of expression she was making, but then she looked away before he could observe her further.

Anthony didn't just tell Calvin about Brianna's attack on him. He also told the younger boy about what he learned in college that day, his essay on magical maladies and how to treat them, and his conversation with Secilia. Brianna had perked up at the mention of his friend. However, she didn't say anything about it.

"I didn't realize incubus could have brothers," she said when he finished speaking.

"Why is that so surprising?" asked Anthony.

"Because everyone knows that incubus are destruction incarnate." Brianna crossed her arms. It had the effect of pushing out her breasts, but Anthony tried not to think about that. "Incidents involving incubus have been well-documented by Custodes Daemonium. Incubus do not have relatives. They arrive in our world through unknown means, create a Magic Catastrophe so destructive it doesn't even have a ranking, and then disappear as if they were a ghost. The only thing we know about incubus is that, aside from being considered one of the most magically powerful creatures in existence, they always have a harem of equally powerful women by their side."

Everything Brianna said lined up with what he knew about incubus as well, which he learned from Professor Incanscino. It didn't surprise him that Custodes Daemonium had information on incubus. He couldn't remember when that organization had been formed, but he believed they were first created sometime in the late 15th or 16th century.

"I can't say anything about other incubus, but I wasn't born this way." Anthony rubbed the back of his neck as he talked. "I was actually born human."

Brianna narrowed her eyes. "You're lying."

"I'm not."

"Humans cannot turn into magical creatures on their own," Brianna lectured him with a stern frown. "They can only do so with the help of a powerful demon. Vampires for example. A vampire can turn a human into a ghoul or even another vampire if they so choose. However, vampires are one of the few creatures in the entire world that have this power—and they can't turn humans into incubus."

"I didn't say anything about a vampire doing this to me." Anthony was silent for a moment as he shifted his gaze to Calvin. "Me and my brother… we grew up in a war-torn part of the Americas. Our parents died when we were young, so I did my best to fend for us both, scavenging for food, fighting off demons and humans alike. One day, we were attacked by a powerful vampire and his gang. We would have died that day if Lilith hadn't saved us."

"Lilith?!" Brianna squawked as her eyes grew so wide and round they looked like they might pop out of her head. "You know Lilith?! The Lilith?! One of the Four Succubus Queens?! The Queen of Accadia?! The most powerful Succubus in the entire world?!"

"Yes," Anthony said simply. "She rescued me and my brother from the vampire, and then made me her bondmate at my request." Brianna sucked in a breath. "I became a part of her harem. Me and my brother began traveling alongside Lilith and her harem. Since you seem to know about Lilith, I'm guessing you know about her harem?"

"I-I do." Brianna took a shaky breath and composed herself. "If I'm not mistaken, Lilith had thirteen bondmates in her harem. It's recorded as the highest number of bondmates any succubus has ever had. No other succubus, not even the other three queens, have that many bondmates."

"You certainly know your stuff," Anthony said with an approving nod. "Yes, Lilith had thirteen bondmates in her harem, and I was one of them. The last one, in fact. It was... odd, but strangely satisfying. I was part of a group, and all of them treated me and my brother well, just like we were a member of their family. Well, Dominique kind of hated me, but he was an ass and hated everyone anyway. In either event, we all got along well, and I had a great time, but..." He sighed. "I'm sure you know our time together didn't last."

"The Lilith Incident," Brianna said with a nod.

"Right. The Lilith Incident." Anthony leaned back and placed his hands on his knees, clenching them into fists. "We were attacked by Cane. I'm not sure what he wanted. I think he was in love with Lilith and wanted her for himself, but I don't really know. In either event, Cane attacked Lilith and we fought back. The battle was... devastating."

Anthony closed his eyes as visions filled his mind. The scent of smoke, the sight of mana leaking everywhere, of spells flying all around, and of the haunting laughter of Cane as he slaughtered his way through Lilith's bondmates like they were simple flesh and he was a laser scalpel caused him to shudder. Even now, he sometimes had nightmares about that battle.

"I won't go into too much detail, but at the very end of the battle, Lilith had managed to successfully defeat Cane by creating that black hole everyone likes to talk about."

"But wasn't that black hole caused by..." Brianna trailed off when Anthony shook his head.

"It wasn't caused by the backlash of their magic clashing like everyone else believes," Anthony said. "Lilith created that black hole and sucked Cane inside." He frowned for a moment. "That black hole is one of Lilith's special attacks. It's her trump card, if you will. It should have disappeared after it ran out of mana, but it hasn't gone away for some reason. I'm not sure why."

Brianna frowned at him, but Anthony had no answer he could provide. The power Lilith had used to defeat Cane was one of her most powerful magics. It was also the magic she had acquired after bonding with him. He wondered if he could use that magic now that he was an incubus, but he dared not try it since that sort of magic consumed too much mana.

"In either event, despite managing to defeat Cane, I was mortally wounded during the battle. I don't quite remember exactly what happened. Everything was so blurry I could barely see straight, but I remember Lilith holding me close to her. She said something to me, and then kissed me. I blacked out after that." Anthony took in a deep breath, ignoring the scent of antiseptics as he tried to recall that time. "When I woke up, I was in a hospital, my brother was in a magical coma, and I was no longer human." He paused, then continued in a much softer voice as he stared at Brianna. "I don't know what Lilith did to me, but I'm almost certain I became an incubus because she gave her life in exchange for mine."

No more words were spoken in that hospital room. The silence stretched on, the sky darkened, and Anthony decided it was time to leave. He'd been there long enough.

Brianna followed him out of the hospital without complaint. It was dark out. Well, the sun was down. It was still fairly bright because of all the city lights, but there weren't many people roaming the street at this time. The two of them walked along in silence for a while as they made their way to the maglev station. As they did, Brianna finally asked him a question.

"I learned earlier today that you attend college," she began. "Is the reason because of your brother? I noticed his mana fluctuations had flatlined, yet his heart rate was normal."

"You catch on quick." Anthony released a deep breath, then smiled. "Yeah. My brother is in some kind of a magical coma, though it's a bit more complicated than that. None of the doctors have been able to figure out what's wrong with him. His brain activity is fine. His heart rate is normal. All of his vitals are functioning as they should. However, he has absolutely no mana inside of him according to the scans. Every living being generates mana, so it shouldn't be possible for him to have none, unless…"

"Unless he was dead," Brianna said.

"Bingo."

They continued on, and Anthony could now see the maglev station up ahead. He glanced at Brianna again. Was she planning to follow him home?

"I promised myself that I would cure Calvin no matter the cost," Anthony continued. "That is why I won't let you kill me."

Brianna said nothing, but the look in her wide eyes, which glimmered like binary stars, said more than enough.

***

It had been a late night at the engineering department and Secilia was just now on her way home. She sat on the maglev's bench and stared at the station as it came into view, her mind wandering all over the place. She wondered what Anthony was doing. Probably visiting his brother. That was what he always did after school. A sigh escaped her lips. Maybe it was wrong, but she was quite jealous of that comatose younger brother of his.

Her thoughts scattered as the maglev pulled into the station and slowed to a stop, vibrating only slightly as the magnetic clamps attached to the tracks. The doors slid open. Secilia stood up and made her way outside along with a few other late night stragglers getting home from either a day of work or a night of drinking.

She stepped onto the maglev station. The maglev began moving again as she walked away. Just as she was about to leave the station, she turned back to look at the maglev as it left—and then she froze. Her eyes widened. It was only for an instant, but in that single second, she could have sworn she saw Anthony standing by the window. That wouldn't have been an issue since he usually took this maglev because it stopped at a station near his house. However, something about this time was different.

Someone was with him.

"Who is that girl?" Secilia asked herself as a soft breeze blew her hair.

Unfortunately, there was no one who could answer her.

CHAPTER 3

Beep! Beep! Beep! Bee—

Anthony slammed his hand onto the alarm clock, shutting the blasted thing off before sitting up in bed and stretching out his arms. He groaned when his bones popped. After making sure all the stiffness was worked out of his limbs, Anthony stumbled out of bed and into the shower.

As he stood under the hot spray of water, he recalled the events of last night, how Brianna had not killed him even though she had the perfect opportunity, and how they had parted ways with her saying she needed some time to think and would likely come back soon. He rested his forehead against the warm tiles as fog swirled around him. Tiny drops of water pelted his back. It felt nice and helped him think. Anthony didn't know how long or short "soon" was, but he was hoping it meant she would be gone forever.

His heart couldn't handle an assassin trying to kill him.

Anthony got dressed after he finished taking a shower, wandered into his living room, and flipped on the holographic TV before making breakfast. It was another simple packaged meal. This time he was having french toast sticks. He sat on the couch, dipped his french toast sticks into the syrup it came with, and chewed thoughtfully as he watched the news.

"And it looks like there's been another attack committed by rogue demons. This time, the demons attacked another Nametech facility. Many people have speculated that the reason they are attacking Nametech is because they are after the company's prosthetics, though no one knows why they want them. A new rumor cropped up recently that Nametech may be involved in illegal cloning. Of course, this is nothing more than a simple rumor and does not explain why the rogue demons would bother attacking the company's. Once again, the Academy Island Private Security Forces managed to put a stop to the attack before any damage could be done."

"There's been a lot of rogue demon attacks," Anthony mumbled around a mouthful of french toast. "I wonder what all of them are doing here…"

A knock at the door suddenly interrupted Anthony's thoughts. He looked at the gray door with a small frown, wondering who could possibly be knocking on his door at this time of day. Very few people he was acquainted with knew where he lived. In fact, only Professor Incanscino knew where he lived because she had been the one who set him up with this apartment, and he couldn't see her coming to visit him at all. Like at all at all. Since Anthony did not get any guests, not ever, he could not stop suspicion from creeping into his gut.

He stood up, walked over, and paused at the door, frowning as he wondered if he should answer it. Matters were taken out of his hands when, whoever was on the other end, knocked again. Then a somewhat familiar and feminine voice spoke up.

"Anthony? I know you're standing in front of the door. Hurry and open up. I need to speak with you."

Gawking as he heard the voice, Anthony opened the door and stared at the person on the other end. She was wearing jeans that conformed to her long and beautiful legs like a second skin. They were tight and wrapped around her well-developed hips. He noticed the combat boots on her feet. A white shirt stretched across her large chest. The hem was lifted slightly, which meant he could see her black battle suit underneath. She'd thrown a jacket over the ensemble. Her red hair was the same as last night, descending to her back in thick and glossy curls, framing her delicate face with its small nose, soft lips, and vibrant eyes. She still had her music case strapped to her back. It was like she'd never taken it off.

Anthony felt like he'd been hit by a truck.

"What are you doing here? Wait. How did you even know where I live?"

"Isn't that obvious? I followed you here last night." Brianna's answer made him gawk. "Anyway, can you let me in? I need to speak with you regarding several important matters."

Anthony felt a headache coming in, causing his skull to throb as he looked at this woman. He glanced at the time on his wristwatch. It was 9:00am. Glancing from his watch to the woman, he pondered what he should do before sighing.

"Actually, I have to get to school right now," he said. "Do you mind if we talk on the way there?"

Brianna's lips turned into a frown, but then she nodded. "I suppose that is okay, though I'd prefer to speak of this matter in private."

"Thank you," Anthony said.

Brianna stepped back as Anthony turned off his holographic TV and walked outside, sealing the door shut with his wristwatch and traveling down the hallway. The redhead fell in step with him as they made it to the elevator and got inside. Neither of them spoke for a moment, but then he looked at the woman beside him, who was looking straight ahead at the elevator door.

"Have you had any breakfast?" he asked. Brianna didn't say anything, but then her stomach suddenly released a rather ghastly gurgling sound. He chuckled as she blushed beet red. "I guess that answers that question. I'll grab you a bite to eat on the way to the station. We can talk about whatever you wanted on the maglev."

"That's fine."

Brianna was still blushing as she spoke, tilting her head down to look at the floor as she twiddled her fingers. It was an unnaturally cute gesture that he didn't expect from a woman who had nearly killed him two nights ago.

There were a lot of convenience stores on the way to the station. In this day and age where convenience and the ability to get something quickly and without hassle was of paramount importance, these kinds of shops had sprung up all over the place. Some of them were specialty shops. They sold specific products. However, most of them were shops that sold just about everything: clothes, food, supplies, and even digital books that could be downloaded to a wristwatch or tablet from each store's library.

They stopped at one of those convenience stores and Anthony let Brianna choose some food for breakfast. There were a lot of options. This store had everything from pancakes to rice balls. It took Brianna nearly ten minutes just to finally end up going with rice balls filled with pickled plum and salmon.

There was no cashier at the register. While there was a clerk on hand to help in case problems arose, all checkouts were automated. Anthony didn't know when this had started becoming the new standard. He couldn't remember the place where he and Calvin grew up having this, but they'd grown up in a war torn part of the Americas, so that could be why.

"Your total is six dollars," an automated female voice said from the register after Brianna scanned the product.

Anthony activated the holographic display on his wristwatch and held it up to a sensor bar. As he did, Brianna's eyes widened.

"I-I can pay for this myself!"

"I'm sure you can, but I've already paid for it."

As he finished speaking, a soft *beep* echoed from the cash register before the female voice spoke up again. "Check out complete. Thank you for shopping with us. Have a nice day."

Anthony grabbed the package of rice balls and held them out to Brianna, whose cheeks swelled at him as she took the rice balls. Her pout was awfully adorable. She looked like a chipmunk with too many acorns stuffed into her mouth.

They left the convenience store and began walking to the station again. Brianna munched on her rice balls as they moved. In keeping with his thoughts of her being a chipmunk, the way she daintily nibbled on the food completely disabused him of the idea that she was an elite War Maiden from an international organization created for the sole purpose of fighting Magic Catastrophes and demons.

There was a lot of traffic on this street. Numerous hovercars flew over the road, their sleek frames hovering several feet off the ground as they moved.

With the advancement in AI technology, all hovercars were now autonomous. They contained numerous advanced sensors and a powerful artificial intelligence that allowed them to sense everything happening around them within several dozen miles, which meant it was nearly impossible for them to get into accidents. Ever since autonomous vehicles became the new standard, car accidents had dropped to .5%. Anthony had even heard a rumor that all cars used feed from satellites orbiting the Earth to get an accurate read on traffic patterns and choose the best routes to avoid being caught in traffic.

"I just noticed something…" Anthony glanced at Brianna as they walked, but she wasn't looking at him. Her eyes were focused on the people around them.

"What is it?" he asked.

She looked at him. "A lot of people are glaring at you."

Anthony didn't respond at first, instead looking at a pair of young men walking in the opposite direction. Both men noticed his presence and glared at him as if he'd committed a grave sin against them. They didn't do anything, and when the two passed him, they ignored his existence and went back to talking about… whatever they had been talking about before spotting him.

He chuckled mirthlessly. "Incubus release a pheromone similar to succubus. It is supposed to draw in members of the opposite sex while keeping members of the same sex from becoming interested in them."

"So your powers are the same as a succubus's powers?" asked Brianna.

"I'm not sure. At the very least, I know incubus share some abilities with succubus." Anthony paused when a middle-aged woman stared at him with a strange look as she walked by them, then sighed. "Unfortunately, I don't have a handle on these abilities, so my pheromones tend to just leak out of me. I'm fortunate my powers are so weak none of the women around me seem to notice it. If they weren't, I'd be in a lot of trouble."

"And why don't you have a handle on your abilities?" Brianna questioned him some more.

"Because I haven't bound anyone to me, I guess." With a small shrug, Anthony continued. "Just like a succubus, an incubus's power comes from his bondmates—or so my professor told me. Because I have no bondmates, I'm not receiving a steady supply of mana, which is necessary for my continued existence. Also, in order to master my abilities, its supposedly necessary to have bondmates. Something about having a connection to others increases my own powers and ability to control them."

Anthony was still relatively new to the supernatural side of the world. While he had dealt with demons in his youth, he'd never really been a part of that world until becoming Lilith's bondmate, and by the time she had met him, Lilith was already considered the world's most powerful succubus. That was why he didn't really understand how bonding worked. All he knew was that Lilith had thirteen bondmates, including himself, and that they were the source of her power.

"And why, um, why haven't you found anyone to bond with?"

At this question, Anthony glanced at Brianna as they made it to the station. There were a lot of people, and the two of them were jostled around a bit, which forced them to shove against the crowd so they wouldn't be separated. They eventually reached the maglev platform. While they were waiting with everyone else, Anthony ran a hand through his hair.

"Sorry, but that's a personal question I don't really feel like answering right now."

Brianna looked like she was going to contest his decision not to tell her about it, but then a strange expression crossed her face. She stared at Anthony for a moment. He watched as she clenched and unclenched her hands. Several seconds passed, and then she looked away.

"I... I understand," she said in a voice so soft he almost missed it.

The maglev soon arrived. As the doors opened, the mass of people—humans, therianthropes, vampires, and other demons—surged forward and entered the maglev.

Anthony and Brianna were among those who entered. Because all the seats were already taken, the two of them were forced to find a spot in the corner where they could stand and talk.

There were a lot of people around. Several different scents permeated the atmosphere; perfume, cologne, BO. Anthony wrinkled his nose as a man with a rank stench wandered past him. Even Brianna looked slightly disgusted as she stared at the strange man who had bloodshot eyes and looked like he might be on several drugs.

"You said you wanted to talk?" Anthony said at last.

Brianna nodded as her expression turned serious. "After we spoke last night, I did a lot of thinking, and I've come to the conclusion that you aren't a monster or a Magic Catastrophe that needs to be eliminated."

"Well... I suppose that is a good thing," Anthony said, slightly startled.

"But you still have the potential to become one," Brianna continued. "Throughout history, incubus have been synonymous with disaster. I can't just let you roam free without supervision."

It didn't take a genius to figure out where this was going. Anthony gave Brianna an incredulous expression as he realized what she meant.

"So, what? You're going to be my watcher?"

"That's right," Brianna said. "I've already contacted HQ and let them know that you currently aren't a threat to be eliminated and should instead be watched for signs of unusual activity. If nothing else, I think you deserve the chance to prove you aren't a threat. That said, do not think this means I won't eliminate you should you become a threat. If it turns out that you are a Magic Catastrophe, I won't hesitate to wipe you out."

Anthony wasn't sure what facial expression he was making just then. His emotions were so mixed up at the moment.

It was good that Brianna had decided he wasn't a Magic Catastrophe that needed to be eliminated, but she also said that might change if he ever became a threat. He guessed he understood where she was coming from. Custodes Daemonium had classified him as an S-class Magic Catastrophe, which was on the same level as the Lilith Incident that wiped an entire city from the face of the map and rearranged the geography of that area. The fact that she was willing to let him live at all could be taken as a huge concession on her part.

On the other hand, Anthony really hadn't done anything to anyone that warranted being considered an S-class Magic Catastrophe to begin with. He was just an incubus—a rare breed of demon that hadn't appeared for several hundred years. True, his predecessors had all without fail caused Magic Catastrophes to happen, but they had nothing to do with him.

As Anthony silently contemplated what he should say, the maglev slowed to a stop. Someone backed into Brianna, who gasped in surprise as she fell forward into his chest.

Anthony froze as two soft swells pressed into him. Brianna's scent, a vaguely floral aroma, addled his mind and caused him to inhale sharply. He looked down at where her breasts were squishing against his chest.

The person who had bumped into Brianna didn't seem to notice and backed up even further, forcing the two of them into even closer quarters. Her chest bulged as they were further smashed against him. Brianna looked up as she placed her hands on his chest, gripping his shirt, her eyes wide and her cheeks stained with a dark shade of red as all the blood rushed to her face. He was sure his face had turned a similar color.

A large number of people exited the maglev at this stop, including the man who'd backed into Brianna, which allowed them more space. Even so, the two remained locked together as if they couldn't be pulled apart. It was as if they hadn't realized there was no longer any need to remain pressed so close together.

Anthony struggled for a moment against his natural instincts. He wanted to lean down and kiss this gorgeous woman whose hair reminded him of fire and whose eyes were like glowing emeralds. He wanted to pull her to him and ravish her, to strip off her clothes and claim her as his own. Closing his eyes, Anthony struggled intensely against his own nature, telling himself over and over that he was loyal to Lilith, that he wouldn't betray her.

"Unbelievable," a voice suddenly muttered, knocking Anthony out of his depraved thoughts.

He looked around and found a pair of older women glaring at him and Brianna. They looked like they were middle-aged

workers. His companion had also noticed and turned her head to look at them.

"Can you believe the youth of today?"

"I cannot. Back in my day, we would never be so bold as to make out on a maglev. Does today's generation have no modesty?"

As the two women carried on, talking about how he and Brianna were a disgrace to society because of their shameless behavior, the two of them jumped apart. It was only after those old crones spoke that he and Brianna realized their close proximity. Brianna's face was burning like an incandescent fire. All the blood had rushed to her cheeks, causing them to become redder than her hair. Anthony glanced at himself in the reflection of a window and noticed his face was of a similar shade.

"S-sorry about that," he apologized.

"N-no… it was my fault," Brianna said. "I should have been… more self-aware."

As the maglev ride continued, an awkward silence lapsed between the two of them, who no longer had any idea what to say or do.

Anthony would eventually get off the maglev and separate from Brianna.

His face would still be red.

***

Even though Anthony diligently took notes from Professor Incanscino's lecture, he couldn't say his heart was really in it—or his mind. In fact, for most of the time within the diminutive professor's class, Anthony's mind was plagued by memories of what happened on the maglev. He tried his best to shut the memories out, but perhaps his body, or maybe his instincts as an incubus, continued to plague him.

He could still remember the feel of Brianna's breasts mashed against his chest.

He could still remember her scent invading his nose.

He could vividly recall his desire to press her against the maglev's wall, to press his mouth to hers and take her right there.

Anthony understood that these desires came from being an incubus. Just like their female counterparts, the succubus, incubus were naturally sexual creatures with a high libido. What's more, Anthony had been resisting these instincts for a long time now. He had never had sex with anyone besides Lilith, and he didn't want to start now. No one could ever replace Lilith in his heart.

Class eventually came to an end. Anthony put his laptop away, slung his case over his shoulder, and was getting ready to leave—

"Stay in class for a minute, Mr. Amasius."

—when Professor Incanscino stopped him.

He turned around and looked at the professor as everyone else left. He wondered what she wanted, but the woman wasn't even paying attention to him as she took small sips from her water bottle. Meanwhile, the other students soon exited the room, leaving the two of them alone.

"You said you wanted to speak with me?" Anthony said when the woman said nothing.

"I did." Professor Incanscino turned around and narrowed her blue eyes at him. Her small lips were set in a stern frown. "I heard from a little birdy that you were spotted talking with that War Maiden from Custodes Daemonium this morning."

Anthony blinked before he narrowed his eyes. "Were you spying on me through a social camera?"

There were a number of social cameras located throughout Academy Island, which were used to monitor the city and respond to crime. Most of the cameras were located only in the busiest sections of the city. There had been a move to place social cameras everywhere, but the people rebelled against the idea of having their privacy so thoroughly violated like that. However, the Academy Island Board of Directors had been able to push a law through that allowed the use of social cameras in stores and heavily populated areas of the city.

"I am your watcher." Professor Incanscino shrugged. "I'm granted access to any and all video feedback that has you in it."

Anthony wasn't sure he liked that, but he knew it wasn't something he could contest either. He was already being allowed to live in this city and attend school like a regular person. This was despite the threat he could potentially pose. He guessed this was just one of the injustices he needed to put up with in order to continue living.

"I was talking to Brianna this morning," he admitted.

"So her name is Brianna?" Professor Incanscino thoughtfully narrowed her eyes and pursed her lips. "I am surprised she told you her name, but I guess if she's been speaking to you, her feelings have changed since she tried to kill you. Regardless, you really should be more wary around that girl."

"I don't think I need to worry right now," Anthony said.

Professor Incanscino's eyes widened. "Ho? And just why is that?"

"Because she told me she's decided I'm currently not a threat that needs to be eliminated but one that should be watched," Anthony said.

"I see." The professor's wide eyes narrowed again. "And was this a decision of Custodes Daemonium or one she came to herself?"

Anthony hesitated. "She decided it herself. She told me she's contacted her leaders and let them know of her decision."

Professor Incanscino snorted. "In that case, you should still be wary of her. She might have decided you aren't a threat, but I doubt the leaders of Custodes Daemonium will feel the same way. I am sure it will not be long before she receives orders to eliminate you anyway. You probably do not know this, but around five hundred years ago, Custodes Deamonium was almost wiped out by an incubus. That girl might have a good heart, but she's also a War Maiden. She's been trained from a young age to follow orders. If she is ordered to kill you, she will."

"I understand that," Anthony said softly.

"If you understand, then be more careful," Professor Incanscino admonished him. "That sword the girl wields is an incredibly powerful weapon known as the Geminus Sword. Aside from being a dangerous double-bladed sword, it uses a form of spatial magic that severs the molecular bonds of anything it touches. It doesn't matter how strong something is. Unless they can also use spatial magic to resist the effects, anybody who is cut with that blade will receive severe injuries no matter how durable their body is." She stared at him with a look that made Anthony turn his head. "Right now, you are weak. You have no bondmates, and you're relying on me to keep you alive. One cut from that weapon will spell your doom."

"I understand," Anthony muttered. "I'll be careful."

"Good. You can leave now."

Anthony didn't say anything as he left the classroom and began heading off to get some lunch. His footsteps were drowned out by the chatter of other students passing him in the hall. However, he barely paid them any attention.

He understood that Professor Incanscino was just worried about him, but he still wished she wouldn't be so harsh, though he could understand that too. He was mooching off her kindness. Anthony's refusal to bond with even a single woman had resulted in her creating a magical ritual that somehow gave him mana. He wasn't sure how it worked, but he did know that it was a taxing ritual to perform every month—and she'd had to perform it twice within the past few days.

If only there was something I could do... he thought as he walked down the hall. *Maybe if I did bond with someone, I wouldn't burden her so much.* He shook his head. *No, I can't do that. It's out of the question.*

"Anthony!"

Just as he was about to reach the end of the hall, a voice shouted from behind him. He turned around to find Secilia, dressed in black tights, jean shorts, and a black sleeveless shirt with a jacket, walking up to him. She was grinning from ear to ear. It didn't look like her normal smile. For whatever reason, Anthony could not help but repress a shiver at the way her lips curled.

There was something off about that smile.

"Hey, what's up, Secilia?"

"Oh, nothing much." Secilia placed her hands behind her back as she walked up to him with deliberately slow steps. He didn't know why, but each step felt like someone was slamming a hammer against his heart. "I was just looking for you."

"Looking for me? What for?"

"Do I need a reason?"

"I… guess not."

Anthony began walking again, this time with Secilia in tow. They chatted about inconsequential matters for a bit. However, as the conversation continued, the strange sense of dread welling up inside of Anthony grew. Nothing about Secilia seemed different from how she normally acted. Even so, he could not help but feel like there was something bugging his friend.

"Is everything okay?" he finally asked.

"Oh, everything is fine. Just fine. However, I do have a question for you." Secilia paused, the smile left her face, and her eyes grew flat as she stared at him. The tension in his heart peaked. "Who was that girl you were with the other night?"

Anthony froze. It was obvious she was walking about Brianna. He hadn't been with any other girl the other night. In fact, aside from Secilia and Professor Incanscino, Brianna was the only girl he had spoken to for any major length of time since becoming an incubus.

"Well…" he began.

Secilia raised an eyebrow. "Well?"

She took a step forward.

He took a step back.

"It's… um… she's…"

"She's… what?"

Anthony had no idea what he should say to Secilia, but he knew damn well that he couldn't answer with the truth. He couldn't tell her that Brianna was an assassin sent by Custodes Daemonium to kill him because he was an incubus. Secilia didn't even know he was an incubus. As far as the general population was concerned, Anthony was just a normal human attending college, and he aimed to keep it that way. There was no need to stir up a hornet's nest.

And so, Anthony thought fast.

"Oh, wow! Would you look at the time! I really need to get going to my next class!"

"It's lunch time," Secilia responded flatly.

"I have some questions I'd like to ask Professor Reno before class. See you later!"

"What?! Hey! Wait! Stop running and answer my question, damn it!"

However, Anthony did not stop running. He took several turns, hopped onto an elevator that took him several floors up, and then hopped on another elevator that took him down one floor. After that, he raced to one of the walkways connecting buildings and entered building #2. Only after he had passed through multiple shops within the restaurant section of the building did he wipe the sweat from his forehead and search for a place to eat.

His stomach was gurgling and he needed some sustenance.

Anthony had somehow managed to dodge Secilia for the rest of the day. He knew he would eventually have to confront her, but he hoped to have a solid story for her by then. There was just no way he could tell her the truth.

After leaving school, he hopped onto a maglev that took him back to his apartment. As he leaned against the elevator wall, he tried to think up a good story he could tell Secilia when he saw her next time. Should he say Brianna was a relative? No. That would never work. Secilia wasn't stupid, and she already knew that Anthony's only living relative was Calvin. What about a childhood friend? That could work. He'd never shared his past with anyone aside from Professor Incanscino, so the childhood friend story could potentially work, but he would have to talk with Brianna about this. A cover story only worked when all parties involved agreed on the story.

The lift slowed to a stop and the door opened. Anthony snapped out of his stupor and was about to walk out of the lift—when a face appeared right in front of him.

"Whoa!"

Anthony and Brianna leapt apart as they nearly collided. The redhead placed a hand against her chest as she stared at him with wide eyes. Meanwhile, Anthony was just shocked to see her again so soon.

"Why are you here?" he asked. "Were you waiting for me?"

"I… no." Brianna calmed down, removed her hand from her chest, and let it drop to her side. "I came here because I wanted to check out my new apartment before buying furniture."

"Oh. I see." Anthony nodded. "I understand. That's a perfectly reasonable—wait." He paused and looked back at Brianna. "Did you say 'new apartment?'"

"Yes," Brianna said.

Anthony needed a moment. The doors tried to close, but he placed his arm between them so the sensors could detect the intrusion and opened again.

"You're… moving in here?"

"That is correct," Brianna confirmed as she placed her hands on her hips. "Because I have decided to watch over you instead of kill you, I needed to find a place to live. It's best if I live close by. That way it's easier for me to keep an eye on you."

"I see." Anthony calmed down and blew out a deep breath. What she said did make sense, though he didn't know if he was happy about it. That said, he was now curious about something. "Does that mean you didn't have a place to live until now?"

Brianna shook her head. "Until today, I was sleeping inside of a playset in Doyle Hollis Park."

Anthony pressed a hand to his face and massaged his forehead. He felt another headache coming on, but he did his best not to respond negatively to the situation. While Professor Incanscino said he should be wary of her, Brianna didn't seem like a bad person, so he'd like to think she wouldn't use their close proximity to kill him.

"So… which apartment is yours now?" he asked.

"Let me show you," Brianna said.

She led Anthony to her apartment, which he realized was the one literally right across from his. Anthony had an apartment located on the outside, so he had a view of Academy Island and the bay several miles out. Hers was located on the inside, meaning it didn't have any windows, but it was also bigger.

Brianna let him inside and showed him her apartment. It was a two bedroom apartment with one bathroom. The living room was about two times bigger than his, and the master bedroom that would be her sleeping quarters was also bigger than his bedroom. Likewise, the bathroom was a lot more extravagant. All Anthony had was a toilet, a sink, and a tiny square shower with just enough room to move around in. Brianna's bathroom consisted of two rooms. The first room was a changing room, while the second was a shower with a bathtub.

In short, her apartment kicked his apartment's ass.

"So… who is paying for all this?" asked Anthony after Brianna finished showing him around.

"Custodes Daemonium is obviously paying for it." The look Brianna gave him made Anthony feel stupid. "They pay for all of my expenses when I travel. I just need to send them the bill each month and they pay it off."

"Must be nice having such a large organization footing the bill." He sighed and ran a hand through his hair. "Anyway, you said something about buying furniture?"

"Yes. As you can see, I currently have no furniture." Brianna paused as she looked around her empty living room, a sort of self-deprecating smile appearing on her face. "I did not expect this mission to involve me finding a temporary place of residence. That's actually why I was sleeping in the park until now. This was supposed to be a one-day trip, so I didn't book a hotel to spend the night in."

"Right," Anthony said. "Well, let's go then. I'll help you find some furniture."

"You don't mind coming with me?" asked Brianna.

"Would I say I'll help you if I did mind?"

"I guess not. Thank you."

Brianna sent him a smile, and despite feeling somewhat exhausted, he smiled back.

Shopping had changed significantly from the time when Academy Island was part of the Americas. The advancement in technology also meant shopping experiences had advanced as well. While many shops still had items on display and even appliances for people to try out, the products they sold were not present at each store. They were located in a warehouse, and when someone bought something, it would be delivered to them.

It made shopping easier, especially furniture shopping.

"Look at this chair, Anthony! It has a massager!"

"I can see that."

"T-t-t-t-t-this f-f-f-f-fe-e-eeels soooo niiiiiice!"

Anthony's lips twitched as he tried not to smile at the redhead, who was acting like a naive kid as she sat on a massage chair, which was apparently doing wonders for her back. He wondered if she realized what else it was doing.

His gaze wandered from her face to her chest, which was bouncing around like a pair of beach balls being tossed through the air. She wasn't wearing a bra because she had that bodysuit of hers underneath her normal clothes, which he could see when her shirt rode up her torso. Was that why her tits were flopping around so much? Did her suit not have an inbuilt bra?

"Are you going to buy that for your living room?" Anthony asked.

Brianna thought about it for a moment, then shook her head. "I-I-I d-d-d-don't t-t-t-think s-s-so."

"Then maybe you should get off. I don't think the clerk glaring at you appreciates what you're doing," he suggested.

Indeed, the store clerk—a young woman with mousy brown hair—was glaring at Brianna like the other woman had murdered her mother. Of course, she could have been glaring at Brianna's breasts, which were around three times bigger than the clerk's. That was always a possibility. The way they were jiggling brought a lot of attention to them.

While reluctant, Brianna didn't remain on the massage chair for long. They soon began searching the store some more.

The store they were in specialized in selling furniture. It was designed with several aisles. Between each aisle were a number of appliances that people could try out to see if they were interested in buying. They had everything from beds, desks, armchairs, couches, love sofas, dressers, and mirrors, to lamps, fridges, microwaves, sonic cleaners, and washing machines. They basically had everything a person looking to furnish their home could ever want.

As they shopped, Anthony was able to see a completely new side of Brianna. Thus far, she had seemed to him like a strong and somewhat stoic but emotionally forthright and honest young woman. Right now, however, she looked more like a child visiting a candy store for the first time. Her eyes glowed with a vibrancy that reminded him of stars. The smile on her face was so wide it threatened to split her face in half. Her new demeanor took years off her appearance, making her look like a teenage girl instead of a mature War Maiden who killed demons for a living.

It made him wonder how old she was.

"You act as if you've never been shopping before," Anthony joked as they sat on a black leather sofa.

"I-I have too shopped before," Brianna shouted with a slight stutter. Her cheeks were red as she looked away. "I've just… never shopped for furniture or anything like that. War Maidens are given assigned rooms that are already furnished, and while we are allowed to decorate them however we want, few of us have the time to go shopping because we're constantly training and going on missions."

"Sounds like War Maidens have it rough," Anthony said. "Speaking of, Custodes Daemonium doesn't just have War Maidens, right? I believe there is also a magic division."

"That's right." Brianna nodded as she stood up from the couch and moved on. She continued talking as Anthony followed her. "Aside from the War Maidens and Magic Warriors, we also have the Assault Magicians. War Maidens like myself and Magic

Warriors specialize in close-range combat magic. Assault Magicians specialize in long-range spells. They're generally used for large-scale Magic Catastrophes that require complex magical rituals to solve, while War Maidens and Magic Warriors are assigned missions that deal with single targets or small terrorist cells."

Anthony guessed Magic Warriors was the male equivalent to War Maidens. It sounded like they divided the two into groups based on their sex. Saying that, it wasn't like he knew much about Custodes Daemonium. His thoughts could be way off the mark.

"Are you sure you should be telling me that much?" asked Anthony.

"It's okay," Brianna assured him. "What I'm telling you right now is common knowledge."

He nodded as they moved on.

They spent several hours in the store, and by the end of it, Brianna had bought two beds (a king-sized bed for her room and a queen-sized bed for the guest room), a table for eating, a coffee table, two chairs, two couches, a shoe rack, a dresser, and a holographic TV display. They also traveled to an appliance store and bought bathroom necessities and even a clothing store.

Anthony learned during their shopping trip that Brianna only had three outfits. She ended up buying several more outfits under the justification that she didn't know how long she was going to stay there. Anthony thought she just wanted to buy cute clothes, but he couldn't complain because he got to see her wear those cute clothes while they were shopping.

It was late by the time they finished. The moon was out and the pair found themselves sitting on the maglev, several bags of clothing at their feet.

"Thank you for shopping with me," Brianna said at last. Her hands were in her lap and she was twiddling her fingers.

"You're welcome," Anthony said simply.

"I just realized…" Brianna began with a small frown. "You didn't get to visit your brother today."

A sad smile crossed his face as he gazed into those vibrant eyes that stared back at him with concern. "I think I can afford to miss a day. It's not like anything will change even if I do go there every single day."

Brianna said nothing to that, and so the rest of their ride passed in silence.

CHAPTER 4

Brianna stood in the shower, her head tilted up, eyes closed as water sprayed her face, chest, and shoulders. Thanks to her training, she had incredible perceptions. Her body was sensitive to touch, which allowed her to feel each and every water droplet trailing down her body, like the one adventurous droplet that moved between her breasts, or the ones sliding along her backside. However, at the moment, her mind was locked in a haze as she struggled to retain her consciousness. Only after standing under the water for several more minutes to completely wake up did Brianna finally begin washing herself off.

She had low blood pressure in the mornings.

Once she finished taking a shower, Brianna wrapped a towel around her torso and headed into the first room of her bathroom, which contained a sink, a toilet, and a clothing rack. She stared at herself in the mirror as she combed and dried her long, red hair. There were many times where she considered cutting it. A friend of hers from the Magic Warriors branch of Custodes Daemonium had said he thought long hair suited her, so she kept it like this. She also thought she looked good with long hair.

"I wonder what Calencio is doing," she murmured as the image of a young man with blond hair, green eyes, and a boyish face flashed through her mind.

She shook her head and finished drying and combing her hair. Brianna walked into her bedroom after finishing up.

Thanks to the shopping she and Anthony did last week, Brianna's bedroom now had a king-sized bed sitting in the middle of it. The bed was incredible, with a mattress that relied on a special foam made of composite materials that conformed to her body for a comfortable sleep. She used standard white and pink bed sheets since she didn't like the more ostentatious designs she'd seen while shopping. A dresser sat in one corner. There was also a vanity mirror and a desk. She didn't have anything decorating her room, no posters or wall scrolls, but she did have a rack to hang the Geminus Sword on the wall.

The first thing Brianna put on was her battle suit. She stepped into the black unitard, grimacing only slightly when she pulled it up until it fit snugly against her body. The clothing was pressing into her crotch, which always felt a little uncomfortable at first, but the fabric was at least breathable, so he didn't have to worry about sweating. Because the unitard was sleeveless and the bottom didn't go past the middle of her thighs, she could also wear normal clothes underneath it and no one would know she had this on.

"Now what should I wear…?"

Brianna wandered over to her dresser and began pulling out several articles of clothing. She selected a number of different outfits, which she placed over herself while standing in front of a mirror to see which one she liked better.

"Would Anthony like this one more… or would he prefer something a little more revealing…?" As she murmured to herself, Brianna realized what she was doing and shook her head. "Wh-who cares if he would like it? This isn't about him. I just need to find a nice pair of clothes that are functional and won't attract attention."

Despite saying that, it still took Brianna several minutes to select what she wanted to wear. She ended up going with jeans, a white shirt with some frills along the hem, and a jean jacket with cuffs at the end of the sleeves. Looking at herself in the mirror, she ran her fingers through her hair and wondered if she should try something different. However, she had never styled her hair before…

"I guess I'll leave it as is," she said with a sigh.

Once dressed, the final thing she did was grab her music case and place the Geminus Sword inside. She closed the case, locked the hatches, and hefted it over her shoulder as she made her way out of her bedroom, slipped on her combat boots, and left the apartment.

There was no one in the hallway as she walked across it and stood before Anthony's door. He was still inside. Anthony didn't seem to realize it, but she had created a familiar to watch him, so she would know where he was at all times. This was a precaution in case she needed to find him for whatever reason.

She placed a hand on her chest and took several deep breaths, willing her erratically beating heart to slow down before she knocked on the door.

"It's open," Anthony's voice came from the other side.

Brianna pressed the button that caused the door to slide open and stepped inside to find Anthony, dressed in black pants and a simple white shirt, sitting on the couch as he watched the news. She slipped out of her combat boots and set them to the side, then slowly wandered into the apartment.

"There's a meal for you sitting on the table," Anthony said without looking away from the holographic TV. "You haven't eaten breakfast, right?"

"I haven't," Brianna confirmed as she looked at Anthony's small table. There was a packaged meal of quiche sitting there, steam wafting from it to show it had just been cooked. She grabbed it and moved over to the couch. Only once she was sitting did she speak again. "Thank you. What are you watching? The news?"

"There's been another attack by rogue demons," Anthony said with a nod.

"Again?" Brianna furrowed her brow as she turned to the holographic TV, which was showing video feedback from a satellite of several demons running through the streets. It wasn't just therianthropes this time but also succubus, vampires, and she even saw a couple of dryads among them. They were all low-level variations, though. For example, she couldn't see any pureblood vampires among them. "There have been a lot of rogue demons showing up. Is this natural on Academy Island?"

"Of course not," Anthony said with a shake of his head. "Academy Island strictly regulates demons entering and exiting at all times. In all the years since its founding, there has never been an incident like this. I really have to wonder what's going on. What are the Academy Island Private Security Forces doing?"

Brianna said nothing as she watched the news, listening as the newscaster claimed the reason so many rogue demons were showing up was because someone had smuggled them in. She didn't know if she believed that. It was true the occasional rogue demon could be smuggled into a place like Academy Island, but Anthony was at least right about the security around the island. It was incredibly tight. Even she was only able to enter because she belonged to Custodes Daemonium.

They finished eating their food in silence. Anthony took Brianna's empty package and threw it away alongside his own. Brianna stood up and followed him. Then the two of them slipped their shoes back on and left the apartment.

As they stepped into the crowded streets, Brianna turned her head and could not help but marvel at how different everything felt. Nothing had changed since she arrived. Even so, Brianna felt like everything was different now, more vibrant, more colorful. It was like the wool had been pulled from her eyes, like she had been color blind her entire life and could now see.

She glanced at the person walking beside and felt her heart accelerate.

A lot of her new thoughts and feelings were caused by this young man, whom she had been sent to kill. Anthony was not like what she had imagined an incubus to be. He was, in many ways, just a normal college student, but there was a quiet strength within him that other people didn't have. More than that, she found his personality endearing.

The faces he made when he was working on his homework were cute.

The solemn yet determined demeanor he showed when visiting his brother tugged at her heart.

His willingness to help her adjust to life on Academy Island made her feel comfortable, but it also caused her heart to flutter.

Brianna raised a hand to her chest as the blood pumping organ resting within began pushing more blood through her veins. All that blood went straight to her cheeks. She could feel them burning.

Anthony noticed as well.

"Is something wrong?" he asked with a curious frown.

"N-not at all!" she squeaked. "Nothing is wrong! Nothing! W-why are you looking at me like that?! I promise, nothing is wrong so just look the other way!"

Brianna felt a cold sweat pour down her face as Anthony continued to look at her. Could he hear the sound of her heart thudding against her ribcage? Was he aware of how much blood was rushing to her cheeks? Did he even realize that his intense stare was causing her body to feel all tingly and strange?

As she worried herself into a tizzy, Anthony turned away.

"Well, if you say nothing is wrong, then I guess nothing is wrong," he said at last.

Brianna sighed in relief.

"By the way, your face is red."

"Meep!"

***

Anthony arrived in class and sat in his usual spot, brought out his laptop, and then quietly waited for Professor Incanscino to arrive and start class. More students poured in as he sat there. A few glanced his way. He received several glares from the men, while the women looked at him oddly, like he was a puzzle they couldn't solve. This was all par for the course, so he wasn't concerned.

Several minutes passed before the teacher arrived. Anthony frowned when he saw that it wasn't Professor Incanscino. This man was tall, had a head of full black hair that looked like a lion's mane, and possessed a sturdy body with broad shoulders, a thick chest, and powerful legs hidden underneath his black suit. He walked up to the podium under the watchful gazes of the students and turned to face them.

He also had black ears on his head; they were shaped like triangles and covered in fur. He was a therianthrope. More specifically, he was a pantherian.

"Due to some unforeseen events, Professor Incanscino is currently unable to teach class right now," the man spoke in a gravelly voice. Despite his tone being a low growl, he spoke in a refined manner that made him seem sophisticated and scholarly. "For those who do not know me, my name is Lionel Heartfert. I'll be your instructor for the time being until Professor Incanscino returns. Now, let us begin class."

As the man began lecturing them on the different methods of curing D and C-rank Magic Catastrophes like standard curses and hexes, whispers broke out amongst the students. Anthony didn't pay them much attention. However, he was certain those whispers were the many students speculating about why Professor Incanscino was not teaching class today.

It must have been the rogue demons.

Professor Incanscino was a member of the Academy Island Private Security Forces—a high-ranked Assault Magician at that —which meant she was occasionally called in to deal with situations that the normal forces couldn't handle. It was her position within their forces that allowed her the power to grant him the opportunity to live relatively freely on Academy Island.

Anthony wondered if the rogue demons were really that big of a threat. Even the weakest demon was far stronger than a regular human, but it wasn't like the Academy Island Private Security Forces fought against demons one on one. When a demonic threat occurred, they worked in units and used advanced magical weaponry to fit any given situation. Unless they were up against something like a Vampire Warlord from the European Federation or the King of Beasts from the Russian Empire, they should have been able to handle anything that came their way.

Or so Anthony thought.

Class eventually ended and Anthony shut off his laptop, stowed it away, and stood up. He left class with everyone else. Professor Heartfert didn't call him to stay like Professor Incanscino sometimes did, so he was able to quickly make his way to Building #2.

Anthony ate his lunch alone that day. Neither Secilia nor her half-brother Alex showed up like they often did. He wondered what they were up to. Maybe they'd both been called into work.

School passed uneventfully, and outside of Professor Incanscino not showing up, nothing truly interesting happened—not until Anthony was walking toward the station.

"Anthony!" a voice called out.

Turning around at the sound of someone calling his name, Anthony found a grinning Secilia running up to him. She was dressed fashionably as always. Her dark hair was styled into ringlets that day. They framed her attractive face and really highlighted her vibrant eyes. The stockings covering her legs were partially translucent. Jean shorts wrapped around her hips, while a sleeveless green top hung loosely off her shoulders.

"Secilia," Anthony greeted. "I thought you were working today since I didn't see you during lunch."

"I was. Now I'm not." Secilia grinned as she stopped beside him. She placed her hands behind her back and leaned over slightly, which allowed him to see a small hint of cleavage. "And you? Heading home?"

"That's right," Anthony said.

"You're going to see that girl again," Secilia accused.

Anthony almost winced but maintained his composure. "That is correct. She lives right next door, so it's kind of hard for me *not* to see her."

"I really don't like how fast that girl is moving," Secilia mumbled.

Anthony had created what he believed was a relatively believable story about how he and Brianna were just acquaintances who had met after she moved in. Everything he told her, like how they had met under unique circumstances, was true. He just didn't tell Secilia that the circumstances were that Brianna had been sent to kill him. Either way, Secilia had accepted his explanation.

"I'm not sure what you mean by that," Anthony said with a shrug.

Secilia rolled her eyes. "Of course you don't. Anyway, I've decided that you aren't going to head home just yet."

"Is that so?" Anthony raised an eyebrow at the woman. "Then what exactly am I going to be doing if not heading home?"

"I am so glad you asked." Gracing Anthony with a seductive smile that he couldn't help but find attractive, Secilia walked closer to him and grabbed his hand with both of hers. Her hands were warm and soft, but she had several calluses that came from working with engineering equipment. "You are going to take me out on a date."

"… Huh?"

✳✳✳

Brianna waited for Anthony to show up at the maglev station like she always did, but when the time he normally arrived came and went, she began frowning as a small niggling feeling entered the pit of her stomach.

She looked at a clock on the wall. 4:25pm. For the past week since she arrived on Academy Island, Anthony had always shown up at the maglev station at exactly 4:15pm every day. That he wasn't showing up now caused her to worry.

Closing her eyes, Brianna chanted a short spell under her breath. A small portion of her mana drained out of her as she connected herself to the familiar she had created. She could track Anthony by using her connection with her familiar to track its movements.

She furrowed her brow when she saw that Anthony was heading in the opposite direction of the maglev station at an incredibly fast speed—too fast for a human to move on their own.

Anthony might be an incubus, but she had already learned that his powers were weak because he hadn't bound a single woman to him. According to him, incubus were like succubus. To gain strength, they needed to build a harem of women who would grant them power. Without even a single woman bound to him, Anthony was barely stronger than a human. He couldn't move that fast even when he was using physical enhancement magic.

That meant he was on a maglev.

Why was he moving away from her?

Brianna thought about chasing after him to see what was going on, but the moment she took a step forward, her body straightened as though it had been zapped by lightning. A strange sensation like an electric jolt hit her mind. Her eyes widened.

Someone had just entered her apartment! They weren't hiding their presence, but they hadn't broken her barrier either.

After biting her lip in indecision for a moment, Brianna hopped onto a maglev that would take her to her apartment. She wanted to know what Anthony was doing, where he was going, and whether or not he was with anyone. However, if someone broke into her apartment, it meant they were a highly skilled individual. Only someone extremely powerful and knowledgeable about barriers could slip through the barrier she had set up without breaking it.

The maglev was crowded, but she ignored the people around her as she leaned against the wall and crossed her arms, impatiently tapping her foot against the floor. The fifteen minutes it took to reach her stop felt agonizingly slow.

When the doors opened, she burst out before anyone else and began running through the streets, dodging pedestrians left and right. She blinked once. As she did, a trickle mana drained from her reserves as she activated a powerful magic known as Foresight.

The world around her seemed to slow. Then afterimages began appearing, though they were not true afterimages. No one was moving at a speed that exceeded light. It just seemed that way.

A person on her left was going to move in front of her shortly, so she stepped to the side and avoided them. Another person was coming in from her right. They would smack her in the face if she didn't do anything. Brianna moved on the balls of her feet, ducked underneath that person's elbow as they shouted into their wristwatch, and continued on.

The afterimages formed from each person were, in actuality, visions of what would happen five seconds into the future. That was the power of Foresight. While Brianna was just a novice at using it and could only look five seconds forward, her combat instructor had mastered Foresight to the point where she could look thirty seconds into the future. She'd even heard that the Priestess could look a full minute into the future.

Of course, for combat, five seconds was really all you needed.

It didn't take more than five minutes for Brianna to reach her apartment, and then another minute to reach her floor. As she walked down the hall, she undid the latches on her music case, grabbed the Germinius Sword as it fell out, and adopted a combat stance as she crept down the hall. She used Foresight to make sure no one would be coming as she moved. The last thing she needed was for a civilian to see her weapon.

Finally reaching the door to her room, Brianna paused as she spread out her perceptions to the other side. She furrowed her brow. She knew someone had entered her apartment, but there was not a single ripple or undulation of mana coming from beyond this door.

The hairs on her arms prickled.

Taking a shaky breath, she unlocked the door, slipped inside, and hit the button that closed the door with her elbow before adopting a combat stance with her feet spread shoulder width apart and her legs bent. She swept her gaze from side to side, looking for an intruder. There was nothing. At least, she thought there was nothing.

Until she saw the owl sitting on her windowsill, that is.

The owl was completely white and possessed yellow eyes. Its pure feathers the color of fresh snow looked quite fluffy. As it stared at her, the claws on its feet clacked against the windowsill.

"I-Instructor!" Brianna gasped as she realized what this creature was.

"Brianna," a voice said. It came from the owl, but it did not belong to the owl. The person speaking to her was simply using this familiar as a medium to speak through. *"It seems like you have settled into your new accomodations quite well."* The owl blinked its big eyes and craned its neck to look around the living room. *"You have even bought furniture."*

"I didn't know how long I was going to be staying here," Brianna said as she slipped out of her boots and wandered over to the owl. She set the Geminius Sword against the couch and knelt on the floor. "I thought it would be prudent to have a place to stay while on my mission."

"Yes... your mission. That is what I am contacting you about." Now that she was closer, Brianna could see the magic circle inside of the owl's eyes. She knew her instructor was gazing at her through those eyes from the Custodes Daemonium headquarters. *"We have read and reviewed your report on the incubus known as Anthony Amasius."*

"Then you understand why I sent it?" asked Brianna, trying not to let on how nervous she was. Her heart was hammering.

"I do indeed. However, the higher ups do not care if this Anthony is a threat or not. The potential for destruction that he represents alone is enough to classify him as an S-class Magic Catastrophe. They believe that if we wait until he becomes a legitimate threat to our world, it will be too late to save the people from disaster."

Brianna's blood turned cold. She sucked in a deep breath. Her heart was pounding in her chest. She felt like she could hear the rushing of blood filling her ears as she stared at the owl.

"But... my report..."

"We have looked over your report. Anthony might not be a threat now, but we cannot afford to wait until he becomes one to act. If you don't act now, he could go on to destroy entire civilizations."

"You don't know that!" Brianna shouted. She clenched her hands into fists as she stared at the owl with a pleading look in her eyes. "Anthony is a good person. The only thing he wants to do is bring his brother out of a coma. He's never harmed anyone. Please, instructor. Let me watch over him instead. If he turns out to be a threat, I will kill him, but we should at least give him a chance to prove that he's not a threat."

A sigh echoed from the owl. Weary. Resigned.

"It seems sending you on this mission might have been a mistake. You are still not ready for something like this." Brianna flinched at the words, but her instructor didn't seem to notice or care. *"You have your orders. Kill the incubus called Anthony Amasius, or we will send someone else to take care of him."*

As her instructor finished relaying the damning orders, the owl suddenly glowed with a bright white light before unraveling right in front of her eyes. It turned into small sheets of paper with numerous magical formulas written on them. As the papers fluttered in the air, they quickly caught fire before burning to a crisp, disappearing so not even their ashes remained.

Brianna didn't know how long she stared in despair at the spot where her instructor, or rather, her instructor's familiar, had disappeared. Her entire body felt cold. A chill swept through her, causing Brianna to shiver as she hugged her arms around her waist.

With stumbling steps, she mechanically walked into her bedroom, hung the Geminius Sword on the rack, and crawled onto her bed. She sat against the headboard. Taking a slow, shuddering breath, Brianna curled her knees into her chest, wrapped her arms around them, and buried her face between her knees. A single sob wracked her body.

What was she going to do now?

Could she really kill Anthony?

Alone in her bedroom, Brianna was plagued with despair and a feeling of intense isolation.

***

Anthony couldn't stop himself from frowning as he wondered how he'd gotten into this situation. He was standing in front of a movie theater, Secilia's arms wrapped tightly around one of his own, while the woman in question looked at the different holographic posters to figure out which movie she wanted to see. It looked like there were several.

"Hmm… I can't decide," Secilia muttered. "I'm tempted to see *Daylight Explosion* because I really love a good action flick, but *Evening Solace* is directed by Gabriel Angel and stars Alexandria Ryker. That's my favorite director and actress in one place." She turned to look at him. "What do you think?"

"Why do we have to see a movie at all?" asked Anthony with a frown. "Isn't a movie kind of cliched for a date?"

"Oh? Then do you have any better ideas?"

"Of course not. I've never been on a date before."

"Then stop complaining about cliches and choose a movie."

"I don't even know what's good."

"Fine. Then I'll just choose at random." Secilia pointed at the *Daylight Explosion* posters. "Ini mini miny moe." Her finger went back and forth from *Daylight Explosion* to *Evening Solace*. "Catch a tiger by his toe. If he hollers let him go. Ini mini miny moe." Her finger ended on *Evening Solace*. "*Evening Solace* it is."

With her decision made in the most banal way possible, Secilia tugged on Anthony's arm and got him moving alongside her. They went up to a line of people who were buying tickets from the automatic ticket booths. They would select what movie they wanted to watch, pay by having the booth scan their wristwatch, and then head off into the theater.

"That was not random," Anthony said.

"Was too," Secilia rebutted.

"No, it wasn't. Ini mini miny moe is a predictable rhyme. When you use it to choose between two options, your finger will always point at the opposite option you started on." Anthony narrowed his eyes at her. "You started on *Daylight Explosion* because you knew it would land on *Evening Solace*."

"You got me," Secilia confessed, smiling in that teasing manner of hers. "I was perfectly aware of what I wanted to see. There's no way I can miss a movie directed and acted by two of my all-time favorites."

"Isn't *Evening Solace* a romance movie?"

"It is. Got a problem with that?"

"Not really." Anthony shrugged, but then stopped when his arm rubbed against Secilia's breasts. She was hugging his arm, so it was nestled firmly within the valley of her twin peaks, which made him very aware of how... soft her assets were. "Anyway, since you are the one who arbitrarily decided on what we are going to do, you get to pay."

"Uh uh. No way. Everyone knows it is the man's duty to pay for the date."

"I believe in true gender equality," Anthony argued in a bland voice. "When a woman asks the man on a date, it is her duty to pay. Consequently, if a man asks a woman on a date, then he should obviously pay. Deciding who pays based on their gender is the basis for gender inequality, and I won't stand for it."

"That's the kind of eloquent bullshit men spout when they're cheapskates." Secilia tossed him a mild glare without any real heat. When she saw the stubborn look in his eyes, however, she smirked. "Okay then. How about we settle this the way we always do when we have a dispute?"

Anthony could feel a strange heat rise up in his chest as he stared at the woman, whose smirk was so sexy he could have pushed her against the wall and claimed her right there. However, this wasn't a heat from sexual desire. He could feel his competitiveness surging. Secilia had lit a fire inside of his veins that needed to be quenched.

"You're on," he said.

Secilia's smirk widened. "Then follow me."

They moved out of line and left the movie theater. They traveled through the bustling streets, merging with pedestrian traffic. Hundreds of sounds and scents assaulted Anthony's ears and nose. The honking of hovercars, the thrum of engines, and the chattering of people filled the air. A person walking on their left smelled faintly of perfume. Someone several feet in front of them smelled like they hadn't bathed in a few days. Combine all the different smells and sounds with the lights from passing cars and street signs, and Anthony felt like his senses were being overstimulated by everything around him.

After a year of living here, he had fortunately grown used to this.

Secilia eventually led Anthony to a large building of about six stories called Aces High Arcade & VR Tag. It didn't look like much on the outside. Most buildings were shaped similarly. However, several people both young and old were emerging from the building wearing large smiles.

"Come on," Secilia commanded as she tugged on his arm.

Anthony didn't resist as the woman pulled him inside, where a large lobby appeared before them. He looked around as they walked across the carpeted floor. There were quite a few people here. Some of them were sitting around holographic TVs that projected images of several people wearing helmets and wielding rifles as they moved through a simulated world. However, a few people were standing near the betting booths. It looked like they were placing bets on which players would win.

"I want to place an order for two people to play exactly one game of virtual reality laser tag," Secilia said the moment she got to the booth.

Unlike the movie theater, where orders were fully handled by computers, Aces High Arcade & VR Tag still used people to deal with customers. The person behind the booth right now was a young man who was maybe 15 or 16 years-old. He had dark skin, brown eyes, and a relatively skinny build. As he looked Secilia over, his nostrils flared slightly and a hungry look entered his eyes.

Anthony pretended he was not annoyed by the look.

"One game for two people will cost forty dollars," the boy said.

"We're paying separately," Anthony said as he and Secilia held out their wristwatches.

The boy nodded as he tapped on a holographic display, selecting from the number of paying options available. He selected the one player option, scanned Secilia's wristwatch, then selected the one player option again and scanned Anthony's. A soft beeping sound issued from the desk. Anthony looked at the holographic monitor floating above his wristwatch as an icon flashed within it.

"All right. You two are ready," the boy looked at them both. "It looks like you both have a membership here, so you probably already know the rules. However, I still am required to inform you both that you two are not playing alone. There can be anywhere from fifteen to forty people playing at any given time." The boy paused, glanced at his holographic screen, and continued. "It looks like your game is going to be on floor four. There are already thirty-one people playing, so with you two, that makes thirty-three."

"Thank you." Secilia smiled at the boy, who blushed bright red, then turned to Anthony and cracked her knuckles. "You ready?"

"Ready to kick your ass, you mean? Bring it on," Anthony said.

"The only ass that will be getting kicked here is yours," Secilia retorted with a confident smile.

Anthony and Secilia traded barbs as they walked into the elevator, and they fired even more verbal shots at each other as the elevator ascended to floor four. When the elevator doors opened, they stepped out and into a large room that had several pod-like stations lined up in four rows of ten. Several people were already present. There were both men and women. Anthony and Secilia received a few glares and appreciative looks from some of the people there, but they both ignored the stares and continued insulting each other as they traveled to their respective pods.

As Anthony stood in front of his pod, he placed his wristwatch up to the scanner. Soft beeping issued from the pod, followed by a hydraulic hiss, and then seams appeared at the top before the pod opened up. What lay inside the pod was a helmet, a vest, and a rifle. The rifle was not real. It resembled an AP4 LR-308, but it was white instead of black.

Anthony first slipped on the vest, then placed the helmet over his head and flipped the switch, activating the helmet's VR system. The darkness that had engulfed him after putting on the helmet suddenly disappeared and revealed the room he was in. However, there was also a heads up display appearing in his vision. It showed a compass, his health gauge, and his ammo bar.

Once he was outfitted, he turned to Secilia. She had also finished putting her equipment on as well. The vest blocked off the view of her chest. Her helmet made her look like one of those old-school anti-demon officers from the early 2100s. Meanwhile, she was wielding two pistols instead of a rifle like him.

When she saw him looking her way, she grinned. "Ready to lose?"

"Ready to win," he corrected her.

It wasn't long before an automated female voice announced that all VR tag participants were to head for the game room. Anthony and Secilia walked inside with all the others. As they entered through a door, which slid shut behind them, their VR helmets activated more functions.

The area around them, which looked like a multi-level room with large geometric objects, places to hide, trenches, ladders, bridges, and everything Anthony could possibly imagine, suddenly turned into a visually appealing world that looked like it came straight out of a sci-fi movie. The towers turned into power plants. The various levels became walkways. Glowing lines of energy raced along the floor and walls. High above his head were several flying ships that soared through a clear blue sky.

"The game will start in 10 seconds and counting. 10, 9, 8…"

As the countdown commenced, Anthony and Secilia glanced at each other one last time and split apart. It wouldn't be any fun if they had to fight each other right off the bat.

"… 5, 4, 3, 2, 1, and 0. Game start."

****

"Ha! I still can't believe you got your ass handed to you so easily!"

Anthony grimaced as he stood with Secilia on the maglev, listening to his companion teasing him. The maglev was mostly empty, which meant there were very few people to hear the woman's mocking comments, but one older gentleman was glaring at them from a distance as if they had disturbed his rest.

"So what? At least you weren't the one who beat me, which means our match ended in a draw."

"Even so… watching as that kid sniped you from a distance really made my day," Secilia continued, chortling as she wiped tears of mirth from her eyes.

During the game of virtual reality battle royale, some young punk had taken a disliking to Anthony, found a perch to stand on, and sniped him from a distance. This had nearly caused him to be taken out of the game early.

Everyone was given 100 points at the start of the match, and they earned points by shooting other players. Consequently, they lost points when someone shot them. The kid who kept shooting at Anthony had sniped him so many times that his points had ended up in the negatives, which forced him to take a penalty. He was honestly lucky he'd managed to win those points back and catch up with Secilia. That meant their game was still a draw.

"Tch." Anthony crossed his arms. "I'm glad someone had fun."

"I had a blast." The grin on Secilia's face widened so much he thought it might split her head in half. "Thank you for doing this with me. It was fun."

"More fun than seeing that movie?" asked Anthony.

"Hmm… yeah, more fun than that. I guess this is the kind of date that suits us best." Secilia stretched her arms above her head, which caused her shirt to ride up and reveal some of her flat stomach. Anthony took a slow breath to steady his heart. His friend continued talking as if unaware of what she was doing to him. "Anyway, it looks like this is my stop."

As she spoke, the maglev slowed to a stop and the doors opened. The old man didn't get up from his seat, but a small group of female vampires did walk out the doors.

Athony turned to Secilia. "All right. I'll see you later."

"Yeah." Secilia smiled, and then surprised Anthony by leaning forward and pressing her lips to his cheek. Anthony was so stunned by the soft, warm feeling of her lips on his skin that he couldn't respond as she stepped back. "See you later!"

With a mischievous grin, the woman stepped off the maglev. As the doors closed behind her, she turned around and waved at him through the window as the maglev lifted off the rails again and began moving.

"That vixen…" Anthony muttered.

Leaning against the wall, Anthony crossed his arms and stared at the city lights arrayed before him. The city seemed to go on forever.

He didn't know what to do about Secilia. She'd given him a lot of signs that she was interested in him, but Anthony didn't really want to enter a relationship with her. It had nothing to do with not liking her. He liked her a lot. But he wasn't human. As an incubus, he didn't do normal relationships the way humans did, and he didn't want to force Secilia into becoming his bondmate. It wasn't something she'd be able to get out of once she got in.

It would also be a betrayal of his feelings for Lilith.

Anthony grimaced. He knew he was using his feelings for Lilith as a chain to keep him from entering a relationship with anyone else, but he just... he couldn't help it. The worry he felt, the feelings gnawing at his heart, and his desire to keep everyone safe by not letting them become involved with him were a force he couldn't break on a whim.

His stop soon arrived, and Anthony got off and traveled the empty streets toward his home. He frowned a bit, however, upon realizing that this area was completely empty. Academy Island had a lot of nightlife. While there were some sections of the city that did become empty after dark like the section where the Academy Island Hospital for Magical Catastrophes was located, the area around his residence should have been fairly active.

A strange feeling crawled up his spine. He did his best to ignore it.

Anthony reached his apartment soon enough, but he stopped when he noticed the figure standing in front of the entrance door. It was Brianna. Her head was tilted down, causing her hair to shift forward over her face, casting it in shadow. He could not see what expression she was making. However, there was a very visible frown marring her lips.

The feeling of wrongness became stronger.

"Brianna?" he called out, walking closer. "Is everything okay?" She didn't say anything. He grimaced. "Listen, I'm sorry for not showing up at the maglev station. A friend of mine dragged me off, and I don't have your comm number so I couldn't call you. Oh! Speaking of which, we really should trade contact information. We can do that right now if you—"

"Just stop it," Brianna suddenly said. "Just stop talking!"

Anthony stopped. He didn't just stop talking. He stopped walking too.

Brianna lifted her face, showing off her bloodshot eyes with red rims. It looked like she'd been crying. Concern shot through him like a bolt fired from a mana rifle.

"Hey… are you okay?" he asked.

Brianna's face twisted into a truly unpleasant expression of anguish. Her shoulders shook. She looked like she was barely suppressing her desire to break down and cry.

"No, I am not okay," she choked out.

"What… what's wrong?" asked Anthony, only now realizing why everything about this situation felt so off.

For the past week, Brianna had been wearing regular clothes, though she still wore her battle suit underneath it. However, right now, Brianna was only wearing the battle suit, which was currently glowing with blue lines of light that ran across it like computer circuits. Her suit had a unique feature called Artificial Physical Enhancement. Those blue lines were basically the same as his physical enhancement magic, except the suit did all the work for her. What's more, she was holding the Germinius Sword in her hand.

"Brianna?" he asked again, feeling the hairs on the back of his neck prickle.

"I just received orders from Custodes Daemonium." Her eyes held an agony that caused his breath to catch in his throat. Her next words sent his mind into a spiral of shock. "They ordered me to kill you."

CHAPTER 5

Anthony felt like he was going to choke. He stared uncomprehendingly at Brianna as she gripped the Geminius Sword in two hands and shifted into a battle stance, right leg sliding forward, left leg back, knees bent. While she looked like she was getting ready to attack him, her eyes contained a sorrow that he couldn't fathom, that made him wonder.

"Do you… really have to do this?" he asked.

"I do," Brianna confirmed.

"You can't disobey them?"

At his question, Brianna's face twisted into a pained grimace. "I… can't. You do not understand what it means to be a part of an organization like Custodes Daemonium. I am an orphan. I have no family. Custodes Daemonium took me in when I was nothing but a child living on the streets. They gave me a home, trained me to become a part of their organization, and gave me a purpose in life. Without them… without that purpose and their training, I might not have lived to see the age of five. I can't just disobey a direct order from them."

Anthony did not know what he was supposed to do or how he should think and feel in this situation. He wanted to be angry that Brianna was about to try and take his life, but he partially understood how she felt. Her feelings for Custodes Daemonium were likely similar to his feelings for Lilith… well, his feelings for Lilith sans the impassioned lust.

Lilith had taken Anthony and Calvin in when they had nothing. She gave them a home and a family even though they could never give her anything of equal value. Anthony was so grateful to her that even now, more than a year after she died, he resisted his incubus nature to stay true to her. Back when she was alive, she could have asked anything of him and he would have done it. He might even be willing to kill someone he was friendly with for her.

So as much as Anthony wanted to be upset at Brianna, he couldn't. That said…

"You know I can't let you kill me," Anthony said as glowing blue lines appeared on the surface of his skin. Mana drained from his body as he activated simple physical enhancement magic. His limbs and core were strengthened. Even his heart felt like it was capable of pumping more blood through the body than ever before.

Physical Enhancement was a very basic skill. It was a spell that simply pumped mana through the body, increasing all physical aspects to superhuman levels. Of course, this magic was more complicated than just that, but that was the gist of it. With Physical Enhancement active, Anthony's limbs became stronger, his body sturdier, and his organs more capable.

As he activated his magic, Brianna gave him a sad smile, her battle suit beginning to glow with the same blue lines as his body.

"I know," she said.

And then she attacked.

Her first attack was a simple stab; there was no extra maneuvering, no feints. She just closed the distance between them in less time than it took to blink and thrust out her sword toward his chest. That said, the attack was so fast a normal human would have never seen it coming.

Anthony stepped aside and twisted his body as the sword pierced where he'd been standing. This wasn't enough to secure him a victory, however, and Brianna proved that when she twisted on balls of her feet and swung at him again. This time her attack was a diagonal slash from the ground up. Anthony leapt away from her, which let him avoid being carved open from his left hip to his right shoulder. Even though he'd managed to avoid her last attack, the woman came at him again, spinning her blade around in a deadly dance as she slashed at him with a strong overhand swing. Her cut was so clean he could feel the air being cleaved.

It was easier to dodge this time than it was the first time they had met. She might have said she was going to kill him, but Brianna clearly wasn't giving this her all; she still felt reluctant to fully commit herself. Her movements were slower, less refined than before. Despite having said she was going to kill him no matter what, her heart was not in it.

As he dodged her attacks, Anthony wondered what he should do, wondered how he could get her to stop trying to kill him. Was there anything? He didn't want to fight her. Even if he had the strength to stand on even ground with her—which he didn't—he would not wish to fight against her. She was too good a person.

While he was trying to think of what he should say and do, Brianna came at him with a powerful overhand slash. Anthony twisted out of the way. Then he had the good fortune of witnessing the wall he'd been backing into get sliced straight down the middle. He gazed at the line she had cut with a grimace. That sword of hers really was dangerous.

As he backed off to gain some distance, Brianna turned around and stared at him with those red rimmed eyes. Her lips were trembling.

"You look like you're about to start crying again," Anthony said.

A sob racked her body, though she did an admirable job of not releasing a single tear. It looked like she was being torn apart from her desire to follow Custodes Daemonium's orders with her desire to not kill him. It re-confirmed his belief that she was a good person. She didn't want to do this, but she was being forced to because the organization she was a part of believed he was too dangerous to let live.

"How can I not be frustrated by a situation like this?" Brianna said through gritted teeth as she readied her sword again. She spun the double-bladed weapon around and adopted a stance with her feet spread apart, knees bent, and body poised to pounce.

"I guess I can understand where you are coming from," Anthony said.

"Is that why you aren't trying to convince me to stop anymore?"

Anthony shrugged. "Maybe I've just realized you won't stop because I ask you to."

Brianna pursed her lips as though she wasn't sure what to make of his statement. Her grip on the Geminius Sword tightened, to the point where Anthony could hear the leather grip creaking. Several magical formulas on the surface of the two blades began glowing bright blue, and Anthony sucked in a breath when he felt an incomparably sharp aura spread from the weapon. It felt like he could get cut from just the aura alone. He could tell Brianna was about to get serious.

And yet, just before she could actually attack him, a massive explosion that was so loud it echoed across the city forced their attention away from each other. They turned toward the source. Several miles away, plumes of smoke rose in the air, and the night sky had turned a slight red as fire spread across several buildings. Anthony sucked in a deep breath when he realized where that fire was coming from.

"That's close to the hospital!"

Anthony stopped paying attention to Brianna as he turned around and blasted off the ground, a foot-shaped imprint left where he'd been standing. He raced through the city streets with reckless abandon. As he ran, the sound of running feet appeared behind him, but he didn't care enough to turn around. Buildings and street signs blurred by.

At some point, people began appearing too. He didn't know why at first, but he realized Brianna must have set up a barrier around their apartment so she could battle against him without any civilians getting in the way. There were a number of different kinds of barriers someone could create to keep people away.

Most of the people were staring and pointing at the fire as they whispered to each other. Anthony ignored them all as he ran. Despite how the hospital was about twenty miles away from his apartment complex, he still made it in less than twenty minutes by pushing Physical Enhancement to the absolute limit.

Gasping as he placed his hands on his knees and hunched over, Anthony ignored the sweat dripping down his body and looked at the hospital. It wasn't burning. The buildings around it were. It was odd, but the hospital seemed to have miraculously avoided being caught in the explosion. He didn't understand how that worked.

Yet even as he stood there, loud screams came from inside of the hospital, and then several people surged out of the front entrance, their eyes wide with terror. Anthony didn't understand at first. However, when several rabid looking therianthropes emerged from the hospital and attacked a nurse, he realized what the problem was.

Anthony didn't think twice as he stomped on the ground and burst forward. He reared back his fist and gritted his teeth as he channeled more mana into it. His target was the therianthrope that had leapt into the air, pouncing toward a young woman in a nurse's outfit who was lying on the ground.

As the woman screamed, he appeared on her left and threw out his fist, which collided with the therianthrope's face. A loud *bang* like the firing of a cannon echoed across the street. An explosion of air spread from the point of impact. Anthony had put enough power into his punch that the therianthrope's jaw broke when he struck it, and the therianthrope, who had no traction to defend against his attack, was sent flying away from the nurse. The creature landed on the ground, rolled for several feet, and struck a light post, which bent and toppled over.

"Ha… ha… you okay?" he asked the nurse, glancing at her.

"I… oh… um… yes?" The nurse blinked several times as though she couldn't figure out what was happening.

"What happened here?" asked Anthony.

"I… we were attacked… demons… they just showed up out of nowhere and began attacking everyone in sight…" The woman's voice was shaky as she explained what was happening. "I don't… I was just doing my rounds when the buildings on either side exploded, and then demons suddenly appeared… and then…"

"I understand." Anthony held out his hand to the woman, who looked at it in shock for a moment before accepting it. He pulled her to her feet and said, "I'm sure the Academy Island Private Security Forces are already aware of what's happening. You should get out of here and find somewhere safe."

"R-right."

The nurse didn't disagree with him, and she was soon running away from the hospital. At about the same time, Brianna showed up, slowing down her run into a light jog as she caught up with him. She still had the Geminius Sword in her hand. However, she wasn't attacking him and instead was staring at the hospital.

"What is going on?" she asked.

"I don't know." Anthony turned toward the hospital entrance. "But I have to make sure my brother is okay."

"I… I understand," Brianna said. "We can hold off on settling the matter between us until after this."

Anthony wanted to return her words with a sarcastic comment, but he didn't have the time. He raced into the hospital. The moment he entered the lobby, Anthony could see the pandemonium that was occurring inside. A pair of demons were located in the entrance lobby. Like the one outside, these two were therianthropes. However, like all the other rogue demons he had fought in the past few days, these ones seemed different… more feral.

The moment he appeared inside of the lobby, the therianthropes turned to him, let out ferocious howls, and raced forward. Anthony gritted his teeth as he moved aside, dodging a leaping therianthropes by the skin of his teeth. He spun around on the ball of his left foot and launched a reverse heel kick into the rogue demon on his right. The creature was already moving past him, so his attack sent it sprawling to the ground.

At that moment, the other therianthrope tried to attack him, but Brianna appeared on his left and swung her Geminius Sword around. Several flashes of light appeared before Anthony's eyes. Each flash created a thin incision line along the therianthrope's body. Nothing seemed to happen at first, but then Brianna leapt back and blood burst from the therianthrope's body as it split apart.

"That weapon of yours really is the most dangerous thing I've ever seen," Anthony muttered, warily eyeing the double-bladed sword in her hand.

"It's the latest and deadliest weapon designed by Custodes Daemonium." Brianna shrugged.

"I really don't want to be cut open by that."

"..."

Brianna said nothing, but her silence was enough.

Anthony and Brianna didn't remain in the lobby for long. They raced into the hallway, found an elevator, and took it to the third floor. Both of them felt a chill down their spines when they stepped out. Even so, they sped through the hallway while keeping an eye out for any enemies.

"This floor is… surprisingly empty," Brianna muttered, her eyes narrowed.

"I don't like this at all," Anthony said.

Anthony was getting bad vibes. The hairs on his arms were standing on end, his scalp was prickling, and his heart felt like it was trying to blast his chest open. He didn't know why, but he was a nervous wreck as he reached room 343.

The door was not locked, which was something else that bothered him. He was certain these doors were locked when visiting hours were over. Only the head nurse on the night shift should have been able to open this door, yet it opened for him when he stepped up to it. He took a deep breath, banished the fear permeating his heart, and stepped inside.

Once inside, Anthony glanced at the bed, but his attention was immediately forced onto the figure standing beside the bed. It was a man. He had skin so pale it looked translucent. He had dark hair that was combed to the side. The black tuxedo he wore created a stark contrast with his skin, but it also lent him the refined air of a gentleman. He was turned away from Anthony and Brianna, staring at the bed, but when he sensed their presence, he turned around.

Red eyes and sharp fangs met Anthony's gaze. He sucked in a deep breath.

"You must be Anthony Amasius." The man turned around, placed his hand against his waist, and bowed, much like a gentleman who was introducing himself to a compatriot might do. "It is a pleasure to make your acquaintance. My name is Frederic Bloodstone."

The sound of feet shuffling against the ground let him know Brianna had adopted a fighting stance, but he was not focused on that right now. First, he checked to make sure his brother was okay. When he saw the steady rise and fall of Calvin's chest, he breathed a sigh of relief. Only then did he fully focus on the man before him.

"What is a vampire doing here? What do you want with my brother?" he asked.

The vampire, Frederic Bloodstone, smiled. "It is not your brother I am after. While he is indeed a curious case, my purpose for this visit is you."

"Me?" Anthony narrowed his eyes.

"Surely I do not need to spell it out for you." Frederic's smile widened, revealing more and more of his sharp, elongated canines. "You are an incubus, a rare breed of monster that has not been seen in centuries, and you are currently without a single bondmate and therefore incredibly weak. It would be a mistake on my part if I did not take advantage of this rare opportunity."

Anthony's heart thundered against his chest as he realized what this man wanted. Blood. His blood. His legs shook, but he tried not to let his fear at this situation get to him. He had faced off against the Vampire Lord Cane alongside Lilith and his fellow bondmates. He had not shown fear then, and he would not show fear now.

"I see. Vampires require the blood of humans to sustain themselves, but they also grow stronger by feeding off the blood of other monsters," Brianna said, eyes narrowing. "So you wish to consume Anthony's blood in order to gain the strength of an incubus. Is that it?"

Frederic finally looked at the woman by Anthony's side, his eyes narrowing slightly when he saw the blade in her hands. He shifted a little. Anthony had the sense that this vampire was wary of the Geminius Sword—not that he could be blamed. Vampire or not, the weapon Brianna wielded could cut through his body like a hot knife through butter.

"I see you are a War Maiden from Custodes Daemonium. You are correct. I wish to consume the blood of this incubus and claim his powers for my own." Frederic's eyes narrowed. "I do not know what you are doing here with this creature, but I'd like to ask that you not get yourself involved. I've no quarrel with your organization."

Anthony didn't know what Brianna would do in this situation. Technically speaking, her best option would be to step back and let this vampire deal with him. If Frederic drained his blood, Anthony would die, which would accomplish Brianna's goal of killing him, and she wouldn't have to lift a finger. At the same time, if this vampire gained his powers, who knew what might happen.

Brianna snorted as she stepped forward. "You must be delusional if you think I'd let you drain Anthony of his blood. The powers of an incubus are dangerous. I cannot allow such powers to fall into the hands of anyone, least of all a person like you, who would turn so many therianthropes into ghouls to do your bidding."

"I would not worry about those therianthropes," Frederic said with a dismissive wave of his hand. "They are not real people—just clones I found to do my bidding."

Anthony narrowed his eyes as he slowly connected the dots. "I see. So those rogue demons that attacked Nametech were actually clones you discovered in their research facility. You turned them into ghouls and let them loose in the city. While the ghouls distracted the Academy Island Private Security Forces, you would locate me and wait for the opportune moment to attack and steal my blood."

"Hmph. You are awfully sharp." Frederic looked disappointed that Anthony had discovered his ultimate goal so quickly, but he must have decided not to let it bother him. "Yes, that was indeed my plan." He spread his arms wide before dark waves of black energy wafted from his body like miasma. "However, knowing what my plan is does not mean you have the ability to stop it."

The black miasma surrounding the man suddenly flew forward, transforming into something that looked like a gigantic beast. It reminded Anthony of a lion's head. The beast opened its jaws as though to swallow him whole, and Anthony found his body frozen as memories of Lilith's battle against Cane filled his vision.

Before the black energy could take a chunk out of him, Brianna stepped forward and swung her blade. The glowing Geminius Sword sliced through the powerful energy. As the energy was separated into two halves, each half slammed into the walls behind Anthony and Brianna, eating right through them. However, they didn't stop at just one wall. They flew through the corridor, devoured the wall leading into the next room, and continued on. When Anthony turned his head, he found that the powerful energy had eaten through every wall within the hospital and traveled out the other side.

Frederic narrowed his eyes and hissed. "I see that weapon of yours really is a Geminius Sword. I'd heard Custodes Daemonium had created a powerful new weapon that could sever space and time to slice through the molecular bonds of every conceivable material known to man, but I didn't think they would give such a powerful weapon to a little girl like you."

Brianna narrowed her eyes at the "little girl comment" and took a step forward, appearing seconds away from attacking this vampire, but Anthony held her back.

"Not here," he said softly. "My brother is in this room. We can't fight him here."

Brianna bit her lip but nodded. Meanwhile, the vampire seemed to hear their conversation and smiled.

"That is right. This boy here is your younger brother, correct?" Frederic moved to stand beside the head of the bed. Dark energy coalesced around his left hand as he brought it to the glass case. He tapped on the case once. "This boy is quite important to you, I hear. Give yourself to me, or I will kill this child."

Anthony clenched his hands into fists. He knew the moment he found out what Frederic wanted that this vampire was going to use his brother as a hostage, but knowing that didn't make the situation any better. What should he do? If he gave himself up, Calvin might live, but there would be no one around to take care of him when he woke up… if he ever woke up.

While he was standing by in indecision, Brianna narrowed her eyes and, quick as lightning, she flung the Geminius Sword at the vampire. Frederic's eyes widened as he jerked his hand away from Calvin. The sword became embedded into the wall just above the boy's head where the vampire's hand had been. If he'd been a second slower, his hand would have been sliced clean off.

Anthony might have been rusty from not training in over a year, but he was not one to let such an opportunity get past him. He raced forward, spun around on the balls of his feet, and slammed the sole of his right foot into Frederic's chest.

Because Anthony did not have any bondmates, he was not very strong, even when using Physical Enhancement. However, that didn't mean he was weak either. His strength was still many times that of an ordinary human. When his foot struck Frederic, the vampire slammed into the wall, breaking through it and stumbling into the other room.

Brianna grabbed her Geminius Sword as Anthony raced into the other room and tried to engage Frederic in hand to hand combat. The vampire snarled as he unleashed a terrifying and dark aura. Black energy surged toward Anthony, who felt alarm causing his heart rate to spike. He backed off, trying to gain some distance, but the energy followed him, transforming into a three-headed snake that snapped at him—at least, until Brianna cut each head off with her weapon. Then the snake dispersed.

"Thank you," Anthony muttered.

Brianna didn't say anything as she turned to Frederic and raced toward him, swinging the Geminius Sword in a series of graceful arcs.

Frederic hissed as he backed off. He seemed to understand how foolish it was to fight against a War Maiden wielding such a weapon in close-quarters combat. He sent a powerful burst of black energy at her. Brianna cut through it with ease, but she was forced to divert her attention, which allowed Frederic to turn around and race out the window.

Anthony ran over to the shattered glass window and looked out, watching as Frederic created a pair of black wings and flew off. A growl escaped his throat. If he let this man go now, there was no telling when he would try to take Calvin hostage again.

"Anthony! Wait!" Brianna shouted as Anthony leapt out of the building, but he did not wait. Landing on the ground, he pushed Physical Enhancement to the absolute limit and chased after Frederic. He could not let this vampire escape!

He didn't know where the man was heading nor did he care. He followed the vampire by leaping onto the roof of a building and jumping across the buildings to keep the man in his sights. Frederic finally noticed him and sent that black energy at him again, but Anthony zigzagged across the rooftops to avoid each attack, which penetrated the buildings and ate through them as if devouring their very existence.

As the chase continued, Anthony wondered how he could bring this vampire down. He didn't have much mana, and his reserves were dwindling fast, which meant he had to act now.

With a soft groan, he used a small portion of mana to create a thread of glowing blue energy, then sent the thread into the sky. It was such a small thread that Frederic didn't notice it until it had latched around his leg. The vampire's startled expression cheered Anthony up as he pushed more mana into his physical enhancement magic, dug his heels into the rooftop pavement, and yanked.

Frederic was pulled down. He struck the roof of the next building over, and Anthony didn't hesitate to leap from his building to this one. The wind whistled around him before he landed on the other building. Frederic pushed himself back to his feet, turned around, and glared at Anthony.

"For such a weak creature, you're awfully tenacious."

"If I'm so weak, why do you want my blood?"

"Hmph. That is obviously because of your potential." Frederic narrowed his eyes. "I do not know what possesses you not to build a harem of bondmates, but you are clearly an idiot. If you bound women to you, your powers could be infinite. You could even gain enough power to rival the Beast King of Russia, the Vampire Lords of the European Federation, the Succubus Queens, or even Hagaromo Gitsune of Japan. Such power is wasted on you, a man who refuses to seek more power, and so I'm going to take it from you."

As he finished speaking, the shadows around him writhed like living creatures before black miasma burst from Frederic's shadow and turned into a ferocious pack of wolves. The creatures raced forward and lunged at Anthony, who tried to backpedal and avoid them. Regardless of his potential, it was true that right now he was weak. A single bite from one of these creatures would probably drain all of his life from him.

Anthony backpedaled, then swerved to avoid a wolf that leapt at him from the left. He gritted his teeth as he dispelled the ethereal creature with a single punch. Yet even after killing that one, there were still many more that lunged toward him. One attempted to take a chunk out of his arm, another his left thigh, and one his right shoulder. There were so many attacking from so many different angles that he couldn't possibly defeat all of them.

Just as it looked like he was about to be overwhelmed, Brianna descended from the sky.

"HAAAA!!"

She swung the Geminius Sword with incredible ferocity. Six flashes of light cut apart six of the wolves. Anthony used that opportunity to channel mana into his fist, which sparked with power as he slammed it into the face of another wolf, blasting the miasma-like energy being apart. Then he raised his foot, blue lightning-like mana racing along it as he kicked another wolf. This one was also blasted apart. Brianna finished the rest with her weapon.

"Ha... ha..."

"Anthony!"

After they finished off the wolf pack, Anthony stumbled forward and nearly fell to the ground. He caught himself at the last second. Even so, his vision was beginning to grow dark.

"It looks like you're nearly out of mana." Frederic gave him a fanged grin. "This is what happens to creatures like you who refuse to seek power. You are weak—too weak to protect even yourself, and for that, you shall die this night. I shall drain your life, gain your powers, and become a supreme being that can rival even the Vampire Lord, Cane!"

"I won't let that happen!"

Brianna stepped forward and brandished the Geminius Sword. Blue lines appeared on her battle outfit before she rushed forward faster than before—faster than when she had been fighting Anthony earlier that night. She was on Frederic in seconds.

The vampire sent a surge of black energy at her, but the redhead cut through it with ease, then stepped forward and swung her blade from the ground up in a powerful horizontal slice. Frederic ghosted backward to try and dodge the attack. He wasn't fast enough, however, and Brianna's blade cut straight through his shoulder.

"Ng! AHHH! AH! AHHHH!!!"

The man screamed as his left arm fell to the ground with a wet thud. Blood gushed from his stump as he stumbled back, his eyes wide in shock and pain. Yet even though he was clearly suffering from what must have been incredible agony, he still had the gumption to push it aside and glare at Brianna.

"You… bitch!" he screeched.

Brianna clicked her tongue and brandished her weapon. "That attack was supposed to cut you down the middle. I won't miss next time."

"There won't be a next time!"

Removing his hand from his now armless shoulder, Frederic snarled as he gathered black energy into his single remaining hand. Swirling motes of power coalesced above his hand, turning into a tiny black orb that seemed innocuous—if you ignored the powerful spatial distortions creating ripples around it.

Brianna's eyes widened. She seemed to realize what he was going to do and rushed forward to stop him.

She was too late.

Frederic slammed his hand onto the rooftop, which exploded with a detonation of dark energy so powerful she was sent flying backward. Her pained scream was drowned out by the roaring of numerous explosions. The dark power blasted through the roof. Then it blasted through the next floor, and then the next, and the one after that. At the same time, the roof collapsed underneath her and Anthony.

As he fell through the building, Anthony spotted Frederic flying off into the distance, but he didn't have time to focus on the escaping vampire. The wind whistled around him as he looked at Brianna. She was unconscious. The dark power had seared her face and body. Some of her battle outfit had been destroyed, revealing several nasty burns on her chest that must have been from the backlash of Frederic's dark mana.

Despite feeling his heart leap into his throat as he fell, Anthony had the sense to act. He used the last of his mana to create a thin thread. He attached it to Brianna, pulled her to him, and hugged her close as he flipped around so he was on the bottom. There was very little he could do now. Brianna had helped him protect Calvin, so if nothing else, he would at least use his own body to cushion her fall.

Brianna shifted against him as he hugged her tight. He smiled just a little as the hole in the roof became smaller and smaller. The wind howled around him. The floors of this building passed by him in a blur. Everything looked like mere streaks of color and shadow. It felt like this moment had slowed down, like he would fall forever, but then he struck the ground. Anthony felt a brief moment of indescribable agony.

Then his world went black.

***

Brianna opened her eyes with a startled gasp. A moment of panic swept through her, but she soon remembered her training and took several deep breaths, calming down and settling her rapidly beating heart. It took longer than she would have liked. Her mind was still locked on what happened to her, on the battle against the vampire called Frederic Bloodstone.

After calming down, Brianna sat up and looked around the room she found herself in. It was a room far more extravagant than her own. More spacious than any bedroom she'd ever seen, this place featured several expensive furnishings and looked like something she'd expect to see in a vampire noble's house. All of the furniture was made from varnished wood. The aesthetic also reminded her of the few times she'd visited a vampire noble from the European Federation with her instructor.

Once she'd taken stock of her surroundings, she looked down at herself, checking for injuries. At present, she was wearing a simple white robe and nothing else. The robe was light and very sheer. She could actually see her nipples poking against the fabric. She parted the front and looked at her chest, expecting to see a large black mark where the vampire's miasmic power had struck her, but she became surprised when all she saw was smooth white skin and light pink nipples.

During the battle against Frederic, the man had created a powerful attack that exploded against the roof and struck her with its full force. She remembered the searing pain of the intense devouring force slamming into her. Brianna didn't know what happened after that. She had been rendered unconscious.

Thinking about it, she was actually shocked to find that she was still alive.

Just what happened?

It didn't look like she had any injuries, which meant someone must have healed her, perhaps whoever owned this mansion. She was curious to know who that was. Whoever they were either had some really deep pockets or a lot of influential connections.

The moment this thought crossed through her mind, a soft clicking sound made her turn toward the door. Someone opened the door and entered the room. Brianna blinked in surprise when she saw a small woman who looked somewhat like a child. She couldn't have been taller than 4'11", had a head of long blonde hair styled into numerous ringlets, which framed a face Brianna could only call cute. Furthermore, she was dressed in an expensive pink and white lolita outfit.

"She looks just like a doll…"

The woman paused, eyes narrowing. "On account of the fact that you were seriously injured, I am going to pretend you didn't say anything. However, I will warn you that if you say I look like a doll ever again, I am going to turn your time so far back it will be as if you were never born."

It was only after the woman spoke that Brianna realized she had said those words out loud. Heat spread to her cheeks.

"I-I'm terribly sorry. I didn't mean to say that."

"Whatever." The woman sighed before walking up to the bed. "I'm sure you are wondering where you are right now. This is my house. You were very injured when I found you, so I brought you here."

"I… I see." Brianna struggled for a moment before letting her curiosity get the better of her. "Thank you for saving me, but, um, who are you?"

"My name is Lucretia Incanscino," the woman introduced herself.

"You're the Time Witch!" Brianna gasped.

Lucretia sighed. "It seems my reputation precedes me."

"Of course!" Brianna placed her hands on her lap and leaned forward, staring at the woman like she was an extravagant painting made by a famous artist. "Everyone has heard of the Time Witch. You are the first magician within the last five centuries to have completely mastered time magic. Custodes Daemonium has given you the same S-class ranking as the most powerful demons in the entire world. It's said you are one of only five humans who are capable of fighting the greatest demons on even terms."

It seemed even a woman of Lucretia's reputation could not help but feel flattered at the high-praise, for her chest swelled ever so slightly after Brianna finished gushing.

"Well, you are not wrong. I am quite powerful," she said.

Only after Brianna finished gushing did she understand how she'd been healed. "I see. So that is how you healed me. Time magic."

"Correct. You are quite sharp." Lecretia nodded. "I didn't heal you so much as turn back your time to before the injury even took place. It's a bit of a pain to use magic that powerful, but it is not beyond my capabilities."

That did not surprise Brianna at all. Her instructor had spoken highly of Lucretia Incanscino, a legendary figure who was currently hailed as the strongest magician in the entire world. She had heard that this woman was living on Academy

Island. There was a report about it that she had read before leaving for her current mission. Even so, Brianna never expected to meet such a famous figure during her mission here.

Her mission…

Brianna's eyes widened as she realized that if she was here, then there should have been someone else beside her.

"Anthony!"

A jolt raced through her system as small fragments of memory returned. She'd been semi-conscious after that blast struck her and she fell through the roof. Everything had been blurring in and out at the time, so she hadn't been able to see much, but she still clearly remembered the feeling of Anthony hugging her close and using his own body as a cushion to soften her fall.

"I'm surprised it took you so long to remember he was with you." Lucretia turned around and beckoned to Brianna. "Follow me."

At the gesture, Brianna stood up, closed her robes further, tightened the belt around her waist, and followed the much shorter woman outside.

They entered a hallway and walked down it. Brianna glanced at the walls that several paintings hung from. They were all landscape oil paintings, and they looked like they cost more money than an office worker's yearly salary.

"You are Sarah Noel's student, aren't you?" Lucretia suddenly asked.

Brianna was startled but nodded. "Yes, that's right."

"How is that old hag doing?"

Brianna almost got defensive at the insulting term Lucretia used to describe her instructor, but then she remembered the orders she'd been given before all this happened and her anger died.

"She is doing well," Brianna muttered as they turned a corner.

"I imagine so. That woman is quite the tough old sack of bones."

"Are you acquainted with Instructor Noel?"

"Just a bit. I had the chance to meet her around one decade ago. She had just been a regular War Maiden at the time, and I was the head of the Magician's Association. I believe it was during the Cordobalt Catastrophe when she and I chanced upon each other."

Brianna shivered at the mention of the Cordobalt Catastrophe, which had been a catastrophic event where a rogue pureblood vampire named Cordobalt Venswick teamed up with a rogue magician to create a large-scale magic circle that consumed an entire city. Instructor Noel had been one of the people sent to stop Cordobalt. She did in the end, but more than a third of the population had been wiped out before she could finish her job.

Before she could ask Lucretia any more questions, they arrived in front of a door. Lucretia opened the door and walked in. Brianna followed her.

What lay beyond the door was a room much like the one she'd woken up in but with different furnishings. However, what grabbed her attention was not the expensive furniture. It was the figure lying on the bed.

"Anthony!"

She raced over to the bed and stopped. Her heart leapt into her throat and her knees turned weak when she saw the man lying there, his eyes closed, face pale and gaunt, and body completely inert. She leaned down and tried to touch him, to see if he was really there, but Lucretia slapped her hand away.

"Don't." The Time Witch gave Brianna a mild glare. "At present, I have stopped Anthony's time, putting him in a form of suspended animation. However, this kind of magic is incredibly delicate. If you touch him, your mana could infect the tapestries of magic I've woven around his body to keep him like this."

Brianna jerked her hand back. She looked at Anthony, and then at Lucretia.

"Why have you stopped his time?" she asked, feeling something unsettling drop into the pit of her stomach. She had a bad feeling about this.

The woman's next words made those feelings increase a thousand fold.

"Because Anthony is currently dying and there is no longer anything I can do to save him," she said with a dim look in her eyes.

CHAPTER 6

"What… what do you mean?"

Brianna was stunned. Lucretia couldn't save Anthony? Surely there was something she could do? She was the Time Witch, a magician of such outstanding power that even the Vampire Lords and Beast King would not fight her unless they had no choice. Her powers over time were incomparable!

Lucretia smiled as if she knew what Brianna was thinking.

"I may have powers over time, but there are rules I must follow regarding such a temporal law like time." She glanced at Anthony and bit her lip, causing Brianna to also glance at the pale-faced man who currently looked even weaker than usual. "For the past year, I have been turning back Anthony's time over and over again to restore what little mana he has inside of his body. However, incubus, like succubus, have an incredibly strong magical resistance. You know of a demon's magical resistance, yes?"

"It's a demon's ability to resist outside magical interference that influences the mind and body," Brianna answered.

"A textbook answer, but you're only scratching the surface." Lucretia sighed as she walked over to the bed and placed her hand on Anthony's forehead. It was an oddly intimate gesture that took Brianna aback and made her wonder about the relationship these two had. "Demons are born with an innate ability to resist any and all forms of magic. Of course, this includes magical attacks like spells, seals, and even natural phenomena like mana storms. Incubus are no different in this regard. However, incubus are also inherently special."

"How so?" asked Brianna.

"Because their magical resistance toward a specific type of magic seems to increase every time you use it on them," Lucretia answered, finally looking away from Anthony to stare at her. "I have been reversing Anthony's time for the past year, and in that year, my ability to help him has slowly dwindled. Anthony himself doesn't seem to realize it, but the amount of mana he has now is only about a third of what it was when I first began helping him. I suspect I would only be able to reverse his time two or three more times before his body became completely resistant to it."

Brianna sucked in a breath. She had no idea such a thing was even possible, but if Lucretia was saying it, then it must be true, which of course meant this woman really couldn't help him.

Biting her lower lip, Brianna glanced at the frail figure on the bed. A sharp pain entered her chest. She rubbed it, but this feeling would not go away no matter how much she tried to massage it out, for it wasn't something she felt on the outside. This was no physical wound.

"So there is… nothing we can do?" Brianna whispered as she felt her eyes sting. She blinked once as a tear fell down her pale cheeks. Reaching up, she wiped at her eyes, then stared at the water on her fingers. Shock coursed through her. Ever since she'd been picked up by Custodes Daemonium, she could not remember crying even once.

"There is nothing *I* can," Lucretia admitted. "However, there is something that *you* can do."

"Something I can do?"

Brianna's eyes widened as she heard this. She glanced at Anthony and remembered what happened during their battle against that vampire, how he had used his own body to save her from the impact of falling from several hundred feet. He had protected her even though she had been trying to kill him.

She closed her eyes and struggled to make a decision, to choose between saving this man and just letting him die. Custodes Daemonium had ordered his death. If she did nothing, he would die and she would accomplish her mission.

But doing so would hurt. It would really, really hurt.

It was only now, at this juncture, that she truly understood what kind of impact Anthony had left on her. She had spent the past week with Anthony, living next to him, seeing him everyday, going out with him and experiencing things she never had before coming to Academy Island. The time she had spent with him had been so much fun. More than that, however, Brianna had come to understand what kind of person Anthony was.

Anthony was a caring person who worked hard, treated others with respect, and didn't seek power for powers sake. He could have built a harem and become incomparably strong, so strong he could probably take over Academy Island, but he didn't. He lived a quiet life as a college student. His only real desire was to bring his brother out of a coma.

Brianna admired Anthony. She respected him. What's more, even just thinking about him made her heart flutter and her chest feel warm. He invoked feelings in her that she did not understand. She had been hoping to explore those feelings until the order to kill him had come…

"What… can I do to save him?" Brianna finally asked, turning her gaze to Lucretia.

The infamous Time Witch smiled, but she didn't answer right away.

"Tell me, how do you feel about Anthony?"

"How do I feel?" Brianna scrunched up her face. "I think he is a great person. I… while I was ordered to kill him, I would much rather see him live. He does not deserve to die."

"That's the kind of answer I would expect from that old hag's disciple." Lucretia sighed and shook her head as though Brianna had said something annoying. "Let me try this in a way even someone dense like you can understand: Do you love Anthony?"

While Brianna initially felt insulted at being called dense, her expression, which had been narrowed in anger, suddenly froze as if someone had cast an ice spell on her. Yet even though her face was frozen, her blood flow was not. Heat rushed to her cheeks.

"W-what kind of question is that?!" She looked away.

"A very important question." Lucretia answered, the frills of her sleeves rustling as she crossed her arms. "Anthony is an incubus. You understand what that is, right? While there are many differences between incubus and succubus, their powers, at least, are quite similar. An incubus's power comes from the harem of women who become bound to him—his bondmates. They are not just the source of his power. Without having several bondmates to constantly provide him with mana, he will eventually die."

It was well-documented knowledge that succubus formed harems, bonding with men in a symbiotic relationship. In exchange for giving a succubus a constant supply of mana through sex, the bondmate also received outstanding benefits like eternal youth, the ability to use one of the succubus's powers, and great sex—or so Brianna had been told. She wasn't so sure about that last one.

An incubus was supposedly the male version of a succubus. All the documents and texts regarding this elusive creature pointed toward this being true. In every historical text regarding them, the incubus who created a Magic Catastrophe on the level that exceeded an S-rank classification always had a harem of powerful women by his side. The last time an incubus showed up was about 500 years ago, and it had resulted in the incubus and three women laying waste to the entire Custodes Daemonium organization. It had required every member of their organization overwhelming this group with sheer numbers, tiring them out by constantly battling day and night for an entire month, just to kill them.

Brianna had read up on this for her mission, but she hadn't really thought about what that would mean for her.

"So you… want me to have sex with Anthony?" Brianna asked hesitantly, her cheeks burning like an inferno. "You are asking me to become his bondmate?"

"If you want to save him, that is the only way." Lucretia shrugged. "Of course, you can choose not to. No one can force this on you."

Brianna felt like she was at a crossroads in her life. On one side was the life she knew, the comfortable life where she was a member of Custodes Daemonium. In this life, she didn't have to think about anything, about right or wrong, about what she had and what she lacked. She just had to follow her orders to the best of her abilities.

On the other side was a life as Anthony's bondmate, a world of uncertainty, a world she didn't understand and even somewhat feared, but also a world where she would get to stay by Anthony's side and explore these feelings she had for him. It might be hard. No, it would definitely be hard. Yet when she pictured herself ten years from now, the images she imagined invoked a pleasant feeling within her chest.

She took a deep breath and came to a decision.

"I'll do it," Brianna said, her eyes hardening in determination even as her cheeks grew increasingly hotter. "Just tell me what I need to do."

When Lucretia heard her answer, the infamous Time Witch, a woman so great she was given the same threat classification as this world's most powerful demons, someone even her instructed respected and feared, gave the first genuine smile Brianna had seen from her since this meeting began.

***

When Anthony felt his consciousness return, he was a little surprised. He'd honestly not been expecting to wake up at all.

His surprise fled moments later when exhaustion hit him. He'd never felt this tired before in his entire life. It was like all of his life essence had been drained out of his body.

He opened his eyes and found himself in a room that was actually vaguely familiar. It looked like one of Professor Incanscino's rooms. As he turned his head to study where he was, the face of Brianna appeared before his eyes.

"You're awake," Brianna murmured with a voice he'd never heard from her before. It was… odd. He couldn't place it, but there was a lot of emotion in her voice. "Thank God. I don't know what I would have done if you had died."

Anthony wanted to ask her if that was something someone who had tried to kill him should say, but something told him now was not the time.

"What… happened?" he asked instead.

"We were rescued by Lucretia Incanscino," Brianna explained. "I believe she found us buried underneath the rubble of that building we fell through. She's the one who healed us after bringing us to her home."

Anthony would have nodded at her words, but he was far too exhausted, his body like lead and his mind sluggish as though he was wading through quicksand. Now that he was thinking about it, he couldn't remember a single time where he ever felt this awful before. Even after he and Brianna met for the first time, he hadn't been in this bad of shape.

"Anthony…" Brianna called out to him again, and Anthony blinked several times to focus on her face, which he only now noticed was filled with worry. She was biting her lip. "There is something I need to tell you. You are currently dying. You exhausted nearly all of your mana when we battled against that vampire. Lucretia healed your physical injuries, but apparently, you have built up such a strong magical resistance to her magic that she can no longer rewind time for you."

Listening to everything she said, Anthony only felt a vague disappointment.

"Oh… so I'm dying. Well, that sucks." He took a deep breath and closed his eyes for a moment. When he opened them again, Anthony looked at Brianna as he spoke. "Hey, I'm sorry to ask this of you, but can you do me a favor? When I'm gone, I want you to ask the people from Custodes Daemonium if they can take Calvin in. I couldn't save him, but maybe they can. Will you do that for me?"

Brianna's eyes widened for a moment, a look of uncomprehending shock on her face, but then she narrowed her eyes.

"I won't."

Anthony felt a brief moment of irritation before his exhaustion swept it away. "But... why? I don't think I'm asking for too much. Is it because I'm an incubus?"

"That's not it." Brianna's long red hair wavered as she shook her head. "I'm not going to do it because you are not going to die. Lucretia told me there is a way I can save you."

Even though Anthony felt awful, like his spirit was already slipping out of his body, he was at least smart enough to understand what she meant. He narrowed his eyes a little and shook his head.

"I can't. I won't."

"Why not?" Brianna snapped, actually sounding angry at him. "Why won't you bind me to you? I'm offering myself to you! I'm willing to become your bondmate! Or is it that you don't think I'm good enough for you?"

"That's not it at all," Anthony muttered.

"Then why?! Don't you want to wake your brother from his coma?! You can't do that if you're dead! If there is a chance to live, why won't you take it?! What are you so afraid of?!"

Anthony's hand twitched when Brianna mentioned him being afraid, but it wasn't like he could deny her words. He closed his eyes. A vision of loveliness appeared in front of him, a woman with hair like midnight, eyes like cobalts, and an aristocratic face reminiscent of nobility that was filled with kindness and warmth. The vision faded, even as he reached out to grasp it, and he opened his eyes again to discover Brianna still staring at him.

"You're right. I am afraid," he admitted. "I'm afraid of losing these feelings I have. Incubus magically bind women to them. These women become the backbone of his entire existence. They don't just provide an incubus with mana. If I bind a woman to me, I will be giving them my body and soul. I will be giving everything to them. I'm afraid that if I do that, if I give myself to another woman, my feelings for Lilith will disappear…"

It was something he had never admitted out loud, his greatest fear and the true reason he refused to bind any woman to him. His feelings for Lilith were something he held closely to his heart. Lilith had saved him and his brother, had given them a place to live, a purpose to live for. She had been his everything. He didn't want to replace her. He didn't want to forget these feelings because of his nature as an incubus.

"You are really loyal to Lilith, aren't you?" Brianna asked with a strange look on her face, a mixture of admiration and pain. "I'm kind of jealous of her, to be honest. I wish I had someone who loved me that much. However, don't you think you are doing Lilith a disservice by giving your life away like this? I don't know what exactly happened, but she is the reason you became an incubus, right? She gave her life and powers to you. If you die right here, her sacrifice will have been in vain."

Anthony blinked several times. Lilith's sacrifice would be in vain if he died, wouldn't it? He had never thought about it like that before, but it was true that she had given up her life and powers for his sake, turning him into an incubus at the cost of her own life. All this time he had shunned female contact because he didn't want his feelings for Lilith to disappear, but dying like this when she sacrificed everything for his sake really would be dishonoring her memory.

"I guess… you do bring up a good point," he muttered. "But I…"

"You're worried," Brianna said, offering him a small smile. "You're not alone in that. I'm worried too, about becoming your bondmate, I mean. I've lived most of my life being trained by Custodes Daemonium to slay demons, and yet here I am about to let myself become bound to one. I'm terrified."

"Speaking of, are you really sure about this?" he asked her. "I don't think Custodes Daemonium will appreciate you going against their orders like this."

Brianna's eyes only wavered for a moment before hardening. It was as if someone had ignited a fire within her.

"I've already made my choice," she stated with complete certainty. "I've decided that you don't deserve to die, and that I… I wish to explore these feelings I have for you."

Anthony sucked in a breath. "You have feelings for me?"

"I-I don't know exactly what I feel," Brianna admitted with a blush that made her seem way cuter than such a buxom woman had any right to be. "But I do feel something, and I want to explore what they are. I want to understand them."

"I understand." Anthony paused. "So… how should we do this? I'm afraid I can't really move right now…"

"Right now, your body is extremely weak because you've depleted all your mana," Brianna explained as she pulled the covers back, revealing inch after inch of his bare skin. It was only now that Anthony realized he was naked under these covers. "At present, you probably can't move at all because of that. Um… I don't have any experience with this sort of thing, but I do know the basics about procreation. And Lucretia gave me a few pointers."

"Professor Incanscino gave you pointers?" Anthony wasn't sure how he should feel about that. The idea of his tiny professor having experienced sex just felt weird to him. It also felt like something inside of him was raging at the thought. How strange.

"Yes. So I should be able to do this." Anthony said nothing as Brianna completely removed the covers. Now his entire body was bared before Brianna, and Anthony suddenly felt self-conscious, especially when her eyes widened in shock. "S-sorry you have to see me like this. I know it's not the most attractive sight."

"Is your body like this because you don't have a single bondmate?" asked Brianna.

Anthony couldn't nod, so he just said, "Yes. My muscles have atrophied, and my body is basically starving for mana, so I've become like this."

Because he'd been running on minimal mana for the past year, Anthony's body was rail thin. His ribs were visible, his stomach looked concave, and his arms and legs were like twigs. This was the reason he always wore baggy clothes. He didn't want anyone to see how badly malnourished his body was.

"I can't believe you would do this to yourself," Brianna murmured as she reached out and touched his chest. Her fingers were gentle and warm as she trailed them across his skin. She stopped after going to his stomach, and then found her true target.

Anthony couldn't say anything in his defense, so he didn't bother, and he wasn't sure Brianna would have listened anyway. She was too busy staring at the spot between his legs.

Climbing onto the bed, Brianna wandered over to his legs before stopping right beside him. She reached out and tentatively touched the long object dangling between his legs. She jerked her hand back when his dick twitched a little, but then she bit her lower lip and reached out again, placing her hands over his cock.

Anthony breathed in as Brianna's soft and wonderfully warm hands rested on his dick. Her gentle touch caused his cock to swell in her grasp. Brianna released a gasp of shock as the thing went from flaccid to fully erect within seconds.

"W-what kind of monster is this?!"

"I'm not sure how I feel about you calling my penis a monster."

"S-sorry." Brianna sounded contrite, but she hadn't taken her eyes off his dick since it swelled up like an oblong balloon. "It's just a lot bigger than I expected it to be. I've seen pictures before during sexual education, but... I don't know. I never imagined they would be this large in real life."

Anthony was actually pretty sure his size was somewhere in the middle. Some of his fellow harem members in Lilith's harem had truly massive cocks, which had always made him feel inferior to them. Hearing Brianna call his dick big was a bit of an ego booster.

"You've never had sex before, right?" he asked.

Brianna shook her head. "I haven't, but I do know what to do."

She didn't give Anthony time to say anything more as she leaned down. She paused just above his cockhead. Her warm breath washed over him and made Anthony's dick twitch as a small shiver ran up and down his spine. She hesitated for a moment, cheeks glowing like a neon sign, then stuck out her tongue and slowly licked his dick.

"This taste…" Brianna muttered.

Anthony wanted to know what she meant by that, but he was unable to speak and could only groan when Brianna pressed her tongue against his shaft and gave it a more thorough lick. Her warm and wet tongue felt like heaven. Once she started, Brianna seemed to become possessed. She licked him from his ball sack all the way to his head. It was incredibly awkward, and Anthony could tell she'd never done this before, but her enthusiasm more than made up for her lack of experience.

Perhaps it was because he hadn't been with anyone in so long. Barely a few seconds had passed since Brianna began coating his dick in her saliva before Anthony felt his balls and stomach tighten.

"B-Bri! S-stop! If you keep doing that, I'm gonna cum!"

Brianna stopped what she was doing and looked up at him. Her eyes were half-lidded pools of seduction. She was breathing heavily and her cheeks were stained a dark red. It looked like she had become lost within a haze of lust, a look he'd never seen on her before, but one he had seen on himself and Lilith's other bondmates plenty of times.

"Clothes…" Anthony croaked. "Take off your clothes please."

He didn't know if Brianna had heard him at first, but then she climbed off the bed and undid the sash tying her white robes together. As the robes parted, Anthony finally saw the first hints of her cleavage. His throat went dry. She was not wearing a bra right now. As she slid the robes down her arms and let it fall to the floor, he got his first gaze at a completely naked Brianna.

Anthony had always known Brianna had a great figure. That battle suit she wore did not leave anything to the imagination.

However, seeing her in a suit and seeing her like this were two completely different things.

Brianna was the possessor of a body that shouldn't have been possible. Her breasts were large, perhaps even larger than Lilith's had been, and they looked so very enticing as they sat on her chest, capped with light pink areolas and nipples.

He let his gaze wander down. She had a very thin waist, almost wasplike, but she also had hints of a six pack. Her abdominals were not completely visible, hidden behind a fine layer of softness. However, he could see her stomach muscles flexing as she rotated her body slightly to the side. Now that they had come this far, Anthony could say he'd really like to some day take body shots off that stomach.

Finally, he looked even further down, at Brianna's wide hips. They complimented her large chest and small waist, creating what many would have called a perfect hourglass. Her hips were muscular like her stomach and well-defined. She also had the thigh gap, which allowed him that perfect glimpse of her pussy. As he gazed at her nether lips, which were just a perfectly smooth line, Anthony swallowed heavily and cursed his inability to move. What he wouldn't give to bury his face between those thighs…

As he admired her body, Brianna stood there and went into a full-body blush. Blood rose to the fore of her skin, granting her a beautiful pink coloration. Anthony realized he was probably staring too hard.

"S-sorry," he said. "I just… I knew you were gorgeous, but I'm still a little shocked."

"You think I'm beautiful?" asked Brianna.

"I don't think there's a single straight man in this entire world who wouldn't think that."

While the color of her skin deepened, a smile did spread across her lips. "I'm glad you find me attractive."

Anthony smiled back. "Come here please."

Brianna took a deep breath as though centering herself, then walked back over, crawled onto the bed, and straddled Anthony's legs. She placed her soft hands on his chest and rocked her hips forward a little. Anthony stifled a groan when her cunt came into contact with his cock. Brianna bit back a moan as well when she rubbed her pussy along his shaft, which moved backward a little from her actions.

It probably had something to do with his pheromones, but Brianna's pussy soon had juices flowing out of it as she ground herself against him. His throbbing erection twitched erratically as it became sandwiched between her pussy lips. Anthony had to grit his teeth to keep from crying out in pleasure.

"Ha… ha…" Brianna's breathing was heavy as she stopped rocking her hips back and forth. She kept her hands placed on his chest. "O-okay… I think… we're ready…"

"Yeah. Make sure you go slowly. I'm told it hurts the first time."

"R-right."

Brianna lifted her hips and removed one hand from his chest, taking his dick in her hand and guiding it to her entrance. She placed his head against her pussy. The juices still flowing from her cunt, which stained her inner thighs, also drenched his already soaked shaft. Once she felt his dick resting against her lips, she moved her hips down.

"Ah…"

A soft groan escaped Brianna's mouth as Anthony's dick was slowly engulfed in her tight passage. Her lips spread apart as inch after inch became buried inside of her. Either it had been too long since he'd had sex, or Brianna's pussy was just particularly extraordinary, because he felt the urge to cum seconds after she began taking him in. He held out, gritting his teeth, until Brianna stopped moving.

His cock was still only half buried inside of her.

"A-are you okay?" asked Anthony.

"I'm… fine…" Brianna said, breathing still heavy. Her body was coated in a small layer of sweat that caused her alabaster skin to glisten. Her face was scrunched up. "It's just… I feel like you're splitting me apart, and you're barely even halfway inside of me."

"Just… take it slowly… if you need to."

Brianna shook her head at his words. "If I did that… we'd be waiting here for a long time. I'm just… I'm gonna do this all in one go."

"I don't think that's a good idea…"

Despite his words, Brianna raised her hips again. Anthony nearly lost it when the tight walls of her vagina rubbed him from all sides. She moved until just his head remained inside of her, took a slow breath, and then slammed her hips down.

Anthony's mind was blown. As his dick became completely buried inside of Brianna, a white haze fell across his vision as the intense pleasure surging through his body swept over him like a hurricane. Not only did he feel an incredible pleasure. He also felt a surge of energy flow between him and Brianna. The energy rushed through him, filling every crevice of his body, which had been deprived of mana for so long it was like giving a man dying of dehydration a lake. His body felt like it was being rejuvenated at super speeds.

There was something else that appeared inside of him as well, though he had trouble describing the strange feeling. It was like… like a section of his heart had suddenly been unlocked. No, maybe it was more like his heart was opening up, or even expanding. A place appeared inside of him, which he understood instinctively was dedicated to Brianna. This space belonged to her and no one else.

He could feel her inside of him. As he focused on that feeling, he understood that Brianna right now was experiencing quite a bit of pain after having broken her hymen in a single go. This made him feel guilty. He shoved that aside, however, and instead focused on Brianna. He didn't want her to experience any pain when she was with him, and so he narrowed down on those thoughts, on his desire to let her experience only pleasure, and sent them into that space inside of himself that had been created for her. It was almost like instinct.

As a soothing feeling spread from this area, Anthony opened the eyes he had unknowingly closed and looked down. Brianna had fallen onto his chest. Her breathing came out in loud gasps, and her shoulders heaved. She calmed down soon enough. Anthony raised his hands, which he now had the strength to move, and rubbed her back.

"Are you okay?" he asked.

"Yes… I just… didn't think it would hurt that much, or feel that intense."

Brianna raised her head to look at him. She looked oddly satisfied. There was a vibrant glow about her that he recognized from somewhere. He frowned for a moment. Where had he seen that expression before… oh. He knew where.

It was the face he made after having sex with Lilith. He'd seen it in the mirror on any number of occasions.

"Did you already cum?" he asked in shock.

Brianna's cheeks turned scarlet. "Y-you came too!"

Anthony didn't remember cumming at all, but maybe that was because he'd been overwhelmed by the pleasure of having sex for the first time in over a year. Now that she had told him, he could indeed tell that he'd had an orgasm, though this knowledge did not satisfy him at all. In fact, his dick was already swelling again.

Brianna squeaked when his cock, still buried inside of her, once more grew fully erect.

"Y-you're growing bigger again?! Already?!"

"I think it has something to do with being an incubus," Anthony admitted as he stared into Brianna's brilliant green eyes. "Can we keep going? I don't want to stop right now."

Brianna looked frightened, and Anthony did not rush or pressure her for an answer. He would never hurt her. That was why he left the decision to her instead of himself.

"We can... um, I don't mind," Brianna said. She pushed herself off his chest, her hands resting firmly on his body, and looked down at him with her scarlet hued cheeks. "D-do you mind if I remain on top?"

"I don't mind at all." Anthony shook his head as he reached out and placed his hands on her naked hips. "I'll let you set the pace."

"Thank you."

Brianna took a slow breath and seemed to center herself before she began moving. The muscles of her stomach tightened as she raised her hips, then slowly brought them back down. Her ass came into contact with his balls for only a moment before she raised her hips again. The frictional sensation of her tight vaginal walls rubbing against his cock made him groan loudly as he helped her along. As he got her timing down, Anthony thrust his hips upward a little, causing Brianna to gasp. A jolt ran through his mind as he felt Brianna's pleasure, which heightened his own experience and created something of a feedback loop.

As they continued, Brianna became much more enthusiastic, and it wasn't long before the loud sounds of flesh smacking against each other echoed around the room. Trails of sweat began appearing on Brianna's flushed skin. Anthony found himself focusing on one particular droplet as it moved between the valley of her breasts, but then he focused on her chest. Those massive mammaries of hers were bouncing with each movement she made. With her hands on his chest, Brianna's breasts were smashed together, causing them to look even bigger than they actually were.

As he stared at those tits, Anthony was unable to stop himself from reaching out and grabbing a handful of them.

"Ah!"

Another jolt of pleasure slammed into him as Brianna released a startled gasp. Anthony marveled at how his fingers sank into her soft bosoms. Her tits were softer than anything he'd ever felt before. As he stared in wonder at her large breasts, Anthony soon found his eyes locked onto her nipples, which were now hard and slightly pointed. He pinched her nipples between his fingers, not twisting them or doing anything that would hurt, but just playing with them. When he did, he felt Brianna's pussy tighten around him.

Brianna opened her mouth wider as drool escaped from her lips. Her enthusiastic hip movements became even faster and more sporadic as she slammed her hips against his and ground her pelvis into him. Anthony kept pace. For every downward thrust of her hips, he would push his hips up, using the returning strength in his legs and back to lift himself off the bed. The

feedback loop inside of his mind sent waves of intense electric pleasure coursing through his body.

It seemed this feedback loop also affected Brianna, who soon lost the strength in her arms and pitched forward into his chest. He felt her drool leaking onto his chest and mixing with his sweat. She was still moving her hips against him, but she seemed to have lost her strength.

Anthony rolled them over, watching as Brianna's chest jiggled. He sat up so his weight wasn't crushing her (though he still only weighed around 110 lbs so it probably wouldn't have hurt her anyway), and began rocking his hips. Brianna moaned as she came to. Her dazzling eyes contained a vivid lustre as she stared at him. He could tell what she wanted from him even before she spoke.

"K-Kiss… kiss me… haa… ahn… ha… please…"

Anthony didn't say anything as he pressed his lips to hers. He kissed her with everything he had, projecting his intense feelings through it. All of the emotions raging inside of him were buried in that kiss, his desire for her, his desire to protect her, his desire to please her, and his desire to make her happy. As these feelings flooded Brianna, she released a loud scream into his mouth as her pussy convulsed around his dick and the juices flowing from her increased.

Despite Brianna having just cum, Anthony found that he was unable to stop himself. Like a starving man who'd just been told he could eat all he wanted, Anthony continued thrusting his throbbing cock into Brianna's sopping wet and incredibly tight pussy. In response, Brianna wrapped her arms around his neck and pulled him down even further as she shoved her tongue into his mouth. The feeling of her tongue pushing and carressing his only fueled his desire for her. They shared saliva between them in a sloppy kiss as he churned her insides with his cock.

Anthony had no idea how long he kept going. His mind became lost in an intense haze of lust and passion. His body seemed to move with a mind of its own. All he remembered was the feeling of being inside Brianna, of her kisses as she held him tight, of her own desires flooding through the connection that had formed between them. He recalled bringing Brianna to several orgasms as his intense need for sex kept him going well after he should have been finished. He believed that Brianna might have actually passed out at some point.

It was only after he and Brianna had experienced several orgasms that he finally found himself unable to continue, and even then, a part of him was raring and ready to go. As he lay on his back, he looked down at his still fully erect dick and sighed.

Brianna was already spent. She lay on her side, her naked and sweaty body fully pressed against him as she rested her head on his shoulder. She was so deeply asleep that he couldn't even feel her thoughts anymore, which had been a constant buzz in the back of his mind ever since they first connected. Anthony honestly felt a little bad for having sex with her for so long without even stopping.

As he lay there, tired but unable to fall asleep, he caressed Brianna's naked hip with his left hand and raised his right one to his face. His hand looked bigger than he remembered. His fingers had been rail thin before, but now they seemed a bit... beefier? No, that wasn't a good word to describe it. However, they did seem bigger and stronger than before.

He let his hand drop to his side. Brianna muttered something under her breath and tried to snuggle even closer, though he didn't think that was possible since there was practically no space left between their bodies. He smiled at the woman as the hand he'd been using to stroke her hip fell still. With a yawn, Anthony closed his eyes as exhaustion finally came over him and he fell asleep.

***

Anthony did not know how long he slept for, but when he woke up, his body felt more refreshed than it ever had before. He couldn't remember the last time he'd felt this good.

Opening his eyes, he glanced around the room. Nothing had changed since he'd gone to sleep. After observing his surroundings, he looked at the woman still sleeping against him. Brianna's red hair was fanned out across the bed, her breasts pressed into his side, and one of her legs hooked around his. She was smiling, which caused him to smile as well.

He began stroking her hip like he'd done just before going to sleep. His plan was to lay in bed for a bit longer, but as he continued, the feeling of Brianna's nipples poking him made it hard to resist. Anthony had not felt such a burning need to have sex in a long time.

Rolling them over, Anthony stared into the sleeping face of Brianna, which looked so cute when fully relaxed. Her face had a vulnerability to it when she was like this that made him want to protect her… though he knew she could probably protect herself and him on top of that.

As these thoughts flashed through his mind, Anthony leaned down and began placing soft kisses on her cheeks, chin, mouth, and forehead. Brianna groaned and stirred awake. He leaned back when she opened her eyes and smiled at her.

"Good morning."

"Morning." Brianna yawned a little bit, smacked her lips, and then paused when she realized their positions. Her cheeks lit up as she looked away. "We really had sex last night, didn't we?"

"We did. A lot of sex." Anthony agreed with a nod.

"It really was a lot of sex," Brianna admitted, her cheeks glowing even brighter.

"Hey, Bri?"

"Bri? Is that supposed to be me?" asked Brianna, frowning.

Anthony froze for a moment. "Not if you don't want it to be."

"I don't mind." Brianna reached up and cupped his face with her right hand. The smile on her face caused him to melt and nuzzle his cheek against her hand like an animal seeking affection from its owner. "I rather like the idea of having a nickname. You can call me Bri."

"Kay." Anthony turned his head and kissed her palm, all the while staring into her eyes. "I know we just had a lot of sex last night, but can we do it again?"

"Right now?" asked Brianna, startled.

"Right now," Anthony confirmed.

Brianna looked a little stunned, but Anthony could feel through his new connection to her that she was not opposed to the idea.

"I… I suppose we could. I mean…" Brianna trailed off. He thought her blush couldn't get any fiercer, but he was wrong. "… I am your bondmate."

As she warmed up to the thought of having sex so soon after last night, Brianna reached down and began stroking his already hard member. The feeling of her soft hand on his dick was electric. She leaned up and claimed his lips in a kiss. Anthony kissed back, applying a light pressure as he placed one hand on her stomach and slid it across her smooth skin until he was cupping her sex. She was already wet, and she became wetter still as he rubbed his fingers across her. Brianna moaned into his mouth as he began playing with her clit. The small bundle of nerves twitched against his fingers.

Just before things could really heat up, the door to the room suddenly slammed open and in walked an irate Professor Incanscino. She was wearing an all-white gothic lolita dress with numerous frills and wore a glare that caused both Anthony and Brianna to stop what they were doing.

"There will be none of that right now," Professor Incanscino told them. "You've already had enough sex for the moment. I need you both to shower and get dressed. Then meet me downstairs. We have a lot to discuss."

As the woman walked out of the room, Alex and Brianna glanced at each other before nervous smiles appeared on their faces.

They both wondered if the professor was irritated at what they were doing or if something else was bothering her. However, neither of them would know what was getting under the woman's skin until they got out of bed.

Getting out of bed, however, was a lot harder than it sounded.

CHAPTER 7

Anthony did not realize anything about him had changed until he stepped out of bed and stretched his arms. His muscles were drawn taut. He could feel them being stretched out, but they felt… felt… denser? Yes, they felt thicker than he remembered. As he brought his arms back down, a thought occurred to him that he felt a lot better now than he ever had before, even when he had been a human.

"Anthony," Brianna suddenly called his name. He turned to find her sitting up in bed and covering her chest with the sheets. It seemed she still had a sense of modesty despite what they had done the previous night.

"What is it?" he asked when he saw the look in her eyes. They were wide and filled with astonishment.

"Your body… it's…"

"What about my body?"

At her words, Anthony looked down and blinked several times when he saw thick pectoral muscles and the kind of abdominal muscles fitness models dreamed of. Below that was his dick, which hadn't changed at all, but his legs were several times more muscular than he remembered.

Feeling a jolt like lightning travel through his body, Anthony rushed over to the vanity mirror sitting against a corner of the room, where he soon found himself staring at someone completely unfamiliar to him. This… was this… really him?

Anthony's body had undergone a complete transformation. It was like the metamorphosis caterpillars went through when they changed into butterflies. Even Anthony was completely stunned by his new appearance.

While he was still able to recognize the face that was staring back at him, his hollow cheekbones had filled out and now looked healthy. His once ragged and worn out features appeared strong and youthful instead of worn and gaunt. Even his skin now had a vibrant sheen. It wasn't just his face that had filled out either. His entire body had gone from being emaciated to something he would expect to see on a movie star who played roles primarily in action flicks.

Anthony stared at his chest, which had become streamlined and muscular, before shifting his gaze down to his waist. He had the powerful V-cut that a lot of men tried to achieve at the gym. The rippling abs of his stomach further enhanced the appearance of strength. Anthony looked down further at his legs, which were equally well-muscled. He was still thin, his body still lithe, but compact muscles now spread across him, making him look like a young olympian athlete.

"What… what is this?" Anthony asked in shock.

"I think the reason you look so different now is because I've become your bondmate," Brianna said as she climbed off the bed. She still had the white sheets wrapped around her body, not that it did much. Anthony could see her nipples poking through the thin fabric. "We can probably ask Lucretia when we talk to her. For now, we should get dressed and meet her like she asked."

"Right…"

Anthony took one last look at himself before suppressing the curiosity filling him. He discovered that a pair of black jeans and a white shirt had been placed on the desk for him. He was surprised when, upon sliding the jeans up his hips, they fit his new body. Given what he'd looked like before, he had been expecting these to be too small. It appeared Professor Incanscino had suspected this would happen.

After he finished putting on his jeans, he glanced over at Brianna as she let the sheet fall to the floor. He sucked in a breath as her perfectly round ass appeared before him. They shifted into a pair of long and beautiful legs with strong thigh and calf muscles. He looked further down at her elegant feet, which seemed almost delicate compared to the rest of her and featured high arches and cute little toes.

Then he let his gaze wander up her back, following the perfect curvature of her spine. As he watched her, Brianna bent over, which had the effect of thrusting out her ass. Her ample breasts swayed as they hung from her chest. Anthony gulped when he saw her pink nipples. His throat went dry.

Unfortunately, Brianna noticed him staring.

"D-do you really have time to stare at me so much?" she asked with an indignant squawk.

"I'm sorry." Anthony smiled as he slipped the shirt over his head. It felt a little tight around his chest and shoulders, but it still fit. "I just can't help but admire you. I've never met a woman who looks more gorgeous."

Brianna's cheeks flushed a little. "W-well, thank you for that, but please focus on the matter at hand. We can't afford to get distracted."

"You're right." Anthony turned his head, almost missing the disappointment that flashed in Brianna's eyes. "I'm sorry. I think something has changed inside of me and not just the outside. I feel a lot different." He closed his eyes for a brief moment, opened them, then smiled at the redhead. "The urges and desires I've always felt are a lot stronger than before. To be honest, it's taking everything I have not to push you against the wall and take you right now."

Brianna let out a slight squeak, but she didn't say anything as she slid on her panties, put on jean shorts that revealed a good amount of thigh, and then began putting on her bra. Anthony noticed it was one that needed to be hooked from the back. He watched her struggle with it for a moment before wandering over to her.

"Do you mind if I help?" he asked.

Brianna hesitated for a moment but nodded. "Please do."

Anthony reached out and helped Brianna by attaching the hooks together. The woman sighed in relief as she adjusted the bra around her breasts, tucking her hand into the padding to fix them to her liking. He looked away. If he didn't, he was going to have problems controlling himself.

With the bra on, Brianna slipped a pink and white spaghetti strap shirt over her head, and the two of them proceeded out of the room and down the hall. They soon emerged into a large room with a set of stairs. Walking down the stairs, they entered the office and living room of Professor Incanscino, who looked like she was impatiently waiting for them.

The diminutive professor was leaning back on one of two couches in a small sitting area with a coffee table. She had one leg thrown over the other. Her left leg, which sat atop her right, bounced up and down in an agitated fashion. Narrowed blue eyes stared at him and Brianna, framed by curly blonde ringlets.

"I was wondering when you two would finish getting dressed." Professor Incanscino narrowed her eyes further. With her arms crossed, she looked like a very agitated but cute middle schooler. "What were you doing? Don't tell me you went for a quickie?"

"O-of course not!" Brianna squeaked.

"Relax. I'm only kidding."

"You don't sound like you're kidding," Anthony said as he took Brianna's hand and pulled her along toward the couch opposite the professor. Brianna gave him a startled look, but she didn't resist him as he sat them both down.

A moment of silence passed as the two parties stared at each other. Professor Incanscino removed her left leg, placed it on the ground, then lifted her right leg and set it on her left. For whatever reason, Anthony found himself staring at his professor's stocking-clad feet, though he looked away when he noticed the smirk on her face.

"I imagine you two are hungry," Professor Incanscino said at last. At that moment, two loud gurgling noises erupted from Anthony's and Brianna's stomachs. As the pair blushed, the blonde woman's smirk widened. "You're lucky I foresaw this. I've already prepared some food for you."

At that moment, a door on their left opened and in walked… another Professor Incanscino?! Anthony gawked as he looked at the woman who was identical to the one sitting across from them. The difference lay only in their outfits. This one was wearing a traditional black and white maid outfit as she pushed a small cart up to the coffee table. Unlike the skimpier variations he sometimes saw at maid cafes, this one was completely modest and did not show any unnecessary skin.

A delectable scent wafted over to Anthony and Brianna, forcing them to get over their shock. Their mouths watered as the woman stopped next to them. Were they going to try Professor Incnascino's homemade cooking? Anthony was really curious to know how her cooking tasted. What if she was a really great chef? The desire to try his professor's cooking suddenly surged inside of Anthony as he watched the woman who looked just like her remove the bell-shaped metal cover, which he believed was called a cloche.

That desire he felt was soon squashed when he saw what was inside.

What lay on the serving tray was not homemade cooking but carefully wrapped burritos that were obviously made from a takeout company. The tin foil wrapping had a logo plastered on it. Anthony was underwhelmed.

As the woman placed two plates in front of Anthony and Brianna, then set the serving tray of breakfast burritos on the coffee table, he glanced at Professor Incanscino. The woman was still smirking at him. That amused expression was really beginning to irritate him, but at the same time, he couldn't help but find it incredibly attractive.

"Are you disappointed, Anthony?" asked Professor Incanscino.

"No," Anthony muttered as Brianna grabbed one of the wrapped burritos and stared at the object with curiosity. "Of course not. Why would I be?"

"I don't know." His professor shrugged her delicate shoulders. "You tell me."

"Tch."

Anthony decided to ignore the woman for now. He grabbed one of the burritos and carefully unwrapped it, mindful of the heat. Steam rose from the burrito and the scent grew stronger after it was revealed. His stomach gurgled again, which prompted him to ignore his small bit of disappointment and begin eating. This might not be something she made, but it still tasted good.

Sitting beside him, Brianna watched what Anthony did and mimicked his actions, unwrapping the burrito before taking a bite. She almost immediately released a started yelp as she bit into the food without waiting for it to cool.

"Careful," Anthony warned. "The food is hot."

"I-I know that now…" Brianna muttered bitterly as she held her hand to her mouth. It looked like she was fanning her tongue.

"Is this your first time eating takeout?"

"Um… yes. I didn't expect it to be so hot." Brianna cast a glance at Anthony as he continued chowing down. "How can you deal with this heat?"

"Don't know." Anthony took another bite, chewed, then swallowed. "Maybe my nerves are deadened to pain and heat."

"That doesn't sound possible." Brianna sighed before blowing on her food to cool it down. When it finally cooled enough, she took a small nibble, swallowed, then took a much larger bite. Anthony watched her become more enthusiastic about eating before turning to watch the woman who looked just like Professor Incanscino leave the room through a large double-door on the other side.

"So who was that woman?" Anthony finally could not keep his curiosity contained. "Twin sister? Evil clone?"

"Neither." Professor Incanscino replied. "That was me from about one hour ago." When all Anthony did was blink, the professor laughed. "Time is a rather interesting thing. Let us just say that my ability to control time comes with a few perks."

He really didn't understand what she meant, but Anthony decided to accept her words at face value.

"I didn't realize you could control your own time," Brianna said with an almost reverent gaze.

Professor Incanscino shrugged and looked away. There was a self-deprecating half-smile on her face.

"I can only control my own time up to a certain extent. Unfortunately, there are some things even I cannot do." The woman was silent for a moment, but then she grabbed a small but expensive-looking cup filled with coffee and took a sip. When she set the cup back down, she placed her hands on her thigh and gave them both an even stare. "Now then, I believe it is time we spoke about the recent events, along with the current changes both of you have undergone."

At those words, Anthony and Brianna straightened their spines and stared at the woman. Professor Incanscino, noticing their looks, lifted her hand in the air. A magic circle appeared over her desk. Then a sleek device floated off her desk and traveled to her. It was a standard black holoprojector. It landed on her palm.

"I'm sure you have already noticed the first big change." As she set the device down, Professor Incanscino glanced at Anthony's body, no longer malnourished. "As an incubus, your body is reliant upon the mana provided to you by your bondmates. When you were stubbornly refusing to bond with anyone, you had a severe lack of mana, which caused your bones, muscles, organs, and everything else to atrophy. Now that you've finally had sex, your body is what it should have been from the very beginning."

"What do you mean by 'what it should have been'?" asked Brianna.

Professor Incanscino set the projector on the coffee table and pressed a button, causing a small light to appear within the center. The light coalesced into an image that appeared over the holoprojector. It revealed the body of a male. It looked like a three dimensional anatomical diagram.

"Incubus are just like succubus in that they are made to be physically perfect," Professor Incanscino said. "Perfect proportions, perfect muscle to fat ratio, perfectly symmetrical. There are no flaws on the body of a succubus or an incubus. Of course, while this perfection might make them unappealing to some, the vast majority of humans and demons find this impossible perfection extremely attractive. I suspect incubus and succubus are made this way to attract members of the opposite sex."

Brianna nodded after her question was answered and leaned back, brow furrowing. She glanced at Anthony out of the corner of her eye. He noticed her look and tilted his head, but she looked away.

Professor Incanscino fiddled with the holoprojector, which caused the three dimensional male figure to suddenly light up. Seven small orbs appeared inside of the body. One of them was over his heart, another close to his solar plexus, one on either hand, one near in his abdomen, one between his shoulder blades and the base of his neck, and another in his forehead. Six of the seven orbs were currently dim and gray, but one of them, the orb right around his solar plexus, was glowing a bright blue.

"This is a representation of your body, taken from a scan I did last night," Professor Incanscino explained. "Until now, all of these orbs have been grayed out. When you and Brianna had sex, this orb right here changed color." While Brianna flushed at being so blatantly called out on her sexual activity, neither of them said anything, allowing the woman to continue. "Each of these orbs represents a specific power that you possess." Professor Incanscino pointed at the only orb currently glowing. "This orb right here represents the power of your body."

Anthony narrowed his eyes as he worked through what all this meant. He considered himself a rather smart individual. He couldn't become a doctor who specialized in Catastrophes and Curses if he wasn't.

"So when Brianna and I slept together, my powers as an incubus became active and transformed me into this? Is that what you are saying?"

"Close. It is true that your body was restored thanks to your powers activating, but your powers are capable of doing so much more than just that. We'll go into how your powers work a little later. For now, I want to focus on what you two must do from this point onward." Professor Incanscino paused for a moment as though collecting her thoughts. "Now that you have activated your powers, I am no longer able to reverse time on you like I had before. That means you will be reliant on Brianna here for mana from now on. You understand what that means, right?"

As Brianna once more blushed, Anthony realized that Professor Incanscino was talking about sex. Incubus were just like succubus in that their bodies produced mana from acts of passion. In other words, sex. This was how they sustained themselves.

"Bri?" Anthony turned to the woman sitting beside him, staring at her hands as they rested on her lap. The woman jumped when he called her by the nickname he'd come up with. "Is this something you are okay with?"

Brianna looked at him with wide eyes, but then she took several deep breaths and calmed down. It seemed she was still embarrassed by what happened last night. Perhaps now that their situation had been settled for the moment, she was beginning to comprehend more about their situation and what it meant for her. Anthony was worried she might be regretting her decision.

"I am okay with it." Brianna hesitated for a moment before reaching out and placing one hand on his. While her cheeks were still pink, her eyes contained a determination that couldn't be masked. "I knew what I was getting into when I agreed to save you. I... um... what I mean to say is that I knew being bound to you would mean we'd be doing that... er... having sex, so I was prepared. You don't have to worry about me." She suddenly smiled. "I told you last night. I want to grow closer to you and explore these feelings I have."

Anthony felt a strange tension in his chest, which he hadn't even realized existed until that moment, unravel. His body relaxed as he turned his hand over in his lap and grabbed Brianna's. As he curled his fingers around her hand, she gripped his back, and he felt like he could feel their connection flowing between them through the contact. It was as if he could sense what she was thinking in that moment, though it was very vague and indistinct right now.

"There are a few other things you two will need to understand," Professor Incanscino said, interrupting their moment. They looked over to see her wearing a serious expression as she stared at Anthony. "The first is that you will need more bondmates if you want to activate all of your powers —and you will want those powers activated." She narrowed her eyes as if she could see what he was thinking. "You might have been able to stay under the radar before because you were so weak, but now that your powers have become active, you are going to draw attention. I don't doubt that many powerful beings will attempt to enslave you or kill you. If you wish to fight against them and keep Brianna safe, you'll need to create a dedicated harem of bondmates who can not only help you grow stronger, but who will be able to grow stronger alongside you."

Anthony had been afraid of this. He knew that if he bound a woman to him, he would have to bind more women. Lilith had thirteen bondmates at the height of her power. Anthony had only been the last of those thirteen.

Brianna's grip on his hand tightened, causing him to look over and see her lips pursed. He decided to speak with her about this matter in private.

"There is another reason you'll want more bondmates besides just increasing your powers," Professor Incanscino continued. "Because of the nature of incubus, you are not going to be able to sustain yourself with just one bondmate. Not only will you be unable to activate anymore of your powers, but you will require more sex than one person can give you."

At those stunning words, the professor looked at Brianna.

"You might be fine now, but as time goes on, Anthony's sexual appetite is going to climb. It will not be long before one person alone will be unable to satisfy him. You can try, but once this happens, he will run you ragged. This is just another reason incubus and succubus have multiple bondmates."

"How do you know all this?" asked Brianna, her brows furrowed as she stared at the woman. "Incubus are so rare that only one more has appeared aside from Anthony in the last five hundred years. How can you know so much about them?"

"It's simple. I don't. This is all just guesswork." Professor Incanscino smiled at the now gawking redhead. "However…" Lifting her hand again, the professor summoned another holoprojector, which she placed beside the one displaying Anthony's powers. She turned it on. An image was projected into the air, this time of a woman with thirteen glowing orbs inside of her body. "Can you tell me who this is a representation of?"

"Lilith," Anthony answered, his eyes never leaving the three dimensional figure as longing surged within his heart. "That's Lilith."

"I knew you'd recognize her even without any facial features being shown." Professor Incanscino chuckled. "Yes, this is a representation of Lilith's power, taken from a scan several months before her battle with Cane. I took this scan myself by the way," she added before gesturing to both the male and female figures. "As you can see, the way their power is represented is nearly identical. What's more, Anthony's physiology is also nearly identical to a succubus's. The only difference between these two lay in their chromosomes. Anthony is obviously male."

"I see," Brianna murmured with a sigh. "I guess that explains why you know so much about incubus."

"Exactly." Professor Incanscino nodded. "What I know about incubus is all based on what I've discovered by comparing Anthony's biological makeup with Lilith's. There are enough similarities that I can formulate a working theory that I believe is, if not completely correct, at least accurate to an astounding degree."

Neither Anthony or Brianna said anything to dispute this woman. What could they say? It was clear that Professor Incanscino had not spent this past year twiddling her thumbs. She had obviously used that time to study his body in great depth.

Now that he thought about it, Anthony had spent a good deal of time with the professor. At least once a month, he would come over to her residence so she could turn back the clock on his body to restore his mana. It was foolish to think she wouldn't also use this opportunity to run tests and scans on him to see what made him tick. Incubus were, after all, a rare breed of demon. Only an idiot would miss out on a once in a lifetime chance like this.

"Do either of you have any questions so far?" asked Professor Incanscino.

Anthony and Brianna looked at each other. As they gazed into each other's eyes, he felt like he could see and feel what she was thinking. She smiled at him. He stroked the back of her hand with his thumb before turning to look at the professor.

He shook his head. "We don't have any questions right now. To be honest, everything you just said is a little overwhelming. I think we're going to need some time to absorb everything we learned in this conversation."

Professor Incanscino looked like she'd been expecting this answer because she didn't press the issue any further. Turning off the two holoprojectors, she floated them back over to her desk, and then turned to them.

"In that case, we should get down to the second order of business." Her eyes narrowed. "The vampire who attacked you two last night."

Brianna sucked in a breath while Anthony frowned.

"We ran a background check on him. The vampire who attacked you is named Frederic Bloodstone." Professor Incanscino placed both feet on the ground, put her hands in her lap, and began tapping her left thigh with an index finger. Her expression was pensive. "He is a pureblood vampire from Germany and doesn't come from any noble lineage, and it seems this Frederic has a fairly extensive criminal record to boot."

"So he's a wanted criminal?" asked Anthony.

The blonde woman nodded. "As you know, the Demonic Covenant prohibits vampires from taking the blood of humans without their consent. Frederic disregarded this law and forcibly drained the blood of several human women, killing them. Their bodies were found in abandoned alleys. The forces under the Vampire Warlord Elizabeth Tepes's command tracked the deeds to Frederic, who fled Germany and vanished. No one had any idea where he was hiding until now."

"How did someone like that sneak into Academy Island?" Brianna asked with narrowed eyes and an intense frown.

"I couldn't tell you." Professor Incanscino shook her head. "I have no idea how he managed to slip past security. What I can tell you is that he likely did not act alone. There might be someone within the Academy Island Private Security Forces who wants to stir up trouble, or it could be a company or research institution who wished to use Frederic for their own purposes. At present, we don't have any leads." She paused, sighed, and then gave them both an even gaze. "I'm only telling you both this because you are directly involved in what happened, and I believe Frederic will come after you again. I want you two to be on your guard."

Anthony could tell this issue was causing his professor a good deal of stress, but she was doing an admirable job of hiding her feelings and emotions, keeping them completely off her face. The only reason he knew she wasn't doing as well as she appeared was thanks to how her shoulders were slouched ever so slightly. No one else would have noticed, but Anthony had spent enough time with her to know Professor Incanscino did not under any circumstances slouch like some lazy bum. Her pride wouldn't let her.

"We understand," Anthony said for the two of them.

"Good. In that case, you two can go home now," Professor Incanscino said. As Anthony and Brianna stood up, the diminutive woman continued. "I know tomorrow is a weekend, but I want you to come to school. Bring Brianna with you. It will be a good idea for you to get a handle on your new abilities, but I need time to prepare."

Anthony and Brianna both agreed to come in tomorrow and left the professor's residence.

The journey down the elevator was completely silent, both lost in their own thoughts.

****

The maglev ride home was quiet, but Anthony considered that a good thing since he had a lot to think about regarding Brianna, his powers, and what he needed to do now.

He was supposed to bind more women to him. If he went by the number of orbs inside of his body, then he needed to bind at least six more. Of course, that was going to be harder than it sounded. Anthony refused to just bind any woman he met, and he refused to bind a woman who didn't want to be bound to him.

He also thought about Frederic. That vampire had somehow known about him, about what he was, and he even knew about

Anthony's younger brother. According to Professor Incanscino, the man was a criminal from Germany. He wasn't a criminal mastermind, however, but a vampire who either became too addicted to blood or power, or both. Someone like him could have never discovered so much about Anthony without help.

Someone had to be providing him with information.

The question was: Who?

It didn't take long before they arrived at their apartment complex, traveled up to their floor, and journeyed to the hallway with their doors.

Anthony turned to Brianna. She was staring at him. He could feel her through their connection, which allowed him to understand what she wanted without her telling him, though he still only got vague feelings and sensations from her.

"Hey, Bri. Why don't you come inside my apartment with me," he said. "I think we should talk about what we learned."

Brianna nodded and followed Anthony into his apartment. The door shut behind her. Anthony used his wristwatch to lock the door, then slipped out of his shoes, placed both his and Brianna's shoes against the wall, and took her hand. He traveled to the couch and sat the redhead down. Then he sat next to her.

"How do you feel about all this?" he asked finally.

"I'm a little shocked, to be honest." Brianna gave him a helpless smile, one that didn't reach her eyes. "I thought I understood what I was getting into when I agreed to become your bondmate, but I don't think it occurred to me at the time that you would need to have more than one partner."

Anthony still didn't know what happened while he was unconscious, but he hypothesized that Professor Incanscino had somehow convinced Brianna to become his bondmate. This young woman must have been so worried about him that she didn't even consider the consequences of her actions when she agreed. That both warmed his heart and worried him.

"Do you regret it?" he asked. "Becoming my bondmate?"

"No." The immediate response, which was followed by Brianna shaking her head, caused the worry in his heart to dissipate. "I don't. I'm shocked, and I'm uncertain about the future, but I don't regret it." She gave him a faint smile. "Were you worried?"

"A little, yeah," he admitted. "But I also wanted to believe in us. I haven't known you for long, and it could just be my feelings as an incubus clouding my judgement, but I like to believe our bond isn't so weak that something like this would tear us apart."

Brianna's cheeks turned a soft pink at his words, but she also nodded.

"I feel the same way."

As he stared into her eyes, Anthony once more felt the overwhelming desire to take this woman into his arms. He didn't resist this time. Leaning over, Anthony slowly moved his head closer to Brianna's, giving her ample time to stop him. She didn't stop him, however. Brianna tilted her head up, and though her cheeks were pink, she leaned toward him as well.

Their lips met and an electric shock jolted Anthony's body. Just the simple contact of her soft lips was enough to make his heart race.

Anthony scooted closer and deepened the kiss, pushing his tongue into her mouth. He was happy when Brianna accepted him, opening her mouth and allowing him inside. He caressed her tongue with his. Her warm, wet mouth was absolutely perfect.

However, it wasn't long into their kiss before Anthony wanted more.

"Bri…" he called her name, his voice heavy. "Can I touch you?"

Brianna didn't hesitate for long. Despite looking more than a little flushed and breathless, she still nodded.

"You can. Just… um… be gentle please."

With her permission given, Anthony went back down, kissing her and stirring the saliva inside of her mouth with his tongue. At the same time, he slid his hand underneath her shirt and undid the hook of her bra. With nothing holding them up, her breasts hung a little lower on her chest, but Anthony fixed that when he slipped his other hand under her shirt and held them aloft. They really were kinda heavy. He could only imagine what sort of back pains this young woman went through on a daily basis.

Brianna released a soft, squeaky moan in his mouth as Anthony fondled her tits. He tweaked her nipples, running his finger around them before flicking the now hardened nubs. Before long, he was pushing both her bra and shirt above her chest, causing her breasts to hang out.

Goosebumps broke out on Brianna's chest, but Anthony moved off the couch and leaned down to suck one of her nipples into his mouth. A loud gasp escaped Brianna's lips as he swirled his tongue around her nipple. More lyrical noises escaped from her when he flicked her nipple with his tongue, then tugged on it with his teeth.

"I-if you do that, I'm gonna lose it!" Brianna exclaimed suddenly.

"Maybe I want you to lose it."

He looked up into her eyes with her nipple still in his mouth. She was staring down at him, her cheeks flushed and her breathing heavy. Her eyes were half-lidded with desire just like they had been last night.

"Anthony... I, um... please continue..."

Anthony didn't say anything, but as he switched from one breast to the other, he maneuvered his hand over her flat stomach, reached her jean shorts, and undid both the buttons and zipper. He slipped his hand into her jeans and panties. As he cupped her warm pussy, he used two fingers to rub her outer labia. Brianna released a stifled moan as she spread her legs apart, allowing him even better access. It wasn't long before Brianna herself was grinding her pussy into his hand.

Because this just wasn't enough, Anthony stopped what he was doing. Brianna moaned in complaint. He merely smiled as he closed her legs, grabbed her jeans and panties and slid them down her hips. Brianna lifted her hips to help out. Her panties were stuck to her vagina thanks to her juices, but he soon peeled them off and slid both articles of clothing down her legs.

Now he was given a perfect view of Brianna's bare pussy and smooth lips. Desire welled up inside of Anthony even greater than before as he placed both hands on her knees and spread her legs apart. Brianna looked a little embarrassed now. Her face had become a brilliant shade of crimson. She had even covered her face with her hands... but she didn't tell him to stop, so he assumed she was okay with this.

Leaning down, Anthony placed his lips against the inside of her thigh. His kiss caused Brianna's breathing to pick up. The sounds of her heavy breathing grew louder as he kissed his way up her thigh, enjoying the way her muscles quivered under his lips. The scent of her arousal was quite strong now. Strong and intoxicating.

It wasn't long before he was kissing her groin, but he didn't kiss her pussy yet.

"Anthony… teasing me… ha… ahn… is not fair," Brianna gasped as she placed her hands on the back of his head.

"Sorry," he said. "I'll stop teasing you if that will make you feel better."

Brianna might have said something. Her mouth was open to speak. But Anthony placed his mouth over her smooth pussy lips and pushed his tongue inside of her warm, juicy cunt.

"Hnnnn!"

As Brianna threw her head back and released a strangled groan, Anthony enjoyed his first taste of her pussy. He wasn't quite sure he could quantify her taste. It was kind of citrusy? Or maybe it was tart? Her flavor was hard to describe, but as he worked his tongue inside of her tight vaginal passage, he could say she might be his new favorite flavor. He was sure that in the years to come, he would become addicted to her taste.

"A-Anthony!" Brianna suddenly released a loud cry as Anthony removed his tongue and pushed his finger inside of her. The walls of her vagina suddenly clenched and pulsated as though it sensed the intrusion of something new. As he began pumping his finger inside of her, curling it in a slight "come here" gesture to find the sweet spot that would drive her crazy, he pressed his mouth against her clit and began sucking on it.

"Gggnnnn! Ha! Ah! Ah! Haaaaan!"

She must have already been worked up too much because her entire body suddenly trembled as though it was being shocked. Anthony groaned as an intense wave of pleasure rushed through their bond, along with a feeling of energy—mana, he realized. Brianna's orgasm had generated a small amount of mana that surged through his body and helped energize him further.

As she slumped against the couch, Anthony stopped licking her clit and removed his finger from her pussy. He stuck his finger inside of his mouth, sucking off her juices as he gazed at the young woman while she slowly recovered.

Brianna's hair had become a bit of a mess. It looked like she'd been grinding her head against the couch and it began sticking up everywhere thanks to static electricity. Her body was coated with sweat. She was still wearing her shirt, which had slid back down to cover her breasts, but that meant her clothing was sticking to her skin. It was slightly transparent as well, so her nipples, which were pointed and stiff, had become visible. Combined with the fact that she wasn't wearing anything on her hips and Anthony didn't think he'd seen a more erotic sight since his last night with Lilith.

"Bri?" he said.

"You... you may." Brianna didn't even let him finish his question. "You... um... you don't need to ask me." She looked away, her cheeks still red. "If I ever don't want to have sex, I'll tell you."

Ah. So she knew what he wanted. He should have expected that.

Anthony stood up, undid his button and pulled down the zipper. Like he did with Brianna, he removed both his jeans and underwear in a single go. His cock sprang free. She eyed his dick at full mast as he leaned over her and used one hand to guide it to her entrance, though he didn't push his way inside of her.

He gazed into her eyes, feeling the slight insecurity she felt through their bond, and he knew that just like him, she was also worried about their future.

"Bri, I want you to know that no matter what happens, I will never abandon you," he said. "From the moment we slept together last night, I became yours, and you became mine. I'm never going to let you go. It doesn't matter if I bind six more women to me or a hundred. You are more important to me than my own life, and you always will be."

Brianna's eyes widened, but her shock only lasted for a second before her lips trembled and water glistened within her eyes, though no tears fell.

"Thank you," she whispered.

Anthony shook his head. That was not something she should thank him for, but he didn't say anything. Actions spoke louder than words.

Brianna groaned as Anthony pushed his dick inside of her, spreading her pussy lips as he filled her up. Her tight passage felt like it was pushing against him. That only heightened the pleasure he felt.

She reached out and wrapped her arms around him. Her hug was so tight he found his nose buried against her neck. The mind-addling fragrance she released, a combination of sweat, soap, and something uniquely Brianna, heightened his lust. He pressed his lips to her neck as he rocked his hips.

A loud cry echoed from the woman as Anthony began slowly fucking Brianna. He used her verbal, physical, and mental cues to tell him what she liked and what she didn't like. Brianna did not like it when he bit her neck. She preferred softer kisses and gentle caresses to anything rough. When he thrust his dick inside of her, she enjoyed it the most when he pulled almost all the way out and slowly pushed his hips all the way in until he was buried up to the hilt. He paid close attention, wanting more than anything for this to be an enjoyable experience for them both.

As they continued with their love making, sweat formed on their bodies. Anthony was still wearing his shirt, so the sweat drenched his clothing, which rubbed against Brianna's nipples and caused her mind to jolt with pleasure. This created a feedback loop. Anthony felt her pleasure, which created pleasure for him. This stimulation was almost too much to bear, but he held on as she locked her legs around his hips and began pulling him deeper into her. As he buried himself completely inside of her, it felt like the tip of his dick was knocking against her cervix.

The amount of time that passed seemed indefinite and yet all too soon. Brianna released a soundless scream as her arms and legs tightened around his body. It felt like her muscles had locked. The walls of her pussy tightened so much that Anthony couldn't move anymore, and the extra stimulation this gave him was more than he could handle. He let out a loud groan into her neck as his cock twitched and released several spurts of semen.

They remained like that, tightly embracing, for a number of minutes. Even after Brianna's legs slumped to the floor, she still hugged him as though basking in the warm afterglow of their love making.

Anthony eventually looked at his wristwatch and saw that it was around noon. He sighed.

"Bri," he called out to her.

"Hmm?" Brianna muttered.

"Why don't we go take a shower together, and then we can go out and do something? We still have half a day left."

Brianna released her hold on him and leaned back, staring into his eyes. She smiled a moment later and nodded.

"Good idea. We can't remain inside all day, and I really need to stretch my legs."

"Me too."

Anthony stood up and helped Brianna to her feet. Her knees wobbled a little before she stabilized herself, and then looked at him.

"We should use my shower," she said. "Yours is too small."

"Ah." Anthony blushed as he was reminded that he had a small shower. "That's a good idea."

Putting on their pants, Brianna and Anthony made their way into her apartment room, where they took a shower before changing into new clothes and leaving the apartment complex together.

CHAPTER 8

Because Academy Island was surrounded by the ocean, the early mornings were always, without exception, incredibly foggy. Today was no different. The early morning sun was barely visible behind a thick layer of fog covering the ground. This dense fog made it impossible to see more than a few dozen yards in any direction.

Fortunately, being able to see was not important when riding on a maglev.

Anthony and Brianna were sitting together on a long bench. Sitting at their feet was the music case that contained the Geminius Sword. They sat so close their thighs were touching, and Anthony had placed his arm around Brianna's waist, hugging her to him as he rested his head on hers. He took in deep, gentle breaths. The scent of her hair, freshly shampooed, relaxed him. He had no idea simply smelling someone's hair could be so relaxing.

"Mornings on Academy Island are really weird," Brianna muttered as she stared out the window. Only the hint of a blush could be seen on her face, yet she did not pull away or tell him to stop, and instead continued talking. "And dangerous. Doesn't that fog cause issues with traffic and such? I imagine there are quite a few accidents."

"You'd think so, but there are surprisingly few accidents," Anthony said. "I think Academy Island has around twelve accidents a year. That's a relatively low number."

"How do cars avoid crashing?" asked the curious Brianna. "That fog should mess with the sensors, shouldn't it?"

"Don't forget where we are," Anthony reminded her with a smile. "Academy Island is a forerunner in the creation of advanced technology, especially in matters of magical engineering and robotics. The AI systems installed in hovercars made here are about five years ahead of vehicles created in any other nation. It's actually because of how scientifically and magically advanced Academy Island is that they are able to maintain their autonomy."

"That is true. I guess I didn't think about that." Brianna pursed her lips. Anthony sucked in a soft breath as he resisted the impulse to claim those lips for himself. Patience. Patience. Patience. He repeated the world like a mantra in his head as Brianna, not knowing of his struggle, kept talking. "I keep forgetting where we are. I've never been to Academy Island before I was given this mission."

At the mention of her mission, Anthony turned a little somber.

"Speaking of, what did you tell the higher ups?" asked Anthony.

Brianna's expression turned sullen as she bit her lower lip. Her shoulders became hunched, like a child who knew she'd done something wrong but didn't know how to apologize. Anthony felt a strong urge to protect her.

"I… haven't told them anything yet. To be honest, I do not know what I *can* tell them." She scooted a little closer to Anthony as if taking comfort in his presence, then continued. "I know that I will have to tell them at some point. If I don't, they will suspect something is wrong and send someone to investigate. At the same time, when I do finally tell them, it is likely they'll banish me and label me a traitor. I wouldn't be surprised if they sent someone to dispose of me…"

When Anthony heard that, his grip on Brianna's hip tightened as a fiercely protective feeling came over him. Blood surged through his veins. A red haze filled his vision. The very thought of someone coming to assassinate Brianna made him angry.

"I will never let anyone touch you," he declared.

Brianna smiled as she tilted her head. She hesitated. Anthony even saw her ears begin turning red like the blood in her face could no longer fill her cheeks and thus spread outward. One second passed, then she suddenly leaned up and placed her lips against her cheek. The contact startled him.

"Thank you," she said. "I'm glad you wish to protect me, but you don't need to worry. I know how to take care of myself."

"Ah." Anthony scratched the back of his head as heat rose to his own cheeks. "I guess you do at that."

He had almost forgotten this simple fact, but Brianna was stronger than him. She could protect herself just fine. Heck, she could probably protect him while she was at it.

It only took around fifteen minutes to reach the college stop. Anthony and Brianna exited the maglev and walked toward the Institution of Magical Sciences.

Despite how it was the weekend, there were still plenty of people located on campus. Some people were present because they took weekend classes. However, most people were likely showing up because they had a class project they needed to complete. There were a lot of projects that could only be done inside of the advanced science labs at the university.

As they walked along the walkway, Brianna glanced around at everything in curiosity, but then she suddenly shifted closer to Anthony. She adjusted the music case around her shoulder as he looked down at her. He blinked when she hugged his arm a bit. A frown marred his face.

"Is something wrong?"

"I just realized we're being stared at."

"Ah." He nodded. "Don't worry about those. Men glare at me all the time. It's because I'm an incubus. Even if they don't know it, they instinctively categorize me as a threat, so most men don't like me."

"It's not the men who are the problem," Brianna refuted his words with a shake of her head.

"Huh?"

Anthony needed a moment to process that, but when he finally did, he looked around. It was only now that he truly understood what she meant.

There were indeed a lot of people staring. Like always, several of the men he walked past sent him a vicious glare as if he had dumped shit on their heads, but it wasn't just the men who were staring at him now. Every woman he passed was also staring at him.

At first, he thought there might be something on his face, but there wasn't. He also wasn't dressed funny. His outfit was the one Professor Incanscino had given him last night.

"This is odd..." he muttered.

"I think it's because you are an incubus," Brianna explained her theory. "Until now, you've been sort of like… like a low-key incubus. Your powers were dormant because you were starving yourself magically by not having any bondmates. Now that I have become your bondmate, the mana inside of your body had been filled up and is leaking out, causing you to produce pheromones that attract the opposite sex."

While Brianna did blush at calling herself his bondmate, the fact that she said it made him oddly happy. He wished he could bask in this feeling of warmth that permeated his chest. Sadly, they had things to do.

"That does make sense." He paused, then sighed. "Regardless of the reason, it just means more people are going to be staring at me. I'm not exactly sure I like being gawked at by twice the amount of people as normal."

"I think I understand how you feel," Brianna said in a soft voice after taking another glance around the campus grounds.

Because neither of them wanted to remain the center of attention for any longer than necessary, Anthony and Brianna hurried into Building #1 and took an elevator to the top floor. They arrived in a nice hallway and walked through until they reached an expensive wooden door.

Anthony reached out and knocked.

The doors opened to admit him and Brianna inside. On the other side of the door was the office and living room of Professor Incanscino. The teacher in question was sitting behind her desk as per the usual, manipulating a holographic monitor. It looked like she was grading papers, though she stopped when her eyes landed on them.

"I am glad you two could make it," she said, shutting off the monitor and sliding off the chair. As she walked around the desk, the diminutive professor continued speaking. "There is a lot we have to do today. Since you have only just found a bondate, Anthony, I doubt you understand the changes happening inside of your body. You will need to learn how to control your newfound power. Also…" Professor Incanscino looked at Brianna. "I would like to perform an experiment to see if incubus bonding works similar to a succubus's bonding process."

Wearing a small frown, Anthony understood the gist of what she was saying.

"You mean you want to see if Brianna can use the power I unlocked when she became my bondmate?"

"Correct."

The professor smiled and nodded like her favorite student had just answered her question correctly, but then the smile slowly left and a frown took its place. Anthony shifted from one foot to the other when she stared at him.

"W-what is it?" he asked.

"I see that you are wearing the clothes I gave you yesterday," Professor Incanscino said slowly. "Do you not have any new clothes to wear? Given that you have filled out now, you should have gone shopping yesterday. It would have been nice if you could have come wearing clothing fit for exercise."

"Er…"

Anthony found himself at a loss for words. He looked around the room as if that would somehow help him figure out what to say, or maybe he was hoping to buy himself some time. He honestly didn't even know what he was doing anymore. Fortunately, he had Brianna by his side.

She had no issues mentioning his shortcomings.

"I don't think Anthony realized that his old clothes wouldn't fit him anymore," she said. "We spent all yesterday at the arcade and didn't once go shopping for new clothes."

"Bri! Why'd you tell her that?"

"W-what? It's the truth."

Anthony could tell that Brianna did not understand how embarrassing her words made him because of the sincere look on her face. He wanted to be angry, or at least rant a little, but he was powerless against that genuinely honest demeanor of hers.

"Is that so?"

Professor Incanscino looked from Brianna to Anthony, who felt a nervous sweat pour down his forehead. The good professor was very short. He didn't know her exact height, but she couldn't have been taller than five feet. He was positive her height didn't even reach that. Despite being positively miniscule, the woman had a terrifying deadpan stare that never failed to leave all her students quivering in fear.

"You are very lucky we have some new clothing you can use," she said at last. "Be warned, it is highly experimental. Don't blame me if you get electrocuted or something." With those words, the woman turned on her heel and marched toward the door. "Follow me, you two."

The pair rushed to catch up with Professor Incanscino. As they did, Anthony sighed at Brianna.

"Way to throw me under the hovertank back there."

Brianna didn't say anything, but she did tilt her head as if she couldn't understand what he meant.

✳✳✳

While Building #1 was the main school building and also served as Professor Incanscino's residence, and Building #2 was dedicated almost entirely to eateries and shops, Buildings numbers 3, 4, and 5 were dedicated to labs and training facilities.

The Institution of Magical Sciences was dedicated to the study of magic and science, and on the combining of magic and science. This included subjects like magical engineering, magic in medicine, the study of Magic Catastrophes, the study of curses, and the application and creation of magical formulas. There were also several medical classes, where students took lab courses that gave them practical experience. Anthony took some of those classes.

Anthony and Brianna found themselves being led to Building #4, which was dedicated to the magical engineering courses. He wondered why they were going here at first, but then Professor Incanscino led them into what seemed like a changing room. The woman looked at him with a deadpan stare before gesturing to something further in.

"There are some unique suits that have been created by the engineering department in that locker over there. It's the big one in the very center of the room. The code number is 3343. We'll be waiting for you outside, so hurry up and get changed."

Professor Incanscino closed the door behind Anthony after he stepped in. He glanced at the door, then looked into the locker room, which had several isles of white lockers sealed shut. All of them looked like they had advanced locking mechanisms. However, one of them looked different from all the rest.

The one Anthony walked up to locker, which looked more like a pod with a bulbous shape, almost like it was a seed sticking out of the floor. Several blinking lights dotted its surface around the middle. There was also a small access panel with a touchpad keyboard and the numbers 0-9 located on it. He reached out and tapped in the code Professor Incanscino had given him. 3343.

A soft hiss escaped the pod. Two seams appeared on the top. One went down the middle, extending to about a third of the way down the pod, while another went around it. The pod peeled open seconds later like a blooming flower, revealing a black and white unitard residing inside. He took the item from the pod.

"She wants me to wear this…?"

With a small frown, Anthony tugged on the suit a bit, watching in fascination as it stretched out before springing back to its original shape. This clothing seemed fairly sturdy. He wasn't sure what it was made from, but it felt almost like a synthetic rubber.

Anthony went over to a bench and began stripping off his clothes. He set his clothes down, and then stepped into the black and white suit. It fortunately zipped from the front. As he pulled up the zipper, he realized the suit was a little baggier than he'd expected. It hung from his body in several places, especially his arms and legs.

"Is this really how it's supposed to fit?" Anthony asked himself.

He studied the outfit for a bit, checking himself over, and only after a few seconds of observation did he notice the small dial located on the left side of his chest. His fingers brushed against the dial. Anthony hesitated for a moment before twisting it. The moment he did, the suit suddenly tightened around him, contracting until it felt like he was wearing tight spandex. He shifted for a second, the material creaking as he adjusted. Then he looked down at the massive bulge in his crotch.

"That's a little obscene," he murmured to himself.

"Hey, Anthony! Are you done changing?" asked Professor Incanscino.

"Yes!" Anthony shouted back as he walked over to the door.

The door slid open to reveal Brianna and Professor Incanscino standing just outside. While his professor checked him over with a scrutinizing gaze, Brianna's eyes went straight towards his crotch. Her eyes widened and a blush lit up her cheeks. He wondered if she was recalling the two nights of passion they'd shared together.

"It looks like the experimental suit those idiots from the Engineering Department created is finally working," Professor Incanscino said, though it sounded like she was speaking mostly to herself. "Good. Let's go."

They walked down a pure white corridor that had several doors embedded into the wall on their left. The other wall featured mostly windows. This corridor was curved, so as they walked down it, Anthony had the vague feeling that it was shaped like a donut.

"Professor, what kind of suit is this?" asked Anthony.

"The engineering students call it the BSS Mark II," Professor Incanscino said. "I've no idea what that stands for, but it's supposed to be a suit that uses magical matrices to strengthen the body. I heard the engineering students created this because they didn't like piloting the Mecha Units when doing on the spot repairs. Admittedly, the Mecha Units are unwieldy and not well-suited to delicate welding work." She glanced at him as they turned down a corner. "That said, you'll want to be careful with that suit. I've heard the Mark I they created exploded during the testing phase and caused serious injury to the student who tried it on."

"Then why did you make me wear this?!"

"Obviously because we can't have you destroying your clothes. What you'll be doing is rigorous and your own clothing isn't durable enough to stand up to it. Do you want to walk around naked for the rest of the day?"

Anthony gawked at the woman. Brianna, who walked on his other side, turned her head and released what sounded like a snort. He turned from his professor to her. When she saw his aggrieved look, her cheeks turned a vibrant shade of red like she was embarrassed to be caught laughing at his expense. He could feel through their connection that she found the byplay between him and Professor Incanscino amusing, which left him conflicted.

They soon arrived in another room, but this one was far larger than the changing room and appeared mostly empty. Shaped like a dome, it had a rounded ceiling and was composed from a different type of material than the rest of the building. Anthony tapped his boots against the floor. It produced an odd clang that made it sound like metal, but he was almost certain this was not any kind of metallic substance.

"This room is made from mana stones," Professor Incanscino explained at his curious look. "I'm sure you know what those are."

Anthony nodded. "It's a type of ore that has the special property of absorbing and releasing mana. Mana stones are generally used in the creation of magic engines and delicate magical circuitry."

"Very good. Yes, you are correct." Professor Incanscino walked over to the far end of the room, where a small pedestal with a screen sat. "Not only can it be used in the creation of magic engines and computer circuits, but it's also used in the creation of many medical devices, and it's currently being used by the Academy Island Private Security Forces in the creation of weapons, barriers, and security scanners."

She pressed a finger against the monitor, which began glowing. Several symbols appeared. It looked like they were written in a form of code. As she fiddled with the device, the floor, walls, and ceiling suddenly lit up with a dim blue glow. It was as if a layer of light had been placed over the room.

"It's a barrier," Brianna muttered as she looked around. She tapped her foot on the ground and watched as a soft ripple spread across it.

Professor Incanscino walked back over to them as she explained. "The magical engineering students test all of their equipment in here. Because of how dangerous some of their equipment is, we have surrounded this room with a layer of mana stones. The mana stones absorb the mana within the atmosphere and can be activated using a premade magic formula to create a barrier that will keep the room from getting destroyed." After a slight pause, the professor pointed to a window located about a dozen yards above the floor. "When testing, students go in there and observe their devices from a distance just in case it explodes."

"I had no idea magical engineering was that dangerous," Anthony said with a frown.

"Magical engineering is easily the most dangerous course we have," Professor Incanscino admitted. "I myself am not a magical engineer, but I understand the basic principles. Mana was never meant to fuel inanimate objects. Trying to do so creates a highly volatile reaction that generally results in the mana overrunning the artificial magic circuits and exploding. I'm honestly shocked by Markus Zauber. That man was either a genius or insane."

"Or both," Brianna said. "I hear Markus Zauber was often considered a mad genius by all the people who knew him."

"Or both." Professor Incanscino admitted her point with a nod, then clapped her hands. "In either event, it is now time to get down to business. Anthony, I want you to activate Physical Enhancement right now."

Anthony nodded, took a slow breath, and then activated his physical enhancement magic.

Physical Enhancement was one of the easiest forms of magic to use, but it was also one of the most dangerous. By filling the body with a mana, a practitioner of Physical Enhancement could increase their physical capabilities up to ten times greater than normal, but they also ran the risk of overloading their magic circuits with mana. If someone shoved too much mana through their body, it could result in their magic circuits exploding. In the best case scenario, their magic circuits would become useless, and in the worst case scenario, they would lose their life.

Anthony let his mana flow through his magic circuits, which lit up with a light blue glow. Because he was wearing the BSS Mark II, it was impossible to see the magic circuits underneath his skin, but if he hadn't been wearing the suit, Brianna and Professor Incanscino would have been capable of seeing the thick blue lines running across his body like the circuits of a computer's motherboard.

"How does it feel?" asked Professor Incanscino.

Anthony raised his left hand and stared at his palm, covered by a thin glove. He curled his fingers. The glove emitted several creaking noises. However, his focus was not on the glove but something else, something lurking beneath the glove, beneath his skin even.

"It feels… great. My mana is flowing through my body far more easily than it ever did before. It feels almost like it's second nature now," he answered.

"That is as it should be." The diminutive professor nodded, blonde ringlets shifting and swaying. "As an incubus, you should have a natural affinity for magic. The reason you couldn't use magic easily before was simply because you did not have any bondmates. Now that you have a bondmate, your physical enhancement magic has been fully activated, which means using it will come far more easily than before." Professor Incanscino went back over to the pedestal. "Now, let us see if you can use that magic in live combat."

"What?" Anthony asked as he looked up from his hand to stare at the professor.

Professor Incanscino didn't answer him with words as she tapped several buttons on the monitor. A large sliding door to his left suddenly opened, revealing a dark alcove, and then several people stepped out—or so Anthony thought. It wasn't until they had stepped fully into the light that he realized what stood before him wasn't people but machines.

The machines were humanoid in shape. They had arms, legs, a torso, and a head. However, their bodies were made entirely of a bright silver metal that gleamed in the room's blue light. They had no facial features whatsoever and looked a lot like mannequins.

There were six of them.

"Aren't these the latest combat drones developed for the Academy Island Private Security Force's use?" asked Brianna, gawking.

"They are indeed," Professor Incanscino answered. "The Academy Island Private Security Forces occasionally asks our faculty to create new combat algorithms for them, so we have several stored away that we can use as test dummies. I hear the magical engineering professors have been using them to help teach their students about magical programming. Anyway, Anthony, I want you to face off against these."

"You want me to fight against six combat drones by myself?" asked Anthony. He felt like he'd just swallowed a lemon.

"Oh, relax," Professor Incanscino chided him with a smile. "Now that you have a bondmate, you cannot compare your physical enhancement magic from before to what it is now. You should be more than capable of defeating six combat drones without breaking a sweat."

Anthony didn't really know if she was blowing smoke in his ears or if she honestly believed what she said, but it wasn't like he had much of a choice.

Brianna moved to stand by Professor Incanscino as the six combat drones surrounded him. Anthony eyed the drones with narrowed eyes as he slid his feet apart and raised his hands in a defensive position.

Unlike Brianna, who had been extensively trained in combat since she was young, Anthony had no combat training. Everything he knew came from the many brawls he got into before meeting Lilith. Of course, after meeting Lilith, his brothers had helped him refine his sloppy brawling style, but it wasn't like his overall combat abilities had changed. He was just a little better at minimizing his movements, blocking attacks, and maximizing how much damage he did.

A moment of silence passed. Anthony felt his heart thundering against his chest. The combat drones remained stationary for a second longer, then launched themselves forward and attacked.

Anthony's eyes widened as one suddenly darted right in front of him. He raised his arm to block the combat drone's fist, expecting the attack to break his limb. Combat drones were made from mana stones just like this room. They had mana filling their bodies, increasing their physical strength, and while they couldn't outdo a therianthrope in physical prowess, they were more than capable of outclassing other types of demons.

That was why Anthony became surprised when the attack didn't hurt at all. He stared wide-eyed at his arm, which was blocking the punch with ease. Then he looked at the faceless head of the combat drone.

A smile suddenly split his face.

What followed was a complete and utter demolishing of the combat drones as Anthony tore through them like they were sacks of flour. His punches shattered heads, his kicks broke off legs. One unlucky combat drone was even torn in half when he launched a powerful kick into its torso and sheared right through its body. It didn't take more than fifteen minutes before all six combat drones were lying in pieces around Anthony, who stood in the center of the room, barely winded and full of excitement.

"P-Professor! I did it!"

He looked over at Brianna and Professor Incanscino with a wide smile. While his bondmate looked stunned by how quickly and easily he had destroyed the combat drones, the professor was nodding her head as if she had expected this outcome.

"Yes, you did." Professor Incanscino eyed the broken body parts scattered across the floor. "I do wish you hadn't completely destroyed these combat drones, but it's obvious you're incapable of fully controlling your newfound strength. We'll work on that later. For now, I believe the first half of this experiment is a success. Now it is time for the second half."

The blonde woman waved her hands. A surge of mana spread through the room like a rippling shockwave. Anthony felt like something had jolted his insides. A wave of heat spread through his body, forcing him to shake his head and banish the sudden and strange thoughts running through his mind. Perhaps it was his incubus nature acting up again. However, Anthony had felt a sudden and intense desire to make love to his professor.

As he was dealing with incubus issues, the numerous scattered parts trembled before they were swept into the air and the drones reassembled themselves. Arms, heads, and legs were reattached to bodies. Magic Circuits fused together as the wounds, terrible rips that looked like someone had shredded them apart, disappeared like they had never existed. Not even a second had passed before all six combat drones looked the same as before Anthony had torn them apart.

"Brianna." Professor Incanscino turned to the redhead. "It's your turn. Now that you've become Anthony's bondmate, you should be able to use physical enhancement magic without the use of a combat suit."

Brianna nodded as she stepped forward, unslung the music case from around her shoulder, and undid the latches. She pulled out the Geminius Sword, currently in a more compact form. It looked like a simple cylinder at the moment. However, as she walked forward, she channeled some mana through it, which caused the two blades to jut out from either side. Each blade was about two feet long, while the grip was one foot long. Brianna slowly spun the blade around in both hands as she walked into the center of the combat drones formation.

Anthony walked over to his professor and turned to watch Brianna. The young woman took a slow breath and closed her eyes. As soon as she did, Anthony felt something tugging at his chest. He looked down, expecting to see something pulling on him, but he was surprised when he found nothing.

"That's not a physical sensation," Professor Incanscino told him. He looked over at her. "It's a metaphysical one. Brianna is pulling on your power and using it for herself. Don't worry. It doesn't adversely affect you when she uses your power, but because it is yours, you can feel when she is using it."

"I understand," Anthony said.

He turned back to look at Brianna, whose skin now had several blue lines like glowing computer circuits traveling along the length of her body. He knew those were her magic circuits.

The battle began and ended even faster than Anthony's. He believed it was because she was using the Geminius Sword. That weapon of hers severed molecular bonds through spatial magic. Even if these combat drones were made of mana stones, which could absorb mana to some degree, they were completely useless against someone who had such an incredible weapon *and* the ability to use Physical Enhancement.

While Anthony was gawking at the woman's incredible abilities and grace, Professor Incanscino crossed her arms and nodded.

"I believe we can say this experiment is a success." She waved her hands and restored the combat drones back to their original state, then ordered them all to head back inside of the storage space. She only continued speaking after the storage door had closed back up. "You two have an incredible amount of power now. However, even though we now know about your newfound power, this doesn't mean you can slack off, especially you, Anthony."

"Why me especially?" asked Anthony.

"Because you are an incubus." The professor rolled her eyes as if the answer to that question should have been obvious. "It won't be long before word gets out about you, and when that happens, you will be targeted. Didn't I tell you this last night? So many people are going to try to use or kill you for their own purposes. I'm sure there are many scientists who'd love to dissect you and see what makes you tick."

Anthony shuddered at her words, imagining himself bound to a table as some mad scientist type split open his chest and pulled out his innards. It was not a pleasant vision. He felt violated just thinking about it.

"We'll work hard," Brianna said in his place. She wore a determined expression. "I promise to train and master Physical Enhancement." She glanced at him. "I'm also going to help Anthony train. He might be strong, but his fighting style is seriously lacking in refinement."

"I rather like my fighting style," Anthony muttered.

But Brianna shook her head. "Being a brawler is all well and good, but you should learn how to properly fight. Right now, you use a lot of wasted movements during combat. That's fine against opponents who are weaker than you, but if you ever fought against someone stronger than you, fighting like you do now will result in your loss."

Anthony scratched the back of his head as heat spread to his cheeks. "I guess... you are right."

"Don't worry." Brianna gave him a confident smile. "You don't need to learn a fighting style from scratch. We just need to further refine your hand to hand combat. That shouldn't be too hard."

"Which you two can do here." Professor Incanscino broke into the conversation. "This particular room is meant specifically to test the combat drones, so you can come in here during the weekends to practice against them. However, you can only come in early in the morning. The students arrive in the afternoon and make use of this testing room until late in the evening."

"We understand," Brianna said with a nod. "We'll come here every Saturday morning, and on weekdays, I will personally spar with him so he can get used to fighting a stronger opponent in one on one combat."

"That sounds like a fine idea." Professor Incanscino agreed. "Just make sure you spar somewhere other people won't notice you."

"Don't worry. I can create barriers to keep people away," Brianna said, puffing out her chest a little with pride.

"Good enough."

The small professor's almost dismissive attitude toward Brianna's apparent barrier creation skills caused the redhead's chest to deflate. It was enough to make Anthony wonder if creating a barrier was supposed to be some great feat. Brianna seemed quite proud of herself, but his professor had the same deadpan expression she usually wore.

Since the experiment was over and it was nearing noon, Anthony went back to the locker room and changed into his regular clothes again. He met up with Brianna outside of the locker room. Professor Incanscino was not there. She had already left them, saying something about how she still had work to do and couldn't afford to spend anymore time with them.

As they were walking toward Building #4's front lobby, Anthony and Brianna discussed the live-fire experiment they just went through.

"It's nice being able to use physical enhancement magic so easily," Anthony said. "I haven't been able to use magic that well since Lilith… well, I haven't been able to use magic this easily in a while."

Brianna had to have noticed his slip, but she chose to ignore it and nodded. "I haven't been able to use Physical Enhancement at all. I've been training hard to use it, but while it is easy to learn, it is hard to master. That's why I have been using a battlesuit."

Anthony frowned. "Doesn't that make it dangerous to send you on missions? What if your battlesuit gets destroyed like it did during your fight with the vampire?"

"That would generally never happen… but War Maidens are usually required to master Physical Enhancement before we are sent out on solo missions like this one," Brianna revealed that piece of information like it was nothing, but Anthony's eyes widened.

"If you're not supposed to go on solo missions until you master Physical Enhancement, then why did Custodes Daemonium send you on this mission?"

"I… I don't know." After admitting this, Brianna's brow furrowed. "I guess it's because I can use Foresight. While it's not an incredibly powerful skill, it is a unique ability that very few people can use. Only my instructor, myself, and the three heads of Custodes Daemonium can use it. My instructor would never be sent on a mission to kill an incubus who cannot wield magic properly, and our leaders do not leave the inner sanctum except in the event of emergencies. I guess, maybe they thought I was the best choice for that reason?"

It sounded more like she was asking a question than answering one.

"Maybe…" Anthony muttered, though he didn't sound convinced.

Just as they reached the front lobby, the doors to the lobby opened and two people walked in. One of them was a woman with curly dark hair and the other was a blond-haired man with a cocky grin. Anthony felt the blood drain from his face when he saw them.

He felt it drain further when they noticed him.

Alex and Secilia stared at Anthony like they weren't sure who he was at first. It was the kind of look people gave someone when they vaguely recognized a person but couldn't place where they had seen them, like looking at an actor who might have played as a background character for your favorite movie. This look only lasted for a second before the pair's eyes widened.

"A-Anthony?!" Secilia shouted in shock.

"Uh… Hey, Secilia," Anthony said with a wan smile.

"Don't 'hey, Secilia' me!" she snapped. "What are you doing here on the weekend?! Why do you look so… so different? What is… going… on…?"

Anthony became worried when Secilia trailed off, but then he realized the woman was giving him a strange look that he couldn't place. It was a hard stare mixed with a blush. Secilia bit her lip, which caused Anthony's still not completely controlled incubus nature to surge up. He brutally pushed it back. Now was not the time.

As Secilia stared at him, Alex walked up to her side, took one look at him, and then took a step back. Anthony didn't know what that meant. However, the cocky smirk had left Alex's face.

"Anthony? Who are these two?" asked Brianna.

Brianna's sudden question caused the two newcomers to realize Anthony wasn't alone. They looked at the redhead. While Alex sucked in a shocked breath at the beauty standing by Anthony's side, the complicated expression on Secilia's face grew even more distraught.

"You are… the girl who moved next door to Anthony, aren't you?" she asked.

"That's right." Now that she was being focused on, Brianna took a step forward, clasped her hands together, and bowed to Alex and Secilia. "My name is Brianna. No surname. I only moved into Anthony's apartment complex a little while ago. He's been helping me adjust."

"And what are you doing here?" asked Alex, recovering from his shock. That said, he still looked sick. His face was twisted like he was struggling with something.

"I expressed an interest in attending this institution and Anthony offered to show me around." Brianna's quick and easy lie was so smooth Anthony was startled. This woman was so straightforward and honest that he didn't think she could lie like that. "He's been giving me a small tour of the facilities."

"If you wanted a tour of Building #4, you should have come to someone who is more knowledgeable about it like me," Alex said with a smile. "I'd gladly show you around."

At his words, Brianna moved closer to Anthony and hugged his arm to her chest. Anthony sucked in a slow breath as his arm became encased between two soft pillows.

"No, thanks," she said. "I'd prefer Anthony show me around."

Another odd look flashed across Alex's and Secilia's faces when they saw this, but it left quickly.

Alex released a strained laughed. "All right. All right. I can see you and Anthony are pretty close. I know when my attention is unwanted. Anyway, Secilia and I need to get going. We have several experiments to conduct on a new piece of equipment our class is making. We'll see you later."

While Alex walked past them, making sure to give Anthony a wide berth, Secilia bit her lip as she stared between Anthony and Brianna. Only after several seconds had passed did she shake her head and walk around them. Anthony turned his head to watch the two as they disappeared down the corridor he and Brianna had just left.

"That was a little weird, wasn't it?" asked Brianna.

Anthony nodded. "Their responses seemed odd. Alex was avoiding me, which he has never happened before, and Secilia… I've never seen her make a face like that."

Brianna shrugged since she didn't know much about his two friends, but even she seemed able to tell that the confrontation just now had been odd.

"Let's go home," Anthony said at last.

"Don't you mean 'let's go shopping for clothes'?" asked Brianna. "You still don't have any that fit aside from this one."

At the mention of how he still needed new clothes, Alex could only groan. He'd completely forgotten about that.

✳✳✳

Secilia continued walking alongside Alex as turmoil plagued her mind. She couldn't believe what she'd just seen! Anthony and Brianna! They… they were…

"They've bonded," Alex suddenly said.

"Yes," Secilia said in a soft tone of voice.

Alex took a deep breath. "What's more, did you feel that aura Anthony was unleashing? I've never felt anything so intense. I'm just a cheap, mass produced human. My magic sense is deadened, which has allowed me to resist Anthony's pheromones, but I still nearly succumbed to feelings of intense loathing just now. I'm afraid I would have attacked him if we didn't leave in a hurry."

"Yes," Secilia said as though she wasn't paying attention.

A moment of silence passed between them. Alex looked at Secilia, but she honestly couldn't be bothered with her half-brother right now. Frustration, hurt, and worry were rolling around inside of her like a storm.

"You know, our… boss is not going to like this," Alex said at last.

"I know," Secilia admitted.

"He might even order us to do something drastic."

"I know."

"Think he might ask us to kill Anthony?"

"Don't say that!" Secilia snapped. "Don't even consider it! There is no way Director Azreal would order us to kill Anthony when he has already invested so much time and effort into acquiring him."

"Hey, I don't want to kill Anthony anymore than you do." Alex raised his hands in a defensive gesture. "All I'm saying is that the boss's original plan has been completely derailed now that Anthony has bonded to someone who isn't you." He gave her a sympathetic look. "You really should have worked faster."

"I-I know that," Secilia stuttered. "But I couldn't."

"Because of Lilith?" When Secilia remained silent, Alex sighed and ran a hand through his hair. "You are way too nice for your own good, Sis." He stopped talking as if waiting for her to say something, but she remained silent, causing him to frown. "Well, whatever the case may be, we'll have to inform the boss and let him decide on what to do. Maybe he will just have us continue to observe Anthony for now."

Secilia didn't say anything as they entered a locker room. Several members of their class were already present.

Their class was rather small, consisting only of about ten people, including them. There was a girl with mousy brown hair, a boy who looked like he had giant's blood in him, two fraternal twins (a boy and a girl), an androgynous male who could have passed for a woman, a vampire girl with pale skin and red eyes, a green-eyed Pantherian boy, and a slightly older woman dressed in a white labcoat.

Alex and Secilia greeted their classmates as they walked up to their lockers. They didn't say anything else about Anthony and his new bondmate. However, even as she pulled out her tools, even as they left the locker room and went to a testing facility, and even as they tested several pieces of equipment, Secilia's mind was plagued by thoughts of Anthony.

CHAPTER 9

Waking up in bed to a warm body lying snuggled against him was one of the greatest perks about having a bondmate—at least, it was in Anthony's mind.

As he opened his eyes, he woke up to the soft breathing of the young woman he was spooning. With his chest against her back, all Anthony could see was her vibrant red hair and a cute little ear. He let his gaze wander down for a moment, toward her bare shoulder, and then he let it wander further. They were both covered by a blanket, but he could feel the nakedness of her back and perfectly round butt pressed up against him.

He also felt his dick trapped firmly between her thighs.

Sitting up a bit, Anthony leaned over, gazing at Brianna's closed eyes, slightly parted pink lips, and small nose. Gentle snores emitted from her mouth. It was so incredible endearing Anthony couldn't resist the sudden impulse that took hold of him.

With a grin, he leaned down and took her ear into his mouth. The woman's soft pink lips parted ever so slightly as she released a gentle moan. However, she didn't wake up. Anthony continued to nibble on her ear until he realized he'd have to take more drastic measures to wake this woman.

He pressed his lips to her jaw, then slowly worked his way across her neck. Brianna's breathing hitched. As he kissed her, mixing hard and soft kisses together, he removed his arm from around her waist and began kneading one of her breasts with his hands. The soft and heavy texture of her tits was truly magnificent. He felt her nipples stiffen as he switched from one breast to the other, then began lightly flicking them with his index finger.

"Nnnhnnn…"

Brianna shifted, her thighs rubbing together, but all that meant was his dick, still trapped between those magnificent legs of hers, became increasingly engorged as his arousal skyrocketed.

He was tempted to rock his hips against her. Anthony wanted it so bad. But he held back. There were some lines Anthony would never cross, and having sex with Brianna while she was sleeping and unable to tell him no was one of those lines.

That said, he had no qualms about giving her a pleasant wake up call.

Removing his hands from her breasts, Anthony slid his hand along her stomach. Out of the corner of his eye, he watched as her tight abdominal muscles twitched under his touch, and he enjoyed the soft feel of her wonderful skin. Very soon, he was cupping her warm sex, which was already wet with arousal.

He pressed two fingers against her lips. As he rubbed his fingers against her, enjoying the way her pussy lips engulfed his fingers, Brianna released a much louder "Hnnn!" that made him wonder if she was about to wake up. Her eyes were closed when he looked at her. However, just as he was about to continue, Brianna rolled onto her back. He removed his dick from her thighs and pulled back before she could snap it in half.

The way her tits jiggled before coming to rest enticed him to lean down and take one of her nipples into his mouth. Brianna bit her lower lip and stifled a moan. Yet even as her brow furrowed in what seemed like frustration, she spread her legs apart, allowing him to better stimulate her pussy with his hand.

Brianna had no hair around her nether lips. He learned a few days ago that she waxed it because she hated how the hair chafed when she wore a battlesuit. She had the cutest little pussy lips he'd ever seen. They were glistening with her arousal at the moment. When he removed his fingers, they came away with some of those juices.

As he swirled his tongue around her hardened nipple, Anthony rubbed her clit. He used slow strokes to get her amped up. While she could sometimes enjoy faster and more hard-paced sex, she generally preferred slower and more tender actions. As he continued his ministrations, Brianna rocked her hips against him, grinding her pussy into his hand.

He felt her end coming when her thigh and butt muscles clenched. A wave of pleasure washed over him through their bond, and a strange feeling of being slightly filled permeated his chest. It was similar to when he ate a hearty meal. That was the mana he received. While having actual sex gave him the greatest amount of mana, even simple acts like hugs, holding hands, and kissing could give him a bit as well.

As Brianna's hips and legs slumped back onto the bed, Anthony removed his mouth from her now wet nipple and looked into the woman's still shut eyes.

"You can open your eyes now. I know you're awake."

Brianna cracked her eyes open a bit, then smiled at him with an only somewhat sleepy expression. She had low blood pressure in the mornings. While this did mean she was slow to wake up, waking up to an orgasm certainly helped her become more alert sooner.

"Good morning," she whispered. Her voice was slightly throaty, but that made her sound sexier in his opinion. There was something inherently attractive about a woman when she first woke up, especially if she first woke up after having an orgasm.

Anthony smiled as he leaned over and kissed her. She returned his kiss, sighing into his mouth before he leaned back.

"Good morning. Do you want to take a shower with me?" asked Anthony.

In response to his question, Brianna curled and uncurled her toes as she sat up in bed. Her eyes remained locked onto him. He didn't turn away from her gaze as she studied him. After a moment, she gave him a wan smile even as blood rushed to her cheeks.

"Shower sex?" she asked.

He shrugged. "Only if you're okay with it."

"I… don't see why not. Sure. It sounds… it sounds fun."

"You sound embarrassed. And you're blushing."

Brianna pouted at him even as her blush intensified.

After agreeing to his request, Brianna climbed out of the bed, and Anthony watched as she walked further from the bed, her gorgeous hips swaying exotically like a dancer's. This woman had always possessed a dancer's grace. He believed it was because she had been trained in sword combat. Her stances and forms were much like those of a dancer.

As she stood there, Brianna twisted her body slightly. Her jiggling sideboob was visible as she looked at him with a half-smile.

"Are you coming?"

"I am. I was just admiring how beautiful you are."

Brianna blushed. Despite how often he complimented her on her beauty, her strength, or even her intelligence, the woman never failed to make that face. It was cute because she blushed even though they had sex almost every day… and sometimes several times a day.

Anthony stood up from the bed and walked with Brianna into the bathroom. Because her apartment was bigger than his, they usually slept at her place. The shower was also bigger. They couldn't have shower sex in his dinky little shower.

After turning on the hot water, Brianna stepped into the shower, and Anthony followed not far behind her. She grabbed a bottle of shampoo, then gave them to him. There was an expectant look in her green eyes as she stared at him.

Anthony got the hint.

They did not have sex after first hopping into the shower. First, he washed her hair. After squirting a dollop of shampoo onto his hands, he began combing his hands through her gorgeous locks of fiery red hair, lathering it in shampoo. He actually enjoyed this almost as much as he enjoyed sex. He believed simple acts like this were a sign of intimacy and trust between them.

It wasn't until after he washed her hair that Brianna slowly spread her legs apart, bent over slightly, and placed her hands against the tub. Now her bare ass was before him, dripping with water and something else. Anthony would have been a fool not to accept such an obvious invitation.

He placed his hands on her hips and lined his cock up with her pussy. A groan escaped his mouth as he slowly pushed his way inside of her. No matter how many times he felt her pussy wrap around him, it always felt just as deliriously good as that first time.

"Have you… gotten bigger?" asked Brianna with a slight grunt as he bottomed out inside of her.

"I don't think so," Anthony said. "Why?"

"N-no reason…"

While Anthony thought her words were strange, he didn't let that bother him as he began rocking his hips back and forth. He had to be careful about not slipping on the wet tiles. However, he'd learned to accommodate for that by bending his knees a little, which actually helped make it easier for him to thrust his hips.

Anthony set a steady pace and alternated his technique as needed. He enjoyed getting Brianna to make different noises. While the sound of his balls slapping against her thighs mixed with the redhead's groans, grunts, and the sounds of running water, Anthony noticed her tits swinging wildly in front of her. Her breasts were large and hung down from her chest. They swung like a pair of pendulums, enticing him, enthralling him.

He removed his hands from her hips and leaned over, grabbing a handful of those large melons and giving them a thorough squeeze before he toyed with her nipples. Brianna threw her head back against his shoulder and screamed. While it could have just been water from the shower, he thought he saw drool escaping her lips and leaking off her chin.

Because it was so blasted slippery, Anthony could not kiss her mouth like he wanted to. If he leaned over too far, he was gonna slip, and then they'd both experience pain instead of pleasure. It had already happened once. Anthony remembered their first attempt at shower sex. They had not been prepared for how slippery the tile got and took a spill. The pain he felt from his dick bending the wrong way while still inside of Brianna remained a vivid memory he never wished to experience again.

Since he couldn't kiss her mouth, he settled with pressing his lips against her shoulders, between her shoulder blades, and the back of her neck. Brianna seemed to like that just fine. He felt a small thrill race through their bond, especially when he kissed between her shoulder blades. It seemed that spot was a bit sensitive.

He didn't just stop there, however. Anthony removed one of his hands from Brianna's breast and reached over to her mouth. He stuck his finger inside of her wet mouth. Brianna closed her mouth and swirled her tongue around his finger, coating it in saliva. While his fingers weren't really sensitive, just the act alone sent a surge of heat racing through his body. She sucked off his finger like she was sucking his dick, and it was so erotic that Anthony almost came on the spot.

As he continued pumping in and out of her, her soft walls clutching him tightened. Anthony held out a bit longer. Only after Brianna's thighs trembled and her butt clenched as she cried out in ecstasy did he allow himself to release his load inside of her. Perhaps it was the angle, but as he pulled out, his seed spilled from her pussy and drenched her inner thighs. It traveled down her legs and mixed with the water.

It was a good thing incubus could not have kids, a fact that he learned only after Professor Incanscino performed extensive scans on him.

"Ha... ha... ha..."

Brianna's breathing was heavy as she leaned over and pressed her head against the tiles. The tips of her ears were red. Anthony smiled. He could feel Brianna's satisfaction through the bond.

He reaffirmed to himself that he would do his best to continue making this woman who willingly bound herself to him happy.

"Hey, Bri?"

"Hmm?"

Brianna recovered enough to stand on slightly wobbly legs and looked at him.

"I love you," he said, wearing a large and joyous grin.

Brianna blushed to the roots of her hair.

***

After taking a shower, the two got dressed, ate breakfast, and left the apartment complex. They journeyed to the maglev station, where they hopped onto a maglev that would take them to Anthony's college.

The maglev was always crowded early in the morning. Anthony and Brianna stood squished together. To avoid potential gropers, Anthony stood behind Brianna and had wrapped his arms around her waist like an overly protective mother bear guarding her cub. That was the excuse he gave at least. In truth, he just wanted to cuddle until it was time for them to part ways.

"We spent way too much time in the shower this morning. You're going to be late," Brianna said as she leaned into him. He couldn't see her face, but her ears were red. There were also a lot of people staring at them. He was certain she was embarrassed, and yet she still didn't try to get out of his embrace.

Anthony shrugged. "Being with you is worth being late."

"T-that's… Is it worth having Lucretia Incanscino upset with you?" When Brianna asked this question, Anthony became silent. He buried his face in her hair. This caused the redhead to squeak like a frightened mouse, but she swiftly mastered her emotions and continued talking as though attempting to distract herself from the feeling of his face against her hair. "You understand that woman quite well, better than me. You should know how she is."

"I'm sure she'll understand," Anthony said after a moment.

Anthony removed his nose from her hair and gazed around the maglev's interior. A lot of people were standing around like him and Brianna.

There were a group of high school girls several meters to his left, wearing the standard blue skirt, collared short-sleeve shirt, and knee-high socks of some academy. When the girls saw him looking their way, all of them blushed and began giggling, though they also glared at Brianna nestled in his arms.

He shifted his gaze from them to the businessman in a suit that was glaring daggers at him. The man looked like he was of middle age. His black and white business suit was sharp, but the man himself appeared slightly haggard. Anthony had heard there were many blue-collar workers who suffered from overwork with little pay. He wondered if that was true…

"I don't think I will be there when your classes end," Brianna said at last.

"Oh? Do you have something you need to do?" he asked.

"Yes…" she hesitated slightly. "There is something important that I need to take care of. Considering how long I've been here, I can't really afford to hold this off anymore. I'll tell you about it later tonight."

Anthony felt a fluctuation through his bond with Brianna and knew it meant she was uncertain about something. The bond they had didn't allow him to receive more than vague feelings. He couldn't tell what she was thinking, but it wasn't like he needed to know exactly what she thought. He trusted her.

"I understand. Tell me about it when you have the time." Anthony paused for a moment, then sighed. "I need to visit my brother anyway. I've been neglecting him for the past week."

Brianna rubbed the hands that were holding her close as though trying to reassure him.

"Don't blame yourself. You haven't had much time to visit him. Also, Frederic is still on the loose and hasn't been found yet. It isn't safe for you to travel alone right now, so you should take extra precautions."

"I know."

Frederic Bloodstone was indeed a big concern to Anthony. The man had nearly killed him once, and even though Anthony now had a bondmate who gave him power, that didn't mean he was strong enough to kill a vampire. This particular one might not be at the top of the food chain among his kind, but vampires were still considered one of the three great demons alongside therianthropes and succubus for a reason.

As the ride continued, Anthony let his curiosity get the better of him. "Has there been any news from Custodes Daemonium?"

Brianna sucked in a deep breath before shaking her head. "None. I don't know if they've heard about what happened yet or have grown suspicious since I haven't sent them a message. In cases like this, protocol would normally dictate sending someone else to investigate the situation, but it has already been a week since I became your bondmate, and they still haven't sent anyone." She bit her lip. "They are also still putting money in my account, which is a little odd. They should have stopped after I cut off all communications. I was honestly expecting them to close the account by now."

"That is odd..." Anthony knew nothing of Custodes Daemonium beyond the basics, but he could at least see how that would be unusual. "I guess we'll just have to play it by ear. Worst comes to worst, you can just move in with me."

Brianna twisted in his grip and gave him a wan smile. "Will your apartment even fit two people?"

"We'll make it work," Anthony said without missing a beat. "I don't mind being in such close quarters with you... in case you haven't realized that."

Brianna's cheeks grew red as she turned around again. He smiled when he noticed her pout in the window's reflection.

As a very forthright young woman, Brianna was determined, straightforward, and honest to a fault, but she also became easily embarrassed. She never took his compliments well. That said, seeing her blush after he made comments like this were one of the highlights of his day.

He wondered if this was because of his nature as an incubus or if it was because of something else. Lilith had also been quite the tease...

The maglev soon reached the stop near Anthony's college. Brianna was not getting off with him this time. She would normally get off and wait for the next maglev to take her back home, but it looked like she was taking this one to wherever her destination was.

He didn't know where that was, but Anthony pushed it to the back of his mind as he leaned down and gave her a kiss. Several eyes landed on them. He could feel them boring holes into his back. Anthony honestly didn't care. Let these people watch if they wanted.

"You should go before the door closes on you," Brianna murmured, her eyes half-lidded and her cheeks stained with color.

"Right. I'll see you later."

Anthony stepped back, turned around, and walked out the door. He paused upon exiting to turn around and gaze at Brianna as the doors closed. The maglev soon lifted off the rail and began moving. He watched until it was nothing but a distant spec, then adjusted the laptop bag slung over his shoulder and walked toward the Institution of Magical Sciences.

His first class of the day was with Professor Incanscino. He entered the classroom to find the professor was already in the middle of her lecture. As the door slid open and he stepped inside, Anthony tried to stealthily move up the stairs without being noticed, which was, of course, impossible since almost every person in class was staring at him.

"Mr. Amasius," Professor Incanscino suddenly called out to him, causing Anthony to freeze. She always used his last name when they were in public like this, but the tone she used when saying it just now sent a shiver down his spine.

"Er… yes?"

He turned to look at the woman, who stared at him with those deadpan eyes set upon that beautiful face. Her doll-like features really were some of the most enchanting he'd ever seen. She was different from Brianna, who was a bombshell with a rocking body. Elegant and refined, but with an incredibly sharp tongue, the woman's young, doll-like appearance was contradictory to her sarcastic nature.

"Why are you late?"

"Uh…"

"Could it be that you had a great morning and didn't want to leave your home?"

"Well…"

"I understand you are a young man with manly urges, but even someone like you should learn to keep those urges in check. Come to class late again, and I will turn back your time to when you were just a child."

Anthony blushed as the class snickered at him. He knew she couldn't actually turn his time back because his body was now resistant to her self-created spell, but the threat still felt very real. Professor Incanscino was not a woman who threatened lightly. While he didn't know if she could turn back his time to when he was just a brat, he did know that she still had a lot of tricks up her sleeves that he hadn't seen yet. According to Brianna, this small woman was an existence so frightening even the greatest demons would not fight against her unless they had no choice.

"I'll do my best, ma'am," Anthony said at last.

"Sit down and get out your laptop," Professor Incanscino instructed. "You missed half the lecture, so ask one of your classmates for notes."

Anthony nodded and sat down next to a young woman who flushed so heavily as she stared at him that she looked like she might pass out. He didn't know who this woman was, though he did vaguely recognize her brown hair and somewhat mousy appearance because they shared some classes together.

"Do you mind if I borrow your notes?" he asked as he brought out his laptop.

"N-n-not at all!" she squeaked.

"Thank you."

Professor Incanscino's lecture that day was on D-rank Magic Catastrophe's, which were Catastrophes that affected individuals instead of groups of people. D-rank Magic Catastrophe's were generally things like curses. Unlike a malady or a magical epidemic, which could be spread to others and was therefore listed as a C-rank and sometimes a B-rank Magic Catastrophe, D-rank Magic Catastrophes could not be spread. Of course, this did not make them any less deadly.

"D-rank Magic Catastrophes come in many different forms," the woman said as she stood on the podium. "From curses that grant a person bad luck to physical defects like involuntary shapeshifting, these Magic Catastrophe's effects are far more ranged and varied than higher ranked Magic Catastrophes. I once met someone who was suffering from a D-rank Magic Catastrophe that made him pass gas every fifteen steps. He was a young magician who eventually found a way around this by creating levitation magic and simply floating himself from place to place instead of walking. However, he often ran out of mana because Levitation requires you to constantly supply it mana, so he became a pretty useless magician."

A ripple of laughter spread through the students at her words, and even Anthony chuckled a little as he imagined the poor young man getting so frustrated with his farting curse he created an entirely new branch of magic. He had actually heard of levitation magic as well. According to one of his textbooks on basic magic, levitation magic had been created by a man named David Levi in the early 1700s...

Anthony frowned as he focused on Professor Incanscino more closely. Everyone else seemed to miss what her words implied, but he understood that she had just admitted to being alive during the 1700s. It made him wonder how old this woman, who looked like she was still in her teens, really was.

Class eventually ended and Anthony ate lunch alone at a small eatery in Building #2, which made his anxiety grow a little.

He had not once seen Alex or Secilia for the past week since they bumped into each other during his and Brianna's first training session. He didn't know what this meant. He didn't know where they were, if they were avoiding him, or if they had some responsibilities that kept them from seeing him. This had never happened before. Even on her busiest day, at least Secilia would visit him during lunch. Sometimes she even skipped out on class and work to see him.

Anthony hoped nothing bad had happened to her.

His worry over Alex's and Secilia's mysterious absence continued into his other classes. After lunch, he had Biochemistry, and his last class was Immunology & Cell Biology.

Biochemistry was the study of chemical processes within and relating to living organisms. It had a heavy focus on how mana affected the biological processes and created chemical reactions within the body, how this could adversely affect or benefit people, and so on. At present, their class was focused on molecular mana genetics, which went into an in depth study on the structure and functions of genes at the molecular level, and how the mana within a person's body could create genetic variations and mutations.

Anthony felt sort of dazed as he listened to his teacher's lecture, though he still did his best to take notes. Most of his thoughts were admittedly still on Secilia.

Now that he was no longer being held back by his reluctance to become intimately involved with women, his thoughts had inevitably turned to how attractive Secilia was. The two of them had been friends almost since the first day he arrived on Academy Island. She had always been beautiful to him, but it was more than just her looks that drew him to her. She was fun to be around, she was fiercely competitive, and she had a quick wit. He loved bantering with her. Now that she had suddenly disappeared, he admittedly felt a little lonely.

When his last class ended, Anthony went to the maglev station. Brianna was not there, so he hopped onto a maglev that would take him to the Academy Island Hospital for Magical Catastrophes.

There were several people inside the front lobby when he arrived. One young boy looked like he was suffering from a curse that caused random parts of his body to swell up like a balloon. They disappeared moments later, but then another part would swell. His mother, sitting next to him, looked both worried and annoyed. There was also a woman in her mid-thirties who kept coughing. Every time she coughed, rainbow colored powder flew from her mouth and crackled like fireworks.

Anthony shook his head when he saw this and walked up to the front desk.

Clarissa was sitting behind the desk again. She looked like she was busy typing something as he walked up.

"Good evening, Clarissa."

Upon hearing his words, Clarissa looked up, a smile curving her lips, but the look left in a flash when she saw Anthony standing before her. Her pupils suddenly dilated as a bright red blush stained her cheeks. He scratched his head awkwardly as he realized she was being affected by his pheromones. Lilith had also emitted them, but she was able to control them so others wouldn't be affected. He currently lacked that control, so everyone he met got a dose.

Stupidly potent chemical secretions…

"A-Anthony?" Clarissa croaked.

"Yes," he said.

"You look…" Clarissa licked her lips as she stared at him, traveling from his face, to his chest, to his broad shoulders, and then back to his face. "You look different."

"I've been working out," was all Anthony said.

"I can tell."

Clarissa took a slow, shuddering breath and placed a hand against her chest. Her breathing had grown heavy, which caused her bosom to heave inside of her sharp business suit.

"You are… um… here to see your brother, yes?" asked Clarissa, who was having trouble focusing.

"Yes, please."

"Okay. Um, let me just add you onto the list of visitors."

Clarissa began typing, though she still occasionally looked back at him. Anthony did his best to ignore her stares. At the same time, he promised himself that he would try to gain control over his pheromones as soon as possible. He didn't like how people stared at him. The women always became hot and bothered, while the men looked hatefully at him like he had shoved a dildo up their ass. It was annoying.

"You're registered now. You can… go see your brother," Clarissa said at last.

"Thank you."

Anthony gave Clarissa a polite nod before leaving the front desk. He noticed when he left that Clarissa heaved an intense sigh as she clutched her chest, but he tried not to let that get to him as he traveled down a hall and entered an elevator, which took him to the third floor.

It was not long before Anthony was sitting on a chair next to his brother's bed. He stared at the figure within the glass tube, which kept harmful bacteria from infecting his brother, whose immune system had grown weak due to being in a coma.

"Hey, Calvin. It's been awhile since I was able to come visit," Anthony said, a self-deprecating smile appearing on his face. "I would have come by a lot sooner, but so much has happened that I haven't been able to until now. I have a lot to tell you, though. This is gonna be quite the story. I hope you're prepared for it."

As always, Anthony spent hours telling his younger brother about everything he had been up to. He talked about how he bonded with Brianna, how he fought against Frederic, how he was training to become stronger, and how he was even thinking about bonding with other women.

"Professor Incanscino says I need to bond with six more women to bring out my full potential," he explained. "I am a little worried about how this is all going to work out, but Lilith was able to have a harem that worked, so I think I can use hers as a base. I remember how kind all... well, how kind *most* of my brothers were."

Anthony reminisced about the past. As the last member of Lilith's harem, he had been the youngest and least experienced. The other twelve men who formed her harem had all taught him what it meant to be part of a polyamorous relationship, so he had some understanding of how they worked.

That said, he also knew harems worked differently for different people. Lilith had never slept with more than one of them at any given time, but Naamah loved having orgies—or so

Lilith would tell him during some of her long winded rants. He wasn't sure how accurate her words were, though. She and Naamah had never gotten along. The few times they met, it devolved into bickering like a pair of children.

His talk continued for several hours, but someone soon arrived and informed him that visiting hours were over. Anthony pressed his hand against the glass case and bid his brother goodbye before exiting from the hospital and beginning his walk back home.

It was dark out now, or it would have been dark if there weren't so many lights.

Anthony watched several hovercars streak by. There weren't that many on the road right now. He then gazed at the signs hanging from buildings.

As he continued walking, a strange feeling caused a chill to run down his spine. It was something he'd felt before. This sensation caused him to stop and look around at the people surrounding him. Everyone had stopped walking and turned in his direction. Their eyes were blank, expressions slack, and a soft red glow permeated their bodies.

He recognized the glow in their eyes.

"These people... have they been turned?"

Anthony only had enough time to ask himself this one question before the nearest person, a young woman, lunged at him. He dodged left, but then an older gentleman tried tackling him to the ground. Anthony spun. His quick actions allowed him to avoid the tackle, which was all well and good, but now everyone was charging toward him with reckless abandon. Several hands reached out as though seeking to drag him to the ground.

Taking a deep breath, Anthony let his mana flow through him like a river and activated Physical Enhancement. Glowing blue lines appeared on his skin, brighter than ever before, and his body became filled with strength. His muscles, bones, internal organs, and even his skin felt far more powerful, more durable, than he could ever remember them feeling.

Anthony bent his knees before leaping into the air. He ascended out of the reach of those people and flew in a parabolic arc before landing on the roof of a nearby building. The people who had attacked him looked up, but they didn't do anything.

They didn't need to.

"I knew it was only a matter of time before you attacked me again," Anthony said as he turned his head to the sky.

Floating several yards above him, his black wings flapping to keep him aloft, was Frederic Bloodstone. He wore the same outfit as before. Anthony also noticed that he had an arm again, though he didn't think it was the man's original arm. He'd heard that vampires had incredible regenerative abilities thanks to their negative life force.

"How many people did you drain of their life to regrow that arm?" asked Anthony. He had not heard of anyone being found dead, but Frederic was a cautious man, so he had probably been careful about letting himself be discovered.

"Do not judge me," Frederic said with a snort. "You and that bitch are the ones who are to blame for anything that has happened to the citizens of this city. Had you not removed my arm, I would not have been forced to drain several people of their blood until their lives expired." Anthony said nothing as he glared at the man, who glared right back with a twisted smile on his face. "You do not know how long I have been waiting for this moment. I knew I couldn't fight you with that woman by your side. I needed to wait until you were alone. Now that you do not have the protection of that War Maiden, I can drain you of your life and add your power to my own. I'll become so strong, no one in this world will be able to mess with me again!"

Anthony stared at the man as he threw his head back and laughed to the sky. Frederic seemed even more unhinged now than he had during their last confrontation.

"Whatever," Anthony snorted. "If you think you can steal my powers, then go right ahead and try."

Anthony had known this confrontation would happen sooner or later since Frederic had not been found by the Academy Island Private Security Forces. He understood this man would wait until there was no one else around and attack him. That said, Frederic seemed to have not realized that Anthony was not the same person now that he had been back then. During their first confrontation, Anthony had been on the verge of dying from Mana Deprivation. That was not the case now.

"Not only will I try to steal your powers! I will succeed!"

A vicious snarl appeared on Frederic's face as dark miasma emerged from his black wings and flew toward Anthony. Each attack took the shape of black crescent blades.

Anthony clicked his tongue as he increased the mana output of his physical enhancement magic, causing the glowing blue lines to increase in luminosity. As the strength of his body increased, the swords reached him, and Anthony punched them. He didn't use any unique abilities. He didn't have any abilities to use. So he simply threw out his fists and slammed them into each dark sword as they arrived.

Loud detonations echoed around them as Anthony demolished every dark sword sent his way. Miasma burst and exploded, then dispersed around him like smoke blown away by a breeze. Frederic gawked at the sight before his eyes narrowed.

"I see. You have bound someone to you." His narrowed eyes turned into fierce slits. "Is it that War Maiden? Have you seduced her into becoming your bondmate? Nevermind. It does not matter if you have a bondmate or not. I will still take your powers!"

"If you want my powers, you will have to catch me first," Anthony declared before he turned around and ran. He leapt over to the next building, and then ran across it and leapt again. As he landed on the next building over, he turned his head to look behind him.

Frederic was giving chase.

In a battle against a vampire who could fly through the air and attack from a distance, Anthony had a distinct disadvantage fighting in such an open battlefield. He simply didn't have the reach to attack. Even if he was stronger now than he had ever been before, physical strength meant nothing if he couldn't use it.

If Anthony wanted to beat this vampire black and blue, he would need to find some method of bringing Frederic down to his level.

Their chase took them far from the hospital. Anthony leapt across buildings at a speed that caused the world beneath him to become a series of blurry images. The wind whistled around him, blowing his hair out of his face, howling in his ears. He was moving faster than he ever had before. Even so, Anthony's eyesight had remarkably adjusted to the sudden shift in speed. This must have been thanks to his abilities as an incubus.

"You cannot run forever!" Frederic shouted behind him.

"Who said I plan on running forever?!" Anthony shouted back.

While Frederic seemed to think he was just randomly running around, the truth was that Anthony had a plan. There was a small sensation burning within his chest. He could feel it pulse like a second heartbeat. Emotions that were not his emanated from this space, and he followed those emenations to their source. Brianna was at the end of those feelings. He could feel her through this bond, and he knew she could feel him as well.

Anthony soon dropped from the building he'd been standing on. He crouched as he landed on the ground, then exploded forward and ran into a six story building with a sign saying Aces High Arcade & VR Tag above the entrance. He bypassed the front lobby and reached a door on the other side. It was locked, but he used his inhuman strength to break it down, revealing a staircase. He would apologize to the owner of this building later.

It didn't take long before Anthony reached the fourth floor, entered, and ran down the hallway until he reached another room. This room contained several pod-like lockers, which he knew held virtual reality equipment. He ran past the equipment and entered a large door on the opposite side of the room, which opened into a massive space that looked like a giant obstacle course.

Large spires jutted from the ground. Ramps appeared everywhere. There were numerous places for him to hide, alcoves where snipers could secrete themselves and take shots at people from above, and barricades for use in urban warfare. This place was like a maze.

Currently, the power was turned off and Anthony wasn't wearing a VR helmet, which meant everything was dark, but he could still see just fine. In fact, he could see even better than fine. The gray material this massive room was made of appeared sharp and defined to him. He didn't know if it was because of his physical enhancement magic or if incubus just had naturally good night vision.

As he raced into the maze-like course, another figure entered the room. Frederic glared into the darkness, his glowing red eyes filled with anger. Anthony would have snickered if doing so wouldn't give away his location.

As he ran through the room, careful not to make any noise, he ascended to the second floor and once more searched inside of himself for those emotions that were his but not his at the same time. He found them easily. Brianna was close. He didn't know how close, but he could feel her emotions stronger than ever through their bond.

"You are very good at running away," Frederic insulted him. "I had no idea incubus were such cowards! Come out! Come out now and face me!"

Anthony said nothing as he hid himself in a small corner and watched the man from a distance. Frederic's face was turning an awfully interesting shade of puce.

"If you will not come out, then I will force you out!"

Anthony didn't know what this man meant by that, but when the shadows inside of the room writhed and twisted, he realized this man was planning to just indiscriminately destroy everything. He wondered briefly if coming here had been a bad idea. It seemed this vampire was an excellent user of shadow magic, but then he shook his head. It was night. Shadows were everywhere, so it didn't matter where he ran. At least in this place, his shadow was so thoroughly hidden by other shadows that Frederic couldn't use it to track him.

Several shadow blades erupted from the ground. They sliced through a number of columns, which fell onto their sides with a rumble. Even more shadows sliced into the ground, creating deep gouges in the floor. However, none of those attacks hit Anthony, who moved swiftly across a bridge several dozen yards above the man.

"DAMN IT! YOU FUCKING INCUBUS! COME OUT NOW!"

Frederic's angry scream rang out across the VR combat zone, but Anthony said nothing as he moved until he was literally above the vampire's head. Only after he confirmed that the burning sensation in his chest was practically on top of him did he act.

Stepping off the third floor ramp, Anthony activated Physical Enhancement again and fell to the ground. Frederic only had enough time to look up before Anthony's two heels slammed into him with the force of a meteor.

The attack was powerful enough that the ground beneath Frederic's feet shattered, and the two of them fell through the floor, though they didn't just stop at one floor. The third and second floors also broke underneath this brutal assault. Anthony's knees jared from each successive impact, but his physical enhancement magic kept him from actually getting injured. When they fell onto the first floor, he leapt off Frederic's face and landed several yards away as the vampire slammed into the ground.

"You must be getting desperate if you fell for a trap like this," Anthony muttered.

"D-damn you..." Frederic stood to his feet. Blood ran down his face and his knees wobbled, but even as Anthony stared at him, those wounds were beginning to heal. "I will kill you... I'll kill you!"

Anthony looked at something behind Frederic and suddenly smiled. "Yeah… no, you won't."

Glaring at him with intense hatred, Frederic opened his mouth to speak—except the only sound to come out was a pained gurgle as something silver erupted from his chest. A shocked expression appeared on Frederic's face as he looked down at the thing protruding from his flesh. It was a sword about two feet in length. As he stared at the blade in astonishment, a beautiful face surrounded by red hair appeared over his shoulder.

"You really made a huge mistake in attacking Anthony while I was away," Brianna hissed. "Did you think I didn't have a means of keeping an eye on him? Do not insult me! I might still be in training, and this might be my first big mission, but a War Maiden isn't a person you can afford to so easily underestimate!"

Frederic tried to speak, but no words came out. The man released several croaking sounds, and Anthony could see the area around his severed skin knitting together.

"He's trying to heal the wound around your sword!" Anthony suddenly shouted.

At that moment, Frederic roared as he whirled around, the sword still impaling him, and tried to swipe at Brianna. He didn't use any magic. He just attacked with a furious battlecry. However, Brianna was not a War Maiden for no reason. She slipped around his claw attack, moved behind him, yanked her blade free from his back, and then spun around with a casual grace as she cleanly removed the vampire's head from his shoulders.

Anthony was silent as the head rolled across the floor and the body fell to the ground with a thud. Blood spurted from Frederic's now headless neck. He bit his lip, but that was all.

Anthony had long since gotten used to violence of this nature—even before Lilith made him her bondmate.

Brianna swung her blade, causing the blood staining it to splatter against the ground. She walked over to him with a soft smile and a worried glimmer in her eyes.

"Are you okay?" she asked.

"Oh, I'm fine." Anthony shrugged and smiled. "You arrived before he could injure me." He glanced at the corpse once more before shaking his head. "Though I have a feeling I could have probably beaten him on my own."

"Maybe, but you aren't a very good fighter yet."

Anthony looked away. "I guess."

"Anyway," Brianna breathed through her mouth. "Let's call Lucretia Incanscino. We'll need to let her know about what happened so she and the Academy Island Private Security Forces can take care of the cleanup."

"Right…" Anthony suddenly grimaced. "I'm not looking forward to informing her about what happened here."

"Me neither," Brianna replied with a pained smile.

With a soft sigh and a prayer in his heart, Anthony made the call to his diminutive and sarcastic professor.

EPILOGUE

Anthony and Brianna were sitting in Professor Incanscino's living room/office space. They had been finding themselves there quite often. It seemed like every other day, they were being called in to see the short professor for one reason or another. Of course, this time, the reason Professor Incanscino demanded they come with her was no small issue.

"While I applaud you for your ingenuitive thinking, Anthony, I really wish you would show more prudence for your surroundings." Professor Incanscino's blonde ringlets jostled as she leaned forward slightly and took a sip of her black coffee. Anthony and Brianna remained silent as they watched her. "Ha… the damage done to Aces High Arcade & VR Tag was extensive. You destroyed one VR room and drilled a hole through four floors. It's going to cost about thirty thousand dollars to repair."

Anthony flinched when he heard about how much the cost of repairs was going to be. Of course, Professor Incanscino wasn't just talking about the cost for repairs but also the materials and manual labor. Even with recent advances in technology, repairing buildings still required a lot of people.

"And I'm guessing I have to pay that off?" asked Anthony, already dreading what he might have to do if he wanted to earn that kind of cash. He'd probably have to get a job, but there was no way he could get an ordinary job. It wouldn't be enough to pay for this anyway. Did he have any special skills that would net him a good job with high pay? Ugh… not that he knew of. About the only thing he was good for was his body, and it wasn't like he could have sex with random women.

How was he going to find a good paying job when he couldn't bring any unique skills to the table?

Professor Incanscino gave him a vague smile as she sipped her coffee, dragging this out for a lot longer than she needed to. Anthony was on pins and needles. Even Brianna was squirming next to him.

"Fortunately, you will not have to pay for the repairs this time," the professor said at last. "An anonymous benefactor heard about what happened and has decided to pay for the repairs themselves."

Anthony sucked in a deep breath and then released it all in one go. His shoulders slumped. He didn't think he'd ever felt so relieved in his life.

However, while Anthony was basking in relief, Brianna narrowed her eyes.

"Who is this benefactor and why are they helping us?" she asked.

"Didn't I just say they were anonymous?" Professor Incanscino shook her head when she saw the fierce expression in Brianna's eyes. "Don't get me wrong. I'm not telling because I don't want to. I don't actually know who they are. When I say anonymous, I mean someone sent us a check with the exact amount needed through an unknown channel. The check was also linked to a bank account with the exact amount of money written on the check, and the account closed the moment we used it to pay for the repairs. We literally have no idea who sent it. We even tried backtracking the flow of money to see what account it came from, but it looks like someone set up multiple dummy accounts, all of which closed immediately after the money was transferred."

Anthony wasn't sure he liked the sound of that. It sounded a lot like whoever this person was, they not only had deep pockets but also knew about him and his circumstances, which he didn't think was a good thing. The last person who found out about him had tried to kill him. Consequently, that was what had resulted in the Aces High Arcade & VR Tag building being damaged.

Come to think of it, Brianna had also tried to kill him. However, she made up for that by becoming his bondmate, so he couldn't really complain.

"Anyway, you two can head home now." Professor Incanscino waved them off. "I have a lot of work to do thanks to you, so I'd appreciate it if you left."

Brianna and Anthony didn't remain there for long. They left the professor's room, exited the lobby of Building #1, and made their way to the maglev station.

"It looks like I can't take my eyes off you for even one second," Brianna said with a slight smile.

"I do seem to be getting into a lot of trouble." Anthony ran a hand through his hair.

Her smile turned wry. "Trouble is an understatement, but I do not believe it is your fault."

The smile soon left and became replaced with another emotion. When Anthony saw the pensive frown on Brianna's face, he felt something unsettling fill his chest.

"What are you thinking about?" he asked.

"I'm thinking about that vampire. Frederic Bloodstone." The frown on Brianna's face grew larger. "Lucretia Incanscino said Frederic was just a regular vampire with no ties to the nobility and he was on the run. How did a man with no connections, who was being chased by the authorities, manage to learn about you? That shouldn't be possible, unless…"

"Unless someone told him," Anthony finished.

"Yes."

Anthony rubbed his jaw as they arrived at the maglev station. He pondered her theory while they waited for the maglev to arrive.

"So someone out there knows I'm an incubus and told Frederic for some reason," he mused.

Brianna gave a slow nod. "Yes, and given what happened between you and Frederic, I wouldn't be surprised if that someone was the same person who anonymously paid for the damage caused by your battle with him."

The maglev soon arrived, but Anthony and Brianna didn't move as it set down and waited for the magnetic clamps to lock into place. As the doors slid open, they made their way inside, the doors shutting behind them.

Perhaps it was because of the late evening, but there weren't many people onboard aside from them. There was just an old man sleeping on the bench several yards away and a vampire couple with dark skin and glowing red eyes. The vampire couple watched them, their glowing eyes containing a strange quality like they were intoxicated, before turning back to whatever they were doing.

"I don't suppose you have any guesses as to who this person might be?" Anthony asked at last. He was joking, of course. There was no way Brianna could know who had given Frederic information about him.

However, his red-haired bondmate took his question seriously. "I don't. I wish I did. The problem is I don't even know who is aware of your existence. There's Lucretia Icanscino, the Academy Island Private Security Forces, Custodes Daemonium… and I'm sure there are several other powerful people or groups who know about you but haven't done anything. For all we know, the person who found out about you and told Frederic is one of those completely unknown factors."

"Well…" Anthony scrunched up his face as he tried to work out his own feelings. In the end, all he could say was… "That sucks."

Despite his words, Brianna gave him a confident look. "It is bad, but you don't have to worry. I will do everything in my power to protect you."

Anthony felt something warm spread from his heart to the rest of his body. "Thank you."

Brianna didn't say anything, but her smile said enough.

The conversation between them grew silent for a moment, and Anthony glanced back at the old man and the vampire couple. Dressed in a trench coat and a large hat, the old man looked kind of like a hobo as he slept on the bench. On the other hand, the vampire couple were dressed in shocking white clothes, which caused their obsidian skin to really stand out.

Since their current topic had been run into the ground, Anthony switched topics.

"So, what did you have to do today? You said it was something you should have done a while ago, but you never told me what."

"Oh!" Brianna's eyes widened before she smiled at him. "Let's wait until we get home. I want your opinion on something."

"O-okay."

Anthony didn't know what Brianna wanted his opinion on, but he was always more than happy to give it to her.

They arrived home soon enough. Brianna led him into her apartment instead of his own, and then asked him to sit on the couch. He did as she asked. Meanwhile, Brianna went into her bedroom.

Taking a glance around the modern living space, Anthony looked at all the new and shiny amenities she had. A lot of her appliances like the holographic TV, the dinner table, the chairs, and the couch he was sitting on were brand new. He remembered helping her buy them. What he was really marveling at, however, was how much space she still had. His own living room had all this as well, but his didn't even have half the leftover space hers did.

Brianna came back into the living room. However, she was wearing something different from anything he'd ever seen on her.

Anthony gawked as the dark blue knee-length skirt swished around her legs, which were also clad in knee-high socks. There was a small gap between her socks and the skirt that revealed her milky white thighs. A white sailor shirt adorned her torso. Because she had a large chest, the shirt looked like it was being stretched a little, and it also caused her shirt to rise a bit more than he believed was intended. When she moved, he could see hints of her stomach. The short sleeves of the shirt allowed him to see her lean arms. Furthermore, her red hair had been tied into a ponytail, which lent her a refreshing and young appearance.

However, all that was secondary to his current thoughts.

"Is this some kind of roleplay you want us to do?" asked Anthony.

"No, silly." Brianna rolled her eyes before she twirled a little. "This is my new uniform. How does it look?"

"It looks great, but again, why are you wearing a school uniform?"

"Because I'll be attending school from now on."

Attending school… she was going to be attending school? Anthony licked his suddenly dry lips as he stared at the girl for what felt like hours. Brianna shifted under his intense stare and looked away.

"W-what is it?" she asked.

"You are… in high school?" he asked cautiously.

"Y-yes? That's not a problem, is it?"

Anthony wasn't sure yet.

"How old are you?"

"I'm eighteen. I turned eighteen last December."

Which meant she turned eighteen three months ago. Anthony released a soft breath as the tension in his shoulders eased.

"Thank mana for that," he muttered.

"It's not a problem that I'm in high school, is it?" asked Brianna, now looking a little worried. "I'm a senior, so I'll be graduating this year."

"No, no. It's not a problem," Anthony assured her with a wave of his hand. "I was just worried that I might be breaking the law for a second there."

Academy Island was fairly lax when it came to sexual relationships, but that didn't mean they didn't have laws. Adults were not allowed to have sex with minors under any circumstances. If someone over the age of eighteen was dating someone under it, they had to wait to have sex until the minor turned eighteen.

Of course, not everyone followed this law. He would even go so far as to say most people who were dating a minor probably didn't follow this law. It also wasn't possible to police every person, and sex was generally not something the authorities on Academy Island concerned themselves with, but Anthony preferred not breaking any laws if he could help it. Being an incubus already meant he was on thin ice.

Thinking on it, though, Lilith had pretty much smashed that law to pieces when she made Anthony her bondmate when he was sixteen, hadn't she? Not that it mattered. The area he lived in had been lawless to begin with.

"That's good." Brianna placed a hand on her chest and sighed as though relieved. Her cheeks soon turned a pale pink as she looked at him. "So, um, do you like it? My outfit, I mean."

"I do," Anthony admitted as he let his hungry gaze roam across her body. "I really, *really* like it. However…"

"However?"

Anthony smiled as he held out a hand. Brianna didn't seem to know what he wanted at first, but then she took the hint and walked over to him. She placed her hand in his, then slowly climbed onto him when he tugged on her hand, until she was straddling his thighs. Her cheeks were beautifully colored as she looked away in obvious embarrassment.

Anthony's erection was already trying to break out of his pants, but he ignored his cock for the moment as he placed his arms on Brianna's hips and tilted his head. Brianna was still embarrassed but leaned down anyway and kissed him. An intense surge of joy raced through his body. Anthony took her lower lip between his teeth and nibbled on it.

"Mmm."

Brianna wrapped her arms around his neck as she moaned into his mouth. Her tongue slipped between his teeth and caressed his own appendage before pulling back. He didn't know how long they kissed for, but Brianna eventually moved back with a soft gasp, her shoulders heaving as she took several deep breaths.

"Hey, Bri?"

"Hmm?"

Brianna looked at him with those half-lidded, seductive eyes, which she only had when they were intimate. He didn't think she made those eyes on purpose. It was like she just naturally exuded sex appeal. Seeing her like this never failed to make Anthony horny.

"Can we have sex while you wear that?"

Brianna blinked. "You want to have sex while I wear my school uniform?"

"Yes."

A pause. Brianna licked her lips for a moment as she considered his request. Then her cheeks inexplicably darkened to a hue of red so vibrant it matched her hair. She looked away from him and coughed.

"W-well, I suppose I wouldn't mind… Just try not to get them dirty. This uniform is brand new."

"I'll do my best," Anthony replied with a gleam in his eyes.

That night, Anthony had sex with Brianna while she wore her school uniform, and it was awesome.

~Fin

AFTERWORD

Hello, everyone! It's Brandon Varnell here, and I would like to thank you all for purchasing my newest light novel. If you enjoyed it, please consider leaving a review. They are the life blood of us authors. Not only do your reviews let us know you want us to write more of this particular story, but they help motivate us to keep writing.

I hope you'll allow me to talk a little about Incubus. I got the idea from the magic high school genre of anime. If you're a weeb like me, then I'm sure you've at least heard of the genre. They are always about a high school student attending a magic academy, where he meets a harem of cute girls who all want him for reasons that you'll never understand, but despite the numerous chicks who want to ride him like a cowgirl, our oblivious protagonist never gets passed second base—and even when he does get to second base, it is usually a result of the accidental boob fall.

I really hate that trope, so I decided to write my own story, one that didn't rely on such a terribly overdone cliche.

Because I wasn't as comfortable writing about high school students in sexual situations, I decided to make them college age. Anthony is a college student and Brianna is eighteen years old. Making them into legal adults allows me to shamelessly write all kinds of gratuitous lewdness.

For those of you who have watched anime or read Japanese light novels, this series is like my version of A Certain Magical Index, Strike the Blood, Absolute Duo, Unbreakable Machine Doll, and Tokyo Ravens. I made sure to include all the tropes found within those series, but I also did my best to subvert them and add more western tropes—like having a protagonist who actually has sex and isn't denser than a box of rocks.

Volume 1 is just an introduction into the series. I introduced my protagonist, a few characters who will join his harem, explored a bit of the world they live in, and gave him a problem that he has to solve. I think it's a decent start, and if you want more, be sure to let me know. I have a lot of ideas on where to take this series.

Before leaving you all, I would just like to give a few thanks to the people who have helped make this all possible.

Thank you Abby for editing my story. I'm grateful to have someone who can catch my mistakes.

Thank you Orendi Laran for doing the art for this series. I really love the visual novel-esque style artwork. I think it works well with this particular story.

And finally, thank you readers. Your support means the entire world to me. I could have never done any of this without you. I hope you will all stick around for volume 2!

~Brandon Varnell

DID YOU KNOW THAT BRANDON VARNELL IS ADAPTING THE AMERICAN KITSUNE SERIES INTO A MANGA ON PATREON?

HAVE YOU EVER EXPERIENCED ONE OF THOSE LIFE-CHANGING INSTANCES? AN EVENT SO MOMENTOUS THAT, YEARS LATER, YOU'RE STILL MARVELING AT HOW IT CHANGED YOUR LIFE?

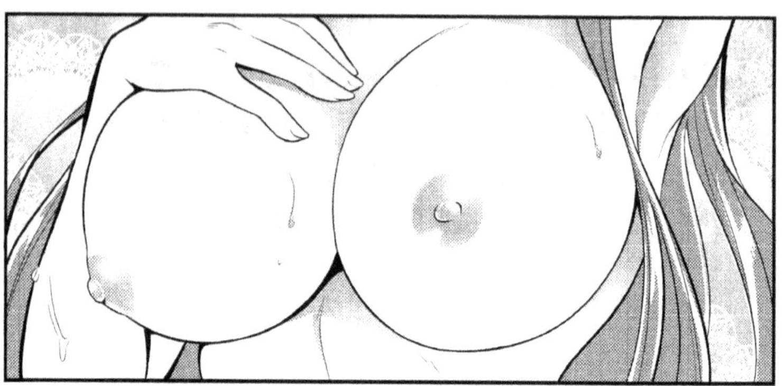

I HAD ONE OF THOSE. IT HAPPENED A WHILE AGO

EVEN TO THIS DAY, THROUGH ALL THE CHANGES THAT HAVE HAPPENED, THROUGH ALL THE EXPERIENCES THAT I'VE BEEN THROUGH, I STILL CAN'T BELIEVE HOW THIS ONE MOMENT CHANGED MY LIFE FOREVER.

NO MATTER WHAT CAME AFTER, OUR FIRST MEETING IS SOMETHING THAT I'LL ALWAYS REMEMBER.

ESPECIALLY SINCE, AT THE BEGINNING OF THIS TALE, I THOUGHT SHE WAS NOTHING BUT AN ORDINARY FOX WITH, UNORDINARILY ENOUGH, TWO BUSHY RED TAILS.

LIFE

.

.

.

.

.

.

.

IT HITS YOU WHEN YOU LEAST EXPECT IT TO.

american kitsune the
manga is coming soon!

Hey, did you know?
Brandon Varnell has started a Patreon
You can get all kinds of awesome exclusives
Like:

1. The chance to read his stories before anyone else!
2. Free ebooks!
3. exclusive SFW and NSFW artwork!
4. Signed paperback copies!
Er... maybe we don't want that last one, but the rest is pretty cool, right?

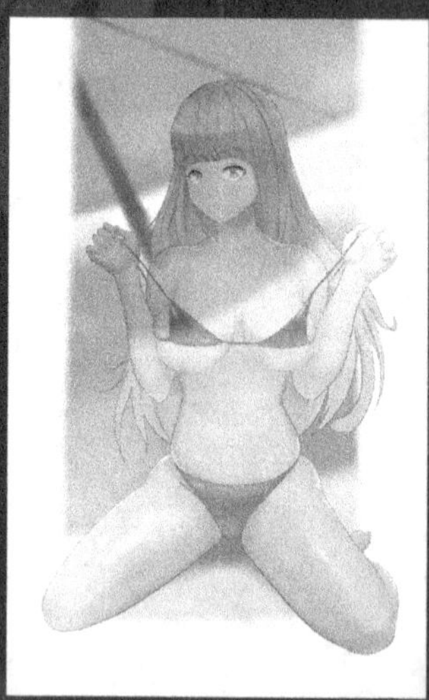

To get this awesome exlusive conent go to:
https://www.patreon.com/BrandonVarnell
and sigh up today!

catgirl doctor
Buy volume 1 on paperback, kindle, and Kindle Unlimited!

American Kitsune
volumes 1-12
are available now!

Volumes 1-7
are available now!

A
Most
Unlikely
Hero

Arcadia's
IgnobleKnight
Volumes 1-6
are available now!

Volumes 1 & 2 are available on
paperback,
Amazon,
and Kindle Unlimited
Swordsman
Of the
Rift 2

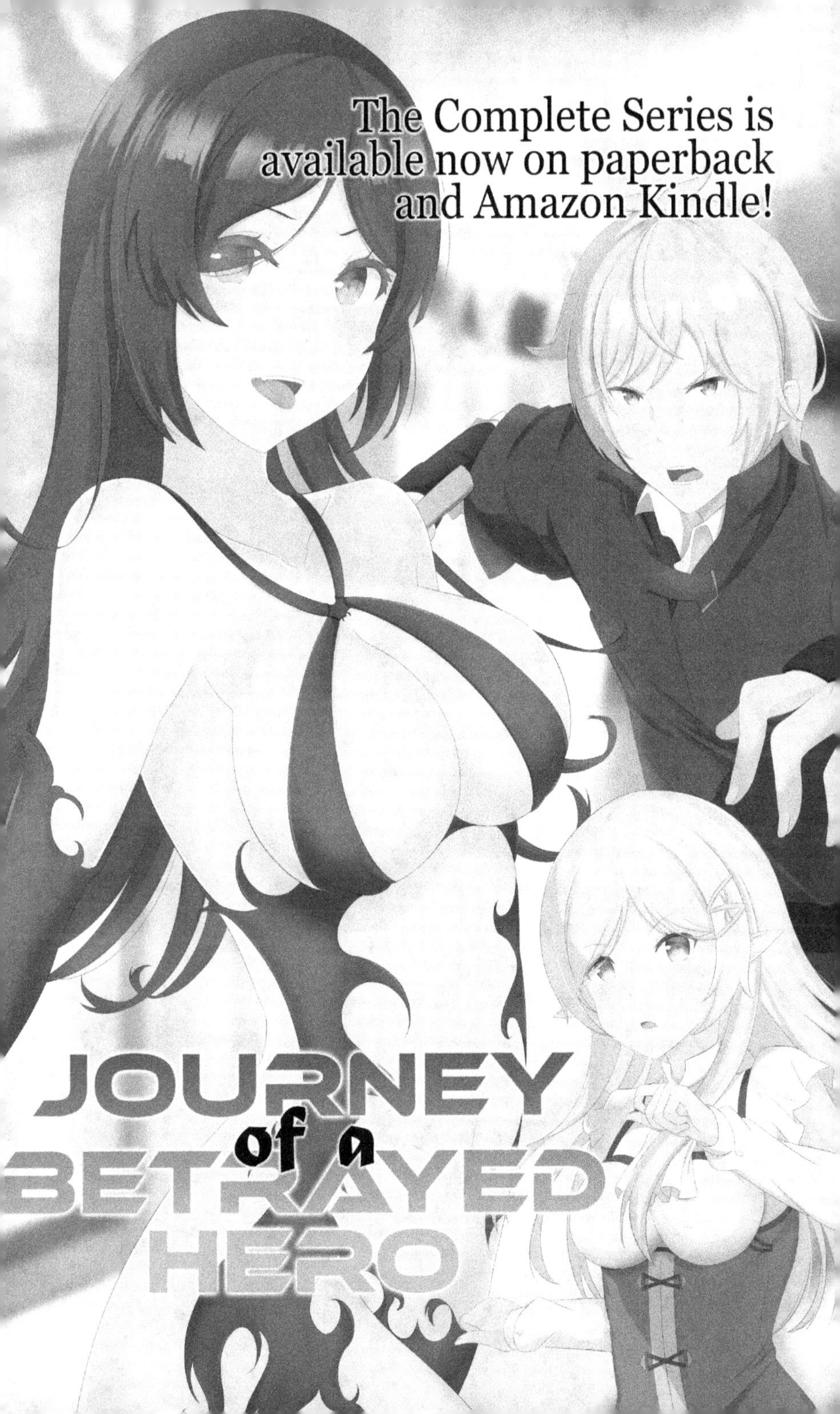

The Complete Series is available now on paperback and Amazon Kindle!
JOURNEY of a BETRAYED HERO

The Executioner Series
The complete series
is available now!

www.ingramcontent.com/pod-product-compliance
Lightning Source LLC
Chambersburg PA
CBHW071746190726
48292CB00003B/882